SECRET INVASION
A Novel by
J. Wesley Buck

ONE

Scattered clouds drifted across the darkening sky offering little hope for a cooling shower in the humid summer evening. The old farmhouse looked forlorn in the red glow of the setting sun. The sisters who lived there were keeping company with special friends. They had been under surveillance and found unique to the intelligence people in nearby Washington D.C. Agency people became quite interested in the sisters' friends after it was discovered UFOs often visited them. Aubrey Blaine had decided it was time the sisters shared what they knew about the aliens. Blaine had gotten warrants to interrogate the sisters. No attorney would be present, as this interrogation had been classified as a matter of national security.

Blaine had been in the intelligence business most of his adult life and it made him seem cold, but he had a sharp, calculating mind under his white hair and behind hard blue eyes, and he kept in good physical form. Will Vaughn, a young man, had black hair and hazel eyes. His physique displayed stamina, the set of his lips a stubborn streak. Blaine had taken him under his wing when Vaughn had come to the agency and was now an up and coming person in the agency. He was to be Blaine's right hand man in the apprehension. Vaughn had one thing a good operative couldn't afford; a conscience. Blaine had been trying to wean him from it for the last couple of years. Vaughn didn't give it up as he considered it an asset. He accepted Blaine's methods, as long as there was no torture or assassination. He had heard unsubstantiated tales about Blaine's method of interrogation, and hadn't cared for what he heard. But he didn't believe the tales, and didn't interfere with special operations Aubrey deemed necessary.

Will crouched beside Aubrey at the hedge along the road. The dew was heavy on the grass as the night kept a grip on the heat of the day. They could see the farmhouse in the light of the rising full moon. It badly needed paint and set off a dirt drive miles from any neighbor. There would be no unwanted witness to the taking of the sisters. All windows were dark and no activity was visible. Aubrey used his radio to make certain his teams were in place.

The heat didn't dissipate as the night dragged into hours of inactivity. There wasn't so much as a breeze stirring, but it was more than heat that had the men sweating.

It was the uncertainty of what might happen if the sister's friends decided to intervene on their behalf. The moon made its arc across the sky, and it seemed to the watching men that the inhabitants of the farmhouse might be in bed. In the west, Will noticed a bright light moving in the sky and tapped Aubrey's' shoulder and pointed. Aubrey alerted the teams to get ready to move.

The object came at an incredible speed and abruptly stopped above the farmhouse without slowing. As it hovered, the interior of the house filled with incredibly intense light that seemed to be going through the roof and spilling out the windows. It was so bright it pained the eyes of the watchers. It abruptly became dark and the object rose slowly into the sky. Aubrey waited until it looked like a star before ordering the teams to close on the house.

The teams approached from four directions, as Aubrey wasn't taking any chance the sisters might escape. He and Will moved toward the house from which no light had appeared. Aubrey alerted his men not to use flashlights as he didn't want to alert the sisters before the house was surrounded. Will and Aubrey quietly went up on the porch and Will tried the door and found it unlocked.

Men began climbing through windows and slipping in the back door. They felt their way through the dim moonlight without seeing any movement, not hearing a whisper. When the teams came together, Aubrey sent two men to the basement, the others he led upstairs.

As Will moved along the hall, he caught sight of a shadowy movement in a room and moved in. The woman's dash made no sound as she leaped from the window and Will saw her hit the ground and run for the nearby woods. He emitted a startled sound as she passed him, bringing Aubrey rushing into the room. They were too late, as she had vanished among the trees. Aubrey stepped away from the window knowing they would find it difficult locating her.

"Goddamnit, Will, why didn't you stop her?" Aubrey asked, angered at her escape. Will turned an annoyed look to him that Aubrey couldn't see in the semidarkness.

"She was out the window before I knew she was here." They went downstairs where they rejoined the men from the basement. Standing between them was a woman. Aubrey had a prisoner.

On the drive to Area C, she sat in the backseat between Aubrey and Will. All she had said was that her name was Janis Randall. He glanced at Will then took hold of her chin and turned her face to him.

"Before this night's over, you'll tell me a hell of a lot more than that," Aubrey said, tweaking her chin. Will saw the expression of pain and felt Aubrey's action had been unnecessary.

Will got his first look of her when they passed under streetlights. She had dark red hair, dark green eyes, and a slim figure. From his first look, Will felt a strong attraction for her, but knew better than to say anything. He would wait and see how Aubrey handled her, but his mind was made up to intervene if Aubrey got rough in his treatment.

The car stopped in front of the gate at Area C. It was a cluster of four one story brick buildings shielded behind a chain-link fence and guarded by men who had no compunction about shooting anyone they were ordered to kill. It was a tight little area, and Will knew its weaknesses. If necessary, he could get Janis Randall out to the civilian authorities, and he was determined not to allow her to be harmed.

The car idled at the gate as a guard came and looked in as another armed man opened the gate and motioned them through. The men in the trailing car had to show identity, and have it verified, before being allowed through the gate. Aubrey ordered the driver to building three. Aubrey took a hard hold on Janis's arm before he opened the door.

"I don't want you trying to sprint out of here, Miss Randall," Aubrey said, coldly. "If you tried, you would be shot. And right now, I need you."

"What do you want with me?" she asked, in a low voice. Aubrey's hard expression didn't change.

"You're going to help me find your sister." Her head came up in a defiant stance and she looked at Aubrey.

"I won't do that." Her words were spoken softly with no trace of hostility.

"I'll change your mind," Aubrey said, looking at Will.

"Think you can get her from the car to the building without her getting away from you?" Will didn't like what Aubrey implied, but he nodded knowing Aubrey was pissed at the other sister getting away.

"Yes," Will replied, in an even tone. Aubrey got out and Will moved his face to Janis' ear.

"I won't let him harm you," he whispered. She turned her head and looked at him with a puzzled expression. Aubrey held the door as she got out followed by Will who stood and took hold of her arm.

It was almost an electric shock when Will touched her bare skin. They followed Aubrey into the building.

They went into a small room with three chairs and a camcorder set on a tripod. Aubrey motioned for her to sit facing the camcorder as he picked up the remote. He pressed the switch and a red light came on below the lens. He said his name and Will's then the name of the interrogation subject and the reason for her being there. Aubrey sat facing Janis as Will leaned against the wall watching Aubrey's face.

"Now, Miss Randall, I want you to tell me about your visitors from the sky," Aubrey began, in a friendly tone. "Then I want you to tell me where your sister is." Her expression remained impassive.

"I'm sorry but I can't tell you anything." Will watched closely but detected no change in Aubrey's expression.

"Why not, Miss Randall?" Will asked. She looked at him with a neutral look.

"Because I'm not permitted to remember anything. Ophelia is the one who does the remembering." Aubrey wasn't pleased with that answer.

"Where's your sister hiding?" he asked, dropping the friendly tone. "And just how the hell do you contact your friends?" Janis turned back to him.

"I have no idea where my sister is." Aubrey had been in this business too long to allow his temper to get the better of him, but Will saw the anger flash in his eyes.

"Miss Randall, I would like to be civil in this matter. But if you don't cooperate, I'll use unconventional methods to learn what I need to know."

"You'll learn no more than I've told you," Janis said, calmly.

"What methods?" Will asked. Aubrey scowled at him.

"Shut up, Will. I'm handling this." The sharpness of his warning wasn't lost on Will. He took a deep breath and looked at Janis, aware Aubrey planned to make it unpleasant for her. For the present, he stood quiet and bided his time. Aubrey nodded.

"That's better, Will. Watch and you might learn how to conduct an interrogation without your fucking conscience getting in the way." The last remark stung and Will didn't like being spoken to in that manner, but there was nothing he could do about it. Aubrey turned back to Janis with a cold expression.

"Don't make this difficult for yourself, Miss Randall."

"I don't remember anything." Aubrey got to his feet, went to the wall, and opened the intercom.

"Dr. Rice, come to room H," he said, looking at Will. "Bring neurophine with you." Aubrey stepped to the door and opened it.

"Tellis, Carlson, get in here." Will knew Aubrey would stand for no interference. If he intervened, he would be thrown out of the room.

"Is this necessary, Aubrey?" Will asked.

"The neurophine or these men?"

"Is this the only way to find out what you want to know?" Will asked, in a level voice. "Neurophine is dangerous shit. It could screw up her mind, and you won't learn anything." Aubrey regarded him for a moment then nodded.

"A good point, Will." Aubrey stepped back to the intercom.

"Forget the neurophine, Dr. Rice. Bring an injection of sodium pentathol." Will felt he had won a minor concession. But knew if sodium pentathol didn't work, Aubrey wouldn't hesitate to use neurophine.

Dr. Rice was short, thin, and balding, with frameless glasses over his brown eyes. He looked small compared to the men who stood by the wall. Tellis had light blue eyes and brown hair, and Carlson had gray eyes and black hair. The doctor looked at Aubrey who nodded to Janis.

"Give her the injection, Doctor," Aubrey said. Rice took the cap from the needle, took a sterile pad from his pocket and tore it open. He bent and swabbed her arm at the elbow and stuck the needle into her vein. He looked at Aubrey and stepped away from Janis.

"You can question her in a couple of minutes," Rice said. Aubrey nodded.

"Stay, Doctor, in case there's an emergency." Will kept his eyes on Janis as her eyelids began to flutter as the drug was carried through her bloodstream. Her eyes closed and Rice bent and lifted one, glanced at Aubrey and nodded. Aubrey leaned down so his mouth was close to Janis' ear.

"Where is your sister?" She moaned softly.

"Ophelia is to make her way to the asfe'lia tse'pi." Aubrey glanced at Will with a puzzled look.

"What the hell is she talking about?" Aubrey asked, looking at Will who shrugged.

"Sounded like Greek to me," Will replied. A flash of anger came to Aubrey, but before he could say anything, Carlson spoke.

"It is Greek, sir. She said safety pocket." Aubrey looked back at Janis with a confused expression. Again, he bent close to her ear.

"Where is the asfa'lia tse'pi, and what is it used for?" A long soft moan escaped her. Will could see she was fighting the drug, but couldn't keep from answering.

"Where is the asfa'lia tse'pi, Miss Randall? I need to know so I can protect your sister." Her eyes popped open and she turned her face to Aubrey.

"You only want to use my sister and me to learn about our friends so you can destroy them." She had spoken in a firm, clear voice. Will looked at Aubrey and saw shock in his expression. Will hadn't suspected that was why Aubrey wanted the sisters. Aubrey looked at Will.

"How the hell can she know that?" Aubrey asked.

"What she said was true?" Will asked, and was rewarded with a scowl.

"They're in contact with ETs that have proven hostile, Will. We could be facing an invasion, and I intend to find out when it might come. And I don't give a rat's ass how I obtain the information."

"Can hurting her do that?" Will asked.

"I'm protecting this country, the goddamn planet!"

"Damnit, Aubrey, think about what you're doing. She's an American citizen!" Aubrey's eyes blazed with anger, but he controlled it.

"These women are being used by the aliens. Get hold of that idea because it's the one thing that will help you through this." Will gave Aubrey a grim, determined look.

"I won't let you hurt her." Aubrey let out an audible sigh and looked at Tellis and Carlson.

"I thought you might try something like this, Will." Aubrey turned to the men as the doctor backed into a corner.

"Throw his ass out," Aubrey ordered. "I mean out of the compound."

"Wait a minute, Aubrey," Will said. "You're not thinking this through. Maybe it's her sister you should be interrogating." Aubrey raised a hand and the men stopped.

"What are you suggesting?" Aubrey asked. Will had to think fast to be convincing.

"Since it's almost daylight, I can take a couple men and return to the farmhouse. We can check the woods. She couldn't have gotten far on foot." Aubrey regarded Will in silence, considering what he said. It made sense, and Aubrey nodded.

"All right, Will. Select two men and search the house." Aubrey wagged a finger at him.

"I want you back here in a few hours, with or without the sister. I'll wait until you return before proceeding with the interrogation."

Will chose two men he had worked with and felt he could trust. Driving to the farmhouse Will briefed them on what to look for.

"What about the woman?" Moore asked. "Do you think she's still in the woods?" Moore was lanky with sandy hair and brown eyes. Will glanced over his shoulder.

"I don't know," Will replied. "But she's on foot and I don't think she's going to stray too far from home." Crist, who was driving, had light brown hair and brown eyes and a swarthy complexion.

"Why does the old man want this woman so badly?" Crist asked, glancing at Will. He wasn't sure how to answer the question, but truth worked best.

"Janis Randall, the woman we brought in, and her sister have been in contact with UFOs. That's got Aubrey paranoid about an invasion." The men exchanged skeptical glances Will noted.

"What do you think, Will?" Moore asked. Will turned a grim look to him.

"Personally, I think Aubrey's full of shit." The rest of the drive was in silence.

Will pointed to the turn off and Crist turned the car down the dirt drive to the farmhouse and stopped in front of the porch. They looked at the house.

"With a little work and paint, this would be a nice place," Moore said. Will silently agreed as he got out of the car. They went to the front door, opened it, and went in. It was as silent as it had been earlier.

"Moore, check the basement. Crist, upstairs, and I'll see what I can find down here." Will went into the kitchen and found everything clean, nothing out of place.

He went into the living room and heard a noise behind him.

He turned and was stunned. He was facing Janis Randall! She smiled and shook her head.

"I'm Ophelia." For a second he didn't understand.

"You're identical twins."

"That's right. I want to make a proposal, Mr. Vaghn." It didn't register that she knew his name.

"What?" She got a mysterious smile.

"I'll give you – or should I say Mr. Blaine? – evidence about the visitors. It should keep him busy for sometime. Rest assured, Mr. Vaughn, they're friendly."

"What do you want?" She got a grim look.

"I want you to bring my sister to me." Will's eyebrows shot up.

"Aubrey will have this place under surveillance." She shook her head.

"I want you to bring her to the asfa'lia tse'pi. I will lead Janis there. She doesn't know anymore than I tell her. Is it a deal, Mr. Vaughn?" Will knew it wouldn't be easy to get Janis away from Aubrey.

"It's a trade, Mr. Vaughn. All the evidence I have for my sister."

"How am I to get your sister after Aubrey has the evidence?" Ophelia got a slight smile.

"Don't give him the evidence until you have Janis. Send him enough to whet his curiosity and he'll agree."

"Once I have her, then what?"

"You accompany Janis to the asfa'lia tse'pi, Mr. Vaughn. There you'll learn the answers Mr. Blaine so desperately wants." Will was thinking of the gauntlet Aubrey would put up to catch them.

"Once we make a run for it, Aubrey's going to have unlimited resources to follow and capture us." Ophelia gave him a confident look.

"You do very well, Mr. Vaughn. That should ensure success." Will knew once he agreed there could be no turning back.

"All right. But where am I supposed to bring your sister?"

"You'll know that when you need to. What you don't know you can't tell." Will felt relaxed and nodded.

"In the closet behind you is an attaché case full of evidence about the visitors. Use it, Mr. Vaughn, to get my sister and return her to me." Will turned to the closet, looked back, and was alone.

He went to the closet and found the attaché case against the back wall. He took it to the large wooden table, put it down, and opened it. There were folders filled with papers covered in an unknown alphabet. He realized these symbols matched the ones described by the people who had seen the I bars from the Rosewell crash. There were hundreds of papers, but how to handle Aubrey? He knew better than to believe he would give her up for this case of papers when he could have both. It would be tricky, but Will could think of only one way.

He called Crist and Moore to join him, knowing it was time to cross the line.

"This is what I want you to do," he said, handing one folder to Moore. "Take this to Aubrey, tell them there's a lot more. He can have it if he brings Miss Randall here. Make certain he understands I mean the woman only." Crist and Moore exchanged glances.

"What are you going to do, Will?" Crist asked. "Get her away from him before he hurts her. After you deliver the folder, there won't be any need for you to be involved."

"It's about time I done something I can feel good about," Moore said.

Aubrey frowned as he looked over the papers in the folder.

"How the hell are we supposed to know what this gibberish is?" he asked, without looking up.

"Linguistics and cryptology might help, sir," Moore suggested. Aubrey turned a cold look on him.

"Why did Will stay at the house?" Crist and Moore exchanged uneasy looks.

"He wants you to bring the woman there, sir," Crist said. "He insists you come alone." Aubrey's eyes blazed as a silent snarl curled his lips.

"I should have suspected he would let his conscience get the better of him. How much more of this material is there?"

"An attaché case full, sir," Moore replied. Aubrey wanted that case, but was loath to give Janis up. He just might have both, and teach Will a lesson.

"You two can go." Moore and Crist left the office. Now it was time to set things up, Aubrey thought.

"Who knows, I might even get the sister," he said, aloud. He was pissed at Will, knowing he would be an expert operative if he could get rid of his goddamned conscience.

TWO

Will was edgy as he waited to see how Aubrey would react to his demand. Demand? He hadn't thought of it as such, but Aubrey would surely take it that way. He moved from window to window, scanning the landscape, alert for any trap. Aubrey liked elaborate traps to minimize the chance of losing what he wanted. He had Janis and wanted Ophelia. What would he do? Will thought through scenarios, and discarded the first as unrealistic. There was no way to surround the house without being seen. That would be too obvious for Aubrey.

He glanced at his watch noting that Crist and Moore had been gone for over an hour. It would be at least another twenty minutes for Aubrey to get here – if he didn't take time to map out a plan. The easiest way for Aubrey to track them would be to have a homing device planted on her or the car. She would be drugged, making it more difficult to get her away. Where would Aubrey plant a tracker? Will knew where to look, but would be shit out of luck if Aubrey had forced Janis to swallow it.

He heard the car before he saw it turn down the drive. Aubrey brought the car to a stop in front of the porch. Will saw Janis, her head lolling from side to side in a drugged state. Aubrey got out as Will came onto the porch. He gave Will a perplexed look.

"Why the hell are you doing this, Will?"

"Two reasons. I don't want to see the woman hurt. It's nothing against you, Aubrey; I just don't see any need to operate like we used to. Second, I'm in a position to get the answers you want – if you allow me to follow through." Aubrey's expression softened.

"We're facing an enemy far worse than the KGB ever was. We don't know what the aliens have done to these women. Think about it, Will. They could easily be using them against us. Even Miss Randall admitted she remembered nothing." Will exhaled knowing what he had to say was a cliché.

"The technology UFOs demonstrate make it clear that we wouldn't stand a chance if they invaded. It's possible I can find out what they're really up to, if you want the truth." Will held up the attaché case.

"If you can decipher this alphabet you might learn why these women have been visited." Aubrey came to the porch and sat down on the steps.

"I've got experts working on those papers you sent. What do you plan to do with Miss Randall?"

"Use her and find wherever the asfa'lia tse'pi is – if you leave us alone." Will knew from Aubrey's expression that wasn't the answer he was expecting. Maybe there's hope for him, Aubrey thought.

"How do you intend doing it?" Aubrey asked, interested in his plan.

"I'll let her sister lead us to the asfa'lia tse'pi. As long as she believes I'm helping her sister, she won't be suspicious." Will kept his gaze on Aubrey.

"How about it, Aubrey? Do you want to get to the bottom of this?" Aubrey leaned back propping himself on an elbow evaluating the plan. He had to admit it seemed to have a good chance of success. He could keep track of Will easily enough. Aubrey smiled mentally as he thought of Will thinking he had him over a barrel.

"All right, Will. I'll give you your chance. Keep me informed and use the scrambler line." Will was immediately dubious, but kept a neutral expression. Aubrey agreed too readily for his liking. Aubrey shook his head.

"I know what you're thinking, Will, but I mean to give you the lead. We have to find the sister if we're to succeed in ascertaining what the hell the aliens' intensions are." Aubrey stood and regarded him.

"Go wherever it is you have to take Miss Randall." Will handed him the attaché case.

"I'll let you know as soon as I have some idea of where we're going, Aubrey. I won't let you down." Aubrey got a slight smile.

"You never have. Maybe I'll know more about what's on these papers when you call in." Will nodded.

"I'll be waiting for your report," Aubrey said, as Will got behind the wheel. He started the car and drove slowly along the drive watching the road, but saw no evidence that Aubrey hadn't come alone. He glanced in the rearview mirror and saw him sitting on the porch looking through the papers. Will shivered as he thought this had been too damned easy. Aubrey didn't cave in like this, and that meant there was a tracker on the car or Janis.

14

Hell, maybe he had a tracker on both. He wanted to put miles between himself and Aubrey. When he felt they were safe, he would check for the tracker.

Ophelia was impressed with Will's boldness. She had watched the encounter from an upstairs window and knew he had no intension of trusting Aubrey. She had to help Janis clear her mind if she was to lead them to the asfa'lia tse'pi. She knew Will would get Janis far from those people, but wasn't aware of what he had let himself in for.

The drug had caused a strong reaction in Janis and Ophelia needed to rid the incoherence from her mind, but it would take time for her to recover. She knew Will would check Janis before she recovered. Until she fully recovered, Ophelia would have to guide Will.

Aubrey called for a car after giving Will enough time to feel free of pursuit. On the way to Area C, Aubrey checked to see how the tracking was going, and was told it was normal. All he had to do was keep a discrete tail on Will until he got to the sister. He would then have both women and to hell with Will's conscience. Yet, Aubrey was curious to learn about the 'safety pocket' Janis had spoken of.

"Which way is he heading?" Aubrey asked.

"South, toward Charlottesville, sir," Moore's voice replied, from the radio.

"How close are you to him?"

"We're keeping a line of sight on him, sir."

"Good. Make damn certain you don't attract attention. Will's going to be watching for a tail."

Crist, driving the tail car, thought this presumptuous of his boss as Will probably already suspected he had a tail whether he could see it or not.

"Yes, sir," Moore replied, and replaced the mike. He glanced at Crist, frowned, and shook his head.

Aubrey replaced the mike and turned to the man in the back seat.

"I want three teams ready to move at a moment's notice. When Will arrives at his destination, I want him and the women taken quickly and cleanly. Understood?"

"I'll see to it, sir." Aubrey turned back in the seat satisfied he had everything under control.

Will turned the car down a dirt road that was parallel to the highway but shielded by trees. He stopped and looked Janis over. She wore no jewelry so a tracker wasn't obvious.

He lightly ran his fingers up her arms feeling for a small lump, but her arms were clean. He didn't feel right as he pushed her dress up and done the same to her legs. The tracker must be on the car, he thought, knowing it wouldn't be easy to find. He had to get a different car, but couldn't rent one as it could be easily traced. That meant he would have to steal one or find another way to travel.

He pulled back on the road and continued south. He would keep an eye out for another car when he got to Charlottesville. He would have to lose the tail he knew was somewhere behind him. But where was he to take Janis? He had a sudden insight to go to New Orleans. He didn't know how he knew, he just knew.

As he passed a wrecking yard, he saw junky looking cars for sale. He pulled onto the lot behind them, got out and went into the office. A grimy looking man with gray hair and brown eyes looked up from a paper-littered desk.

"What can I do for you?"

"I want to buy one of those cars," Will replied. "I'll be leaving mine for someone to pick up shortly."

"I don't give a shit about your business, Mister. If you want one of my cars put the money down and I'll give you the keys." Will took out his wallet and laid three one hundred-dollar bills on the desk.

"Will that cover it?" Will asked. The man glanced at him as he picked up the bills and nodded.

"Which one of those fucking wrecks do you want?" Will looked out the window.

"How does that blue Olds run?"

"Like shit! The best is the green '53 Ford. You can drive a stick, can't you?"

"I sure can. Thanks." Will left the office with the keys to the Ford. He opened the passenger door on the Ford and went to get Janis. He carried her over and put her on the seat and looked for a seatbelt.

"Christ! What am I thinking? This relic's from '53," he mumbled, and closed the door. He got behind the wheel and turned the key in the ignition. For being so old, she sounded like a new car and moved gracefully. He glanced at the fuel gauge and knew he would have to stop for gas.

He didn't know how closely he was being followed, but had no doubt they were back there somewhere.

"He's stopped," Moore said. "Pull over."

"Better inform the boss," Crist said. Moore grabbed the mike and reported to Aubrey. This was something Aubrey hadn't expected. Will was still too close to Washington to be stopping. He recalled the sister had been on foot, and maybe Will was picking her up. Aubrey acted immediately.

"Have all teams converge on the location of the car," he ordered. He wasn't going to count on having the sister until he held her arm. He knew Will wasn't so stupid as to lead them to her without some sort of diversion. Aubrey suddenly understood what his stopping meant.

The man looked out the window when he heard tires squealing to a stop. Four cars were around the one that had been left. He wondered what was going on when Aubrey, followed by three men, came into the office.

"How long has that car been here?" Aubrey demanded. The man decided he didn't care for his attitude and kept his eyes on Aubrey.

"About an hour, I guess. The guy who left it bought a clunker. Oh, you must be the people he said would be by to pick it up." The man felt good at the expression that came to Aubrey.

"Son of a bitch! What kind of car did he buy?" The man also didn't care to help a man with Aubrey's tone.

"A '67 Chevy."

"What color?" Aubrey asked. "Which direction did he go when he left?" The man felt the hundred-dollar bills in his pocket, and knew he would get nothing from this asshole.

"Red and white two tone. I seen him turn north."

"I saw a Chevy like that pass us a short while ago, sir," Crist said. The man got a slight smile when Aubrey slammed his hand on the desk.

"Find him! I want the son of a bitch brought in," Aubrey shouted.

"Who the hell did the guy murder?" the man asked. Aubrey gave him a sharp, angry glare.

"Why we want him is no concern of yours," Aubrey snapped. The man shrugged, feeling good.

"Just asking." Aubrey leaned forward, his palms flattening on the desk, staring at the man.

"Was anyone with him?" The man cocked an eyebrow and rubbed the stubble on his face and nodded.

"A drunk woman he had to carry to the car." Aubrey scowled and stormed out with the men scrambling after him. The man grinned and turned back to his adding machine.

As they went to the car, Aubrey glanced at Crist.

"I think that bastard was lying," Aubrey said. "At least, we know the woman's still under the influence of the drug." At the abandoned car, a man climbed out and faced Aubrey.

"Find anything?"

"No, sir." The other men stood around waiting for Aubrey to give his orders. He was enraged that Will would do such a damn foolish thing, but he also felt a grudging respect. It was just the sort of thing he would have done had he known he was being followed, and now the trail was growing cold. Aubrey began pacing and rubbing the back of his neck.

"If he headed north, he must be going back to the farmhouse," Aubrey conjectured. "That's it! The sister must have been hiding there all the time, and he's gone back for her."

"What do we do, sir?" Moore asked. Aubrey turned to him.

"Get the hell back to that farmhouse, and keep an eye out for that Chevy."

As Will drove southwest toward the Tennessee state line, he began to worry about Janis. She should be showing signs of the drug wearing off, but she remained unconscious. That wasn't good. Aubrey must have given her another dose before getting to the farmhouse. But what had he given her? Will didn't dare stop until he was out of Virginia. Only then could he feel they were safe, for a time at least. He kept glancing at her and noticed she had a peaceful expression. It didn't appear she was in pain or any mental distress. There was nothing he could do for her just now. He would stop at some small motel and see what he could do for her.

It was getting dark when he saw the motel. He pulled off the road and stopped in front of the office. He got a room and pulled the car to a stop in front of it. He unlocked the door and left it open and went for Janis. He lifted her from the seat and carried her inside.

He put her on the bed and closed the door. He bent over her raising an eyelid. She seemed to be in a light sleep and her pulse and breathing were steady. If he only knew what Aubrey had dosed her with. From the state she was in, Will thought of at least three drugs that could have been used.

He had to be certain which one before he tried any stimulant to revive her. One thing he knew was safe might help her. He left the motel and walked to a convience store a block away and got coffee for them both.

Sitting on the side of the bed, he slid his arm under her shoulders and lifted her. He tipped the cup slightly to her lips and some coffee ran down her cheek. Will wiped it off with a washcloth.

"Wake up. We need each other right now." A few more sips and she seemed to be coming around. Janis moaned as she lifted her hand to her head.

"Come on back," Will said, in a soothing tone, relieved. She seemed to be regaining conscieneness and her eyes fluttered and opened. She saw him, a startled cry escaped her, and she tried pulling away from him. He laid her down and took hold of her hand.

"It's all right. You're away from Aubrey, safe." Janis glanced around, her eyes stopping on Will.

"Where are we?"

"In a motel in Tennessee. Your sister told me she would guide us to her. Can she do that?"

"Of course. When did you talk to her?"

"Earlier today at your home. I had Aubrey bring you there so I could get you away from him." She gave him a puzzled look.

"Why are you doing this?" Will wasn't certain he could answer her.

"I don't like seeing innocent people hurt." She kept her eyes on him but didn't try taking her hand from his. She sensed something much deeper in him.

"That's pretty vague." That made him uncomfortable. He hadn't intended to have a face off with Aubrey over her, but it had come to that. He could only go with her and hope to find the answers Aubrey wanted. He shrugged.

"Damned if I really know," he said, shaking his head. "Getting to your sister is the problem. Have you any idea where we're going?" She felt safe – comfortable – with Will.

"Call me Janis. I didn't think you knew why you're helping us." He frowned, knowing she was reading him like a book.

"Where the hell are we going, Janis?" As she watched him, she began to feel why Ophelia trusted him. He got an impatient frown.

"Why are we headed for New Orleans?" She got a wan smile.

"That's where we must go." Will's tension broke and he smiled.

"Where do we go once there?"

"Ophelia hasn't told me yet."

"She hasn't told you?" Will was surprised at the answer.

"Being identical twins gives us a close telepathic bond." He got a baffled look.

"I know you're twins, but I didn't know about any telepathic bond."

"How do you suppose Mr. Blaine intended using me to find my sister? He knew I had no idea where she was, but knew I could use my telepathic link to find her." That was something Aubrey hadn't mentioned.

"I had no idea he knew about such things." She took her hand from his and sat up.

"Mr. Blaine destroyed the Soviet's research on telepathic communications between twins."

"I've worked with him for five years and never heard anything about that."

"You know he's going to try and catch us once we get to Ophelia, don't you?" Will knew, and nodded.

"Yeah. Maybe we'll find out tomorrow." She patted the bed beside her.

"Then we better rest, Will."

Finding nothing at the farmhouse, Aubrey put out the word to local law enforcement to look for the Chevy. Hours passed with no word from Will. Aubrey believed the junkyard man had sent him in the opposite direction Will had gone. He sent a man back to check businesses around the junkyard and see if he could learn anything.

He reported to Aubrey there had been no Chevy, but a green '53 Ford heading south. Aubrey sent out the change in car description and decided to concentrate his search to the south. He felt he would have Will, Miss Randall, and her sister in his hands before another day was over.

It was almost dawn, and there had been no report indicating what direction Will was moving. Aubrey was impatient with inaction and it irritated him. He put down his coffee and went to a map of the southeast and scrutinized it, moving a finger south from Washington. Will could be anywhere. Where would he go if he were looking for a safety pocket that had connections with UFOS? The Bermuda Triangle? Aubrey shook his head. There had been no indication that Will was heading toward the Atlantic Coast. An idea popped into his mind. What if the safety pocket also had some connection with ancient gods? That took his mind to the Yucatan Peninsula. The ancient ruins would be perfect for concealing a base. Hell! Aubrey thought. They might have a weapon under construction there. Aubrey was now certain Will and the woman were heading for New Orleans. No telling what sort of story she had given Will, and he was privileged to classified material. They had to be prevented from leaving the country.

Aubrey quickly issued orders to concentrate the search south to New Orleans. It dawned on him, that in Will, he was dealing with a person who was his intellectual equal. Aubrey smiled.

"He has one flaw," he said, aloud, to himself. "He's got a fucking conscience and I can bust his ass with that."

THREE

Ophelia Randall looked up at the jungle growth on the temple. Her friends had given her swift transport here so she could bring Janis to safety. She was aware the asfa'lia tse'pi lay within this temple. It had been here millennia and she had to find the way to it. Her friends didn't know exactly where it was. She was apprehensive knowing there was only one way she was going to find it. She would have to enter this foreboding structure and search for it.

She had the special light and high potency food supplement tablets given to her by the friends. Going into the dark temple was something she had been told she alone could do. The longer she looked at it, the more hesitant she became. She wasn't certain why none of the friends had come with her, and they hadn't told her why. They had given her a vague explanation as to why she could enter the temple and they couldn't. Ophelia felt what she had been told was inadequate for her understanding. Looking at the structure, she knew she had no alternative but to go in.

She inhaled deeply, plucked up her courage, and began climbing the weed-covered steps. It was precarious, and she had to grab vines and pull herself up the slippery surface. After some minutes, she stood at the top looking into the black square that was the entrance. She didn't feel confident about entering that dark domain, but knew she had come too far to turn back now. People like Blaine had to be stopped before they ruined everything. He had already ruined the attempt to understand how twins could communicate telepathically. With that in mind, Ophelia turned on the light and its intense beam stabbed into the dark interior and moved it over walls covered with symbols. They meant nothing to her, and had been told they were unknown to the friends. She came to a passageway leading to the left and Ophelia stepped into the dark unknown.

Will and Janis were on the road shortly after dawn heading southwest through Tennessee.

"Where do we go in New Orleans?" Will asked.

"We need a boat to head into the Gulf. I'll know which way to go once we're at sea." He glanced at her with a worried expression.

"We have to get rid of this car, Janis. Aubrey probably knows about it by now." She gave him a quizzical look.

"How could he possibly know?" Will got an annoyed frown.

"He isn't stupid, and he knows me. That works against us unless I start thinking differently, which I don't think is possible." She was silent for a moment.

"Can't we rent one?" Will shook his head.

"It can be easily discovered and traced."

"What if I rented it, Will?" He glanced at her. It was a long shot, but Aubrey would be expecting him to do everything. If Janis rented a car it would buy them time.

"That could give us an edge," he said. "It would be something Aubrey wouldn't expect. What sort of ID do you have?" She reached into the pocket of her dress and took out a small wallet.

"Driver's license. I never carry a purse that can be stolen."

In Nashville, they had breakfast and Janis rented a car. Will drove to the airport parking lot and left the Ford. Sadly, he patted its fender knowing he was going to miss this car, but it would remain here for days before anyone checked on it. Janis pulled to a stop and he climbed into the silver-gray Cougar and they headed out of town.

Either they hadn't been recognized by any local police or Aubrey was holding them back. Will knew the latter to be a dream.

"Couldn't we head for Mobile and get a boat there?" Will asked. Janis shook her head.

"We've got to sail over open water, and don't want to increase the distance. We have to leave from New Orleans."

"I'm a pilot. We could rent a plane and fly there." She looked at him with a cocked eyebrow and disbelieving look.

"How long until Blaine knew we were flying?" He frowned, realizing how dumb that idea was.

"It is a bad idea." She glanced at him with a slight smile.

"We still have to reach our destination, Will." He had already worked out how to do that.

"We've got to keep to backroads as much as possible. The Interstate will have local and state police watching for us."

"Won't they cover the backroads too?" He shrugged.

"Probably. But not as carefully as the Interstate. Keep an eye out for police cars."

"I have been. I know Blaine wants us both." She got a troubled look.

"I don't want to be in his company again. Those drugs weren't a pleasant experience." As she finished speaking, a highway patrol passed going in the opposite direction but didn't slow down. Will wondered if Aubrey had guessed wrong about the direction they were traveling. The highway patrolman who passed might have been ordered only to report. But report what? The car they were driving, or the Ford? A man and woman traveling together? Will knew Aubrey would have them all covered and couldn't risk it.

"Turn onto the next road, Janis."

"Why?"

"That patrolman might have reported a man and woman in this car, and we can't take the chance he didn't. Turning onto the road is a precaution."

"What are you concerned about, Will?" He considered that for a moment.

"If he got the license number, it won't be long before Aubrey knows where we are."

"How?"

"He probably knows our direction of travel, and won't pass up any report that could lead him to us." The next road was a few miles on and Janis turned onto it heading south.

Aubrey didn't learn of the rental until late afternoon, and was furious the information had taken so long to reach him.

"Why the hell wasn't I notified earlier?" he roared, at the man who brought the information.

"It took time to check the plate number, sir. It was then traced to a rental company in Nashville." Aubrey knew his people weren't responsible; that it had been bungled at state level.

"What way were they going?" Aubrey asked, in a calm tone.

"Southwest, sir. The patrolman thought they might be headed for Memphis and alerted his HQ." Aubrey made his decision.

"Alert the Tennessee, Mississippi, and Louisiana authorities to watch for them. I want a plane and three teams. I've an idea they're headed for New Orleans." The man got a confused look.

"Why, sir?" Aubrey glared at him.

"If I knew that, I would know where to be waiting for them. As it is, we can hope to apprehend them before they leave that city." The man nodded.

"Yes, sir. I'll take care of it." Aubrey lifted a pen and pointed it at him like a weapon.

"When you speak with the state authorities, tell them it's vital there be no more delays in reporting to me when they've been sighted. Make it damned clear I don't want any of their people trying to stop them. That would really fuck things up."

"Yes, sir." He hurried from the office. Aubrey wondered how Will had thought to trick them into backtracking to the farmhouse. Reluctantly, Aubrey admitted it had been a smart move and had bought them time. But what was in New Orleans? How are they planning on leaving there? He knew Will wouldn't take a plane. They could drive – if their destination was in the country. He concluded they planned to leave by boat and go to wherever the hell they're going, he thought.

"And I think I know what that destination is," he mumbled, hoping he was right. There were so many places in New Orleans where they could get a boat! It would be impossible to cover them all. Aubrey had to start thinking from Will's perspective, if he was to have any chance of getting them.

Spiders! They frightened Ophelia more than anything did. Touching webs with her bare skin was almost too much for her. Yet she kept moving resolutely into the dark temple. The passageway looked the same as when she turned into it. If there was anyway leading deeper into this place it was cleverly hidden.

Ophelia abruptly stopped when she stepped into a section where there were no more spiders and clinging vines.
The hairs on the back of her neck began to stir and a prickling rode up her spine. She turned the light around her. Everything looked the same, except for the absence of spiders and vines, but she felt she wasn't alone. She turned the light back in front of her into the unending passageway. She was surrounded by rock, leaving no place for anyone to hide. But she felt certain she wasn't alone.

The only thing she could do was go on. She didn't consider going back because she didn't want to go through that nest of spiders again.

What lay ahead couldn't possibly be worse than those spiders, she thought. Walking along, she wondered how the passageway could be so long. The top of the temple hadn't been anywhere close to the distance she had came. She halted and pictured the temple as she had seen it from outside and turned the light to the floor. She saw she had been moving down a gradual slope. How much farther can it go on? she wondered. With her next step, the floor gave way under Ophelia's feet.

By taking the road south, they quickly crossed into Mississippi.

"Head for Vicksburg, Janis. We can make it to New Orleans by tonight but we've got to get another car. We can't take the chance Aubrey doesn't know about this one."

"Are we going to rent another one?"

"No. When we get to Vicksburg, stop at the first used car lot you see. Buying one will give us the time we need." Janis blinked and shook her head. Will noticed.

"What's wrong?" She glanced at him with a puzzled expression.

"I don't know, Will. I keep thinking of the names Rogen and Penguin. I'm not certain what they mean." Will recalled Ophelia's words, so the names could mean only one thing.

"I believe you've gotten the name of a marina and boat." She glanced at him with a frown.

"How can you know that?"

"Your sister would have set up a way for us to leave New Orleans." It made sense and she nodded.

"Then we look for the Rogen Marina and a boat named Penguin. He patted her shoulder.

"It's the only thing we have to go on. Let's hope we can get to the marina before Aubrey finds us."

They wasted no time buying a car and getting carryout food. They ate as they went on. Will was driving and found it distracting to watch every car coming toward them. The road they were on didn't have the heavy traffic of the Interstate, but was consuming time slowing at every car that looked like a police car.

The closer they got to New Orleans, the safer they felt, but Will had an apprehension he kept to himself. He couldn't be certain Aubrey hadn't already figured out their destination and was waiting for them. That makes no sense, he thought. They didn't know where they were going in the city, so there was no way for Aubrey to know.

"Let's stop for coffee," Will said. "You want anything else?"

"Coffee will do," Janis replied. He pulled in at the first convience store they came to. While he was getting the coffee, Will heard the TV blaring out the news that was definitely not good for them. He paid for the coffee and hurried back to the car. When he got in, Janis sensed he was apprehensive.

"What is it, Will?" He inhaled deeply as he looked at her.

"There's a tropical storm in the Gulf. I just heard a report that it's expected to become a hurricane and New Orleans will be on the fringe." This wasn't something she wanted to hear, but storm or no storm, knew they had to go on.

"Maybe we'll be able to go around the storm," she said. He got a grim look.

"If it becomes a hurricane there won't be anyway around it." She looked frustrated.

"What do you suggest we do, Will?" He felt helpless and shook his head.

"We've got to risk it, Janis. We've got to get into and out of New Orleans as quickly as possible. We can't afford to fall into Aubrey's hands now." She stared at him with wide eyes. He took hold of her hands in what he hoped was a reassuring gesture.

"We don't have a choice, Janis." He felt her relax and saw her exhale. She had thought he might suggest they hold up somewhere until the storm had passed.

"I agree, Will." He started the car and pulled back on the road.

There had been no further reports of Will and Janis, and it made Aubrey impatient for a solid lead to their whereabouts. Will should have contacted him by now, but felt he might not have had the chance knowing local authorities would be looking for them.
He believed they were coming to New Orleans, and the storm would give him time to locate them. He still hadn't a clue as to where they would go in the city, and that bothered him. Aubrey was sure what Will would do.

His biggest uncertainty was where they would get a boat. He felt they had gotten rid of the rental and were in a different car.

He had to figure out which route they would use into New Orleans. That might be his only chance before they became lost in the city. Will wasn't one to be trapped easily as he had an uncanny instinct for danger. Aubrey had trained him and knew how he thought, but Will had surprised him.

Knowing Will was his greatest asset; he had to know how to use that to his advantage. But there was no easy answer.

Crist came in.

"Still no news, sir." Aubrey had hoped to hear something different. Had Will used another surprise? He nodded to Crist.

"Get a map of New Orleans showing all, and I do mean all, roads leading into the city."

"Yes, sir." If Will was coming in on a backroad, maybe he could be surprised. Aubrey decided to have highway patrol cars along the roads. He wanted no local officers to interfere with them, just report their location. He knew, when asked for help, locals got an ego boost and itched to get into the act. That they were to watch only had to be made explicit.

Crist returned with a map and spread it out on the desk. Aubrey looked it over and glanced at Crist.

"This is the most up to date?"

"Yes, sir." Aubrey pointed to the thin blue lines.

"I want patrol cars concealed along these roads. They're to report only. Make that damn clear."

"Yes, sir." Aubrey went to the window and looked out as rain began to fall. He glanced over his shoulder.

"Make certain they understand I don't want any interference from the good old boys, Crist. Will should be arriving anytime."

"Yes, sir." All Aubrey could do was wait. He began to suspect something more than Will's conscience was compelling him to protect the woman. She certainly was attractive. No! There had to be more to it than that. Aubrey became annoyed at speculating. Yet he couldn't understand Will's motivation.

Opehlia wasn't falling but sliding through a metal tube. She kept twisting and couldn't turn the light on anything.

Then she slammed against the floor, the light flying from her hand and spinning away. The impact had knocked the wind out of her and she lay stunned.

She began crawling toward the light, smarting from the impact. She didn't think she had broken any bones as she reached the light, picked it up and rolled onto her back.

She moved the light around a metal room stopping it on a door. She got to her feet and went to it looking it over. It looked like a hatch in a submarine, having a wheel in its center. She ran her fingers over its smooth, cold surface.

Could this be the way to the asfa'lia tse'pi? She wondered. There was only one way to find out.

She sat the light on the floor, gripped the wheel with both hands and tried turning it to the right. It didn't budge. She tried turning it to the left with the same results. She picked up the light and began moving it over the wall looking for any mechanism. She covered the wall surrounding the door and quickly moved it over adjacent walls. Turning it to the ceiling, she saw no indication of where she had fallen through.

She turned back to the door knowing there had to be a way of opening it, but she didn't know what to look for. Bewildered, and growing frightened at being in a sealed room, she moved the light over the wheel and saw the glint of something on top of the axle. That might be what she was looking for and had to figure out how to manipulate the switch. She took a deep breath and pressed her finger against the yellow switch.

FOUR

Janis turned a surprised look on Will as he made a sudden turn. "What are you doing, Will?" He replied without looking at her. "Taking the Interstate."

"Any particular reason?"

"A better chance to avoid detection. If Aubrey is in New Orleans – and I believe he is – he'll have the backroads covered." He looked at Janis and smiled.

"He won't be expecting us to come this way." She got a slight smile and accepted his reason. There wasn't anything she could do since he seemed to know how to get them to the boat. He glanced at her.

"Do you have another way?" She shook her head.

"I'm trusting you to get us to Ophelia. And you certainly seem to know how to do that." He gave her a surprised look.

"I still have to get past Aubrey, and that's not going to be easy. I'm hoping we can get to the boat and be gone before he learns we're in the city."

"How can he know we're here?"

"He knows we can't fly without him finding out. If we keep driving, he's bound to catch up with us. He knows we need a boat to get away from New Orleans."

"He can't know where the boat is, Will. We're not even sure of that."

"I'm not taking anything for granted. When we get on the Interstate, we could pick up an unmarked police car and wouldn't be any wiser until we found ourselves surrounded." Janis turned and looked out the rear window. Will nodded, pleased.

"If I change lanes and a car behind us changes lanes to keep behind us, let me know."

They slipped into traffic on the Interstate. A sharp-eyed state trooper saw their faces in the glow of the sunset and checked the photos. He reported that he had located them. He was told to follow, but maintain a distance so he couldn't be spotted.
This was fine with the trooper, as he had no idea why these two were wanted. He just wanted a crack at arresting them.

Will hadn't expected to be seen so quickly and had no idea they had been targeted. His attention was focused on the traffic, which was heavy, and relied on Janis to keep watch. He changed lanes when he could, but Janis wasn't sure any car behind did the same. She wasn't used to watching for police cars and failed to see the highway patrol car four cars behind them. Rain began falling making Will all too aware of the storm in the Gulf.

When Aubrey got the report, he quickly swung into action. He looked at Moore and ordered the thought foremost in his mind.

"Make certain the local cops know their orders." Moore nodded.

"They've all been told to follow and report only, sir." Aubrey had a less than confident expression as he pushed the chair from the desk and stood.

"Will got fooled trying to throw us off track. Make certain a team can block any cowboy who thinks he can get a high profile out of this collar."

"All teams have been alerted, sir." Aubrey looked at the map.

"Let's see where Will's going."

Reports of Will's location were coming in every few minutes. He hadn't yet turned into the city, and this began to worry Aubrey. Half an hour after the first report, Aubrey was informed Will had left the Interstate. The patrolman, who had made the initial report, was still with them, but coming into the city made it harder to remain indistinguishable. Will pulled over to a pay phone and pulled the phone book in the car. The patrolman pulled over and turned off his lights, feeling they were unaware they were being followed. He saw Will replace the phone book and pull back into traffic. He turned his lights and windshield wipers on and let two cars pass him.

Janis was anxious and glanced at Will.

"I can't tell if we're being followed, Will. All the headlights look the same through the rain."

"It doesn't matter. We're going straight to Rogen's Marina. When we get there, you locate and get on the boat. I'll join you after I drive around the block to see if we've been followed."

"But if someone is –" He glanced at her and shook his head.

"Don't worry. Just get on the boat and get the motor running. We may have to make a quick exit." Janis wasn't sure but knew what had to be done when she got to the boat.

"Where are they now?" Aubrey asked.

"Along the waterfront, sir," Moore replied. Aubrey nodded.

"I want two teams a quarter of a mile ahead of them. We'll come in behind them with the other team. Tell the locals to break off."

"Yes, sir," Moore said. He left Aubrey alone and puzzled as to why Will had stopped to look at a phone book. Maybe he's doing exactly what he said he would do; find the other sister. Was it possible Will was sending a message by boldly coming in on the Interstate? For a moment, he considered calling off the teams, but then thought Will had no way to contact him. Maybe he was letting Aubrey know he had gained the woman's trust and was carrying out his mission. Aubrey decided to give Will the leeway he needed to lead them to the sister.

The patrolman wasn't about to break off now. They still didn't know he was behind them and reported where he thought they were going. He continued to follow them, knowing this was too good an opportunity to pass up.

"We're almost there, Janis. I'll stop and let you out, drive around the block, and make my way to the boat." She gripped his arm and he saw her anxiety.

"I don't want to be left alone." This was unexpected. He put his hand over hers.

"I'll only be a few minutes. You find the boat and get it ready to go." She took her hand from him with a hesitant look.

"All right, but hurry." He smiled and nodded.

"There's the marina. This heavy rain should give us some cover." Will pulled the car to a stop and she was quickly out moving along the pier. He pulled away and drove to the intersection where he made a left turn.

The patrolman missed Janis' exit from the car. As his attention was too focused. He saw Will make the turn and accelerated so he wouldn't miss seeing another turn, but he made the turn fast, and Will became aware of him.

Will made a sharp turn into an alley pulling the car against a building. He piled out and headed back toward the marina.

Glancing over his shoulder, he saw the patrol car setting behind his and quickened his pace keeping to the shadows until he emerged on the street. Will hurried to the pier and saw Janis waving from a boat. The rain became heavier as he heard rapid footsteps behind him and ran for the boat.

The patrolman stopped his car, jumped out drawing his sidearm, and fired twice. One of the bullets caught Will in the lower right side and he fell beside the boat. As the trooper started after him, Janis desperately pulled Will onto the boat, threw off the ropes, and pushed the throttle forward. Foam spewed from the boat's stern as it raced into a night filling with wind. The patrolman stood silently swearing as he watched the boat head for the open sea. He also saw bright flashes far out to sea he thought was lightning.

Ophelia hesitated before pressing the yellow switch, wondering what she would find beyond the door. She pressed it, and turned the wheel so fast she was thrown off balance and almost fell. She flattened her hand against the wall and looked at the open door for minute. It was just as dark on the other side of the door. She picked up the light and turned its beam through the door. She could make out vague shapes and hoped there weren't any spiders out there.

Aubrey was enraged when heard the patrolman had shot Will.

"What did the stupid son of a bitch think he was doing?" Aubrey shouted.

"He believed he was in pursuit of a felon, sir," Crist replied. "He was trying to prevent his escape." Aubrey glared at Crist.

"Where the hell did he get that idea?"

"It was a matter of his not knowing who he was following, or why, sir." Aubrey was silent for a moment.

"Was he informed to break off?" Aubrey asked, in a calmer tone.

"Twice, sir." Moore came rushing into the room.

"There's more bad news, sir," Moore said. Aubrey turned a frustrated look to him.

"What the hell else can go wrong?" Aubrey asked.

"The storm has been upgraded to a hurricane, sir," Moore replied. "The boat Will and the woman was on is heading straight into it." Aubrey slowly sat down.

"Get the radio frequency of that boat," Aubrey said. "Contact the Coast Guard and see if they can get a ship or helicopter out." Moore shook his head with a glum look.

"I already have, sir," Moore said. "They can't do a thing without knowing the boat's position."

"Goddamnit!" Aubrey said, slamming his hand on the desk. "Will's wounded and heading into a hurricane. Didn't he know about the storm?"

"I think he knew, sir," Crist said, grimly. "He didn't let it stop him."

Will was just beginning to feel the pain. It cleared his mind enough to realize they were heading into a dangerous storm. He saw Janis fighting the wheel and got to his feet. It was clear this was her first time driving a boat. With the sea becoming rougher, her task was becoming more difficult. He stepped under the covering tarp and put his hand on her shoulder as he pressed the other against his wound.

"Go below and get the first aid kit. I need a band aid." When she turned, her hand brushed against his side and he almost doubled in over in pain. She looked at her hand and saw it was covered with blood. She looked at him as she brushed rain from her eyes.

"You're hurt bad. Can you make the boat run itself? You have to come below and have that wound tended to." He wiped rain from his face and looked over the dimly lit instrument panel. He found the autopilot, switched it on, and fell against the wheel. Janis stepped beside him and pulled his arm around her neck. She slipped her arm around his waist and slowly walked him to the hatch. Both were soaked and getting pelted with rain from rising wind. Janis' only thought was to tend his wound.

"You would be unlucky enough to get shot. I'll see what I can do for you." In the cabin, she helped him down on a bunk and he fell on his back with a painful moan. Janis went to the bathroom, grabbed a towel and began wiping rain from her face. She got the first aid kit and returned to the bunk. She wiped the water from his face and opened the kit. She pulled his jacket open and saw the sticky bloodstained shirt clinging to the hole in his side.

Janis unbuttoned his shirt and pulled it away from the wound. She saw she would have to clean it before she could tell how serious it was. She used the wet towel to clean the blood from the wound.

"How big is the hole, Janis?" She turned an alarmed expression on him.

"I could stick my thumb in it." Will nodded and looked relieved.

"Good." Her eyes widened at his calmly spoken word.

"What's so good about it?"

"It's only a flesh wound. It feels a hell of a lot worse than it looks." The boat rolled hard throwing her on top of him. She found her face next to Will's and kissed him. When she took her lips from his, Janis wanted him to make love to her. He smiled weakly.

"We've got to keep the boat from sinking, Janis. Bandage me so I can get back up on deck."

As he pulled himself up on deck, the wind almost pushed him back. He turned his head and shouted.

"Get on the radio and find out about this storm and be ready to send a mayday." He staggered, trying to keep his balance on the pitching deck. He made it to the wheel with rain stinging his face. Waves, much taller than the mast, crashed over the deck almost washing him overboard. He turned off the autopilot and took the wheel, turning the boat into the wind. It seemed to stabilize the boat, but holding it steady was causing him pain. Will persevered until Janis came on deck and staggered to his side. She put her face close to his ear and shouted to be heard above the wind.

"I couldn't get anything on the radio, Will. What can we do?" His mind clouded for a moment then regained clarity. He leaned close to her.

"The force of the wind is whipping up waves that could break this boat up. We've got to be ready to abandon ship." She gave him an anxious look.

"What do you want me to do?" She had taken hold of his arm for balance. He was about to tell her to stay below but thought better of it.

"Stay with me. If we have to go in the water it will be better to do so together." The wind and waves intensified, one wave almost turning the Penguin on her side. Will wasn't certain how he had been able to keep the boat upright. A massive wave crashed down drenching them and snapping off the mast.

Janis held desperately to Will, fearful of being washed overboard. The waves were filling the boat with water as Will looked at Janis and shouted.

"Put on a life jacket." Janis was shivering as she pulled the life jacket around her and fastened it tightly.
She helped Will get his on and grabbed his arm as a wave came crashing down, knocking them off their feet and carrying them over the side. They lost sight of the boat in the rain and darkness as they fought to keep afloat in a world filled by assaulting waves.
The salt water quickly had Will's wound feeling like it was on fire, and he fought to stay conscious. Janis felt the spasms his pain was causing and held him upright.

"Hold onto me, Will. I think I can keep us afloat if you pass out." It was the last thing he heard before unconsciousness overtook him.

Ophelia cautiously stepped through the door. This place must be huge, she thought. The light showed a wide corridor and the only way she could go. The urge to step back through the door became tempting. She heard a whirring sound and saw a pale blue light coming toward her. Ophelia wanted to run, but waited.

A little cart came to a stop in the cone of light. It was the size of a child's wagon, and she smiled as she looked at it.

"What am I supposed to do with you?" The cart turned making it clear it wanted her to follow. She wasn't too certain, but had no place else to go. She kept it in sight as she trailed behind it.

"You're the guide. Show me around this place." The cart moved and Ophelia followed until it made an abrupt ninety-degree turn and stopped. She raised the light and found she stood before a door identical to the first one. She checked for a switch but found none. She set the light down and gripped the wheel. It turned easily and she pushed it open and looked into a dark room.

She retrieved the light and stepped into an immense room filled with panels and gauges. While Ophelia looked around, the cart moved away giving her a feeling of loneliness. She turned her attention to how this place had been lit. She stepped to the nearest panel and moved the light over it stopping on an odd looking switch. She moved the light over other panels, but this was the only one with the odd switch. Ophelia put her thumb against the plastic handle and slid it to the right.

The room filled with light, and there had been no flickering. Ophelia couldn't determine where the light came from as it seemed to be overhead and in the walls. The place seemed made of stainless steel, shiny, flawless, and surrounding her.

She wondered what she should do as she turned off the light in her hand. She walked around touching the cover of the gauges and marveling at their perfection.

Ophelia stopped before a screen on the wall. Beneath it was a dial that had graduated lines on a green disc but nothing to align it with. She turned the dial and the screen filled with colliding colors that began forming a shape. An attractive woman appeared with auburn hair and eyes a shade of gray Ophelia had never seen before. The woman regarded her with a serious expression.

"Welcome to Earth Complex," she said, in a smooth voice, and bowed her head. "I've been waiting for the descendant of Athena to appear and let us know she has returned to the company of the gods."

FIVE

Aubrey turned from the window the rain was pelting. It had become so heavy it was hard to see the lights along the street. Crist came in with a somber expression. Aubrey turned to him.

"Any news about Will and Miss Randall?" Crist shook his head.

"I talked with a Coast Guard meteorologist, sir. If the boat held the same heading as when it left the dock, she ran headlong into the hurricane. The patrolman said the woman didn't seem familiar with handling a boat." This wasn't unexpected to Aubrey, but disappointing.

"When will the search begin?"

"As soon as the storm tracks to the west, sir. About eight hours." An impatient expression washed over Aubrey's face, as he knew he could do little.

"Why can't they try now?"

"Winds have been reported at over 135 mph, sir. The waves are such as to swamp anything sailing or battering it to pieces." Aubrey's shoulders slumped and he rubbed his eyes. It seemed Miss Randall and Will may be dead, especially since he had been wounded and had no medical help. There wasn't much of a case for their survival, Aubrey thought. All they could do was hope their bodies would wash up somewhere in a condition to be identified. He looked at Crist.

"Where's the storm tracking?"

"Southwest, sir. It should brush the Yucatan sometime tomorrow." Aubrey cocked an eyebrow finding that interesting, and giving him some small hope.

"I want a plane standing by to fly us and another team to Mexico City when the weather permits, Crist."

Janis had no idea how long they had been in the water. She was numb from the waves crashing over them. They had a close call when a wave almost dropped the boat's mast on them. Janis had been thankful for something solid to hold onto. She took a rope from the mast and tied it around Will and herself and lashed them to the mast. Her mind was foggy and it seemed as if this night would never end.

Completely exhausted, Janis knew she couldn't remain conscious much longer. She became aware of a bright blue glow beneath them. It was deep and she didn't connect it to their plight.

She hadn't long to consider it for the darkness of unconsciousness was flooding her mind.

The next thing Janis was cognizant of was she and Will, still tied to the mast, were lying on a beach. The storm hadn't abated, but it felt reassuring to be on land. Rain was drenching them and the wind pressed her against the sand. She felt strength flow through her, and reached over and pressed her fingers to his throat. Feeling a weak pulse, Janis knew she had to find help for Will before it was too late.

She untied herself, rolled over and untied Will. She wasn't certain she could lift him to drag into the jungle. The jungle would provide some shelter against the rain, she thought. The force of the wind made her more uncertain, but determined her not to let him die. She had to get them off the beach before she could go for help. Slowly, she struggled to her feet against the force of the wind and shed the life jacket. Janis could only stand with difficulty on weak legs and dropped to her knees. She pulled the rope from Will, rolled him on his bank, and loosened the life jacket. His breathing was shallow, but it was the look of the wound that caused her anxiety.

A wave washed them further up the beach and had Janis coughing and spitting water, but the wave had helped her. She took his arm and slipped it around her neck and struggled to get him up, but the wind almost knocked her over. This brought Will to consciousness and he was able to give her some help getting them into the jungle. Fronds lashed at them causing painful stings, until Janis moved them into a close crop of trees where they collapsed. It wasn't much shelter against the rain, but they were less assailed by the wind and not beaten by leaves. Janis lay down beside Will and wiped rain from her face. She looked at an ashen face that was beginning to tremble. She had to get help! But had no idea where to go. She rolled against him so she could be heard over the roar of the wind.

"Can you hear me, Will?" She saw no reaction to her question.

"I'm going to try and find help. I'll be back as soon as I can." He slowly opened glazed eyes and looked at her. She kissed him, stood and started making her way through the dense foliage. She lifted her arms to protect her face against the slapping leaves as she started an aimless trek into the jungle.

Ophelia stared at the image of the woman on the screen.

"What do you mean?" The woman bowed her head again, and Ophelia wondered if it was a form of greeting.

"I will clarify. You are a descendant of one called Athena by the ancient Earth people. The ones referred to as gods are returning to your planet. They mean no harm, only to check on their experiment." Ophelia was puzzled.

"What's that got to do with me?" The woman showed a flash of impatience.

"There is one among your people who is a direct descendant of Zeus. Zeus expects the two of you to assure his visit is a peaceful one. He trusts you to prevent the people of Earth from attacking when we land.." Ophelia wasn't certain what she could do as she had no idea who Zeus' descendant was, or even how to locate the person. Right now, she needed Janis. She was the one with the logical mind, and would know what needed to be done. But where was Janis? Ophelia hadn't been able to sense her sister's thoughts for some time. Had she and Will been killed? Ophelia closed her eyes and opened her mind and sensed Janis was nearby. She looked back at the woman.

"Can you help me locate my sister? I sense she's very close."

"I will guide her here, but you must go out and bring her in." Ophelia frowned.

"How do I get out of here?"

"The guide will show you the way." As the image faded, Ophelia heard a familiar whirring sound and turned to see the cart come to a stop. Its blue light was flashing rapidly as it turned and headed down the now bright corridor. Ophelia followed.

Aubrey wasn't pleased at the route the plane had to take because of the hurricane. Not only that, he was still waiting for the State Department to get him a clearance to land in Mexico. He was anxious to search for Will but had no clue as to where to start. As the plane flew north, before turning southwest, Aubrey was beginning to suspect the hurricane might not have been a coincidence. The sisters may have had their friends cause it to cover Will and Miss Randall's escape. If that were true, what Will had said about their technology was even more true. Earth had no defense against them. That idea haunted Aubrey.

"We have clearance to land in Mexico City, sir," Moore said, coming into the cabin. "Anything you need will be provided through the embassy." About time I got a fucking break! Aubrey thought.

"Contact the embassy and have two ATVs and someone who knows the Yucatan standing by. I want to move as soon as possible after we land."

"Yes, sir," Moore said, and went back to the cockpit. Aubrey would begin his search along the coast. Crist came in with a glum look.

"What is it?"

"The boat's been located, sir. It was driven onto a beach at Galveston. Its mast was gone and there was no one on board. Will and the woman must have been washed overboard." Aubrey frowned as he inhaled. This wasn't going to make finding their bodies any easier – if they were dead. If they were alive where were they? Floating at sea? Or had they been washed up on a beach? For the first time Aubrey could remember, he had no idea where to begin. The coast of Yucatan would take days to search. He needed some point he could focus on. He rubbed his chin as he regarded Crist.

"I want a plot of the course of that boat from the time it left New Orleans. I want a projection of it through the storm, and if it came anywhere near Yucatan. Have it run through the computer at Langley as soon as possible." Aubrey faced the impossibility of the task and shook his head.

"We've got to have a point to begin the search." Crist nodded.

"I'll see to it right away, sir."

Janis' arms were covered with red welts from striking leaves as she moved among the trees, holding on to keep from being pushed by the wind. She wiped rain from her face and looked around. It seemed the same everywhere, but felt certain she was going in the right direction. She realized she might not be able to find her way back to Will. She was lost! Even if this was the correct direction, she had no way of knowing how far help was. Janis felt helpless against the jungle, but began to sense Ophelia nearby. Janis thought about Will and a reassuring thought came to her. She slumped against a tree and slid to a sitting position to await her sister.

It was a few minutes before the cart came to a stop in front of Janis. She was so weak Ophelia had to help her to her feet.

They wiped the rain from their faces, as they stood shielded by a large tree. Janis leaned close to Ophelia.

"We have to find Will. I don't know the way back to him." Ophelia looked down at the cart and it blinked its light. That told her it could lead them to Will.

"We'll follow our little friend, Janis. It will take us to him. How is he?"

"He was shot before we got away. His condition isn't good. He's going to die if he doesn't get medical help soon." Ophelia took hold of Janis' arm to support her as they stepped back into the wind and stinging leaves. The cart moved through the jungle, the women following as fast as possible.

Janis was surprised to find she hadn't gone far from him. As she wiped rain from her face, she knelt beside Will. Ophelia dropped beside her and checked his pulse, looking at Janis with an alarmed expression.

"He's almost dead," Ophelia said. "We've got to get him inside if we're to help him." Each woman took one of his arms and lifted him from the ground and followed the cart back to the complex. The wind pushed them, and that made it easier to bare his weight as Will hung limply between them.

They moved along the corridor glad to be sheltered from the wind and rain. They took him into the room Ophelia had been in and put him down. Janis sat down beside him as the image of the woman appeared on the screen.

"What can we do to help this man?" Ophelia asked. The woman looked down from the screen at the soaked, unmoving Will. She stared with widening eyes and looked back at Ophelia.

"Please stand away from him," she said. Ophelia helped Janis to her feet and they stepped away from Will. A pale yellow glow covered the screen and projected down to envelope Will.

"Is he alive?" Janis asked. Ophelia hadn't thought to check his pulse. She assumed the image of the woman was a computer-generated image.

"I'm not certain," her voice, said from the glow.

The glow was a soothing balm to Will, erasing pain and restoring energy. He was beginning to feel alive again. The glow began to retreat to the screen and vanished. Will opened his eyes and looked from the screen to the sisters.

"He'll be fine now," the woman said, from the screen. "His wound is healed and his lifeforce restored." Ophelia stepped before the screen.

"Are you a real person?" Ophelia asked. Janis went to Will and lifted his head so it rested on her arm. He smiled thinking this was a delusion and he would wake up and find them back in the storm tossed sea.

"Of course I'm real," the woman replied, indignantly. "This is a transmission from a ship on its way to Earth. What did you think I was?" Ophelia was embarrassed, but relieved to be speaking to a real person and not a machine.

"I thought you might be a computer image," Ophelia replied.

"We thank you for restoring our friend," Janis said. "Who are you?"

"I am Raeta. What are your names?"

"I'm Ophelia Randall and this is my sister, Janis. The man is Will Vaughn."

"How did you come to this place at this time?" Raeta asked. Ophelia went into some detail about the friends, but the more she said the grimmer Raeta's expression became. Janis noticed.

"Is there something wrong?" Janis asked. There was silence before an answer was forthcoming.

"Those you call friends could be your enemies," Raeta finally replied. "They've used you to gain access to the complex."

"But they wouldn't come here," Ophelia said, wondering if what they had told her was true. Raeta nodded with a deep frown.

"They know they can't enter the complex," Raeta said. "Only our descendants, humans, can enter the complex without being destroyed. I fear we may need the help of the people of Earth. It's possible your friends may be planning on taking over your planet. To do so, they will need many slaves." Ophelia glanced over her shoulder at Will and Janis, alarmed at what she had been told. Janis turned her eyes to the screen.

"What can we do?" Janis asked, and Will looked at her with surprise.

"Remain where you are," Raeta replied.

"We've got to find a way to contact Aubrey," Will said. "He's the only one who can get something done about this.

I feel like a dumbass for not believing what he said about UFOs."
Janis shook her head with a helpless look.

"How can we get in touch with him stuck here in the jungle?"
Ophelia asked. Will got to his feet, with a little help from Janis and
faced Ophelia with a determined look.

"I don't know," Will replied. "I do know he's probably looking for
us and that could make it a lot easier."

"Blaine wanted to use us for his own ends," Ophelia said.

"I don't believe he would have harmed you," Will said. "He just
wanted to find out what you knew about UFOs. He suspected we were
facing an invasion."

"How can the Earthman know that?" Raeta asked. Will shook his
head.

"I'm not certain," he replied. "But he found out somehow." A
fatalistic look came to Raeta.

"Then we, and the three of you, must prepare for the crisis," Raeta
said, grimly. "Our ship won't reach Earth for another seven of your
days."

"Whoa!" Will said. "Just what the hell can we do?" Raeta kept her
eyes on him.

"If the Kraken are coming," Raeta said. "They may not wait for us
to arrive before attacking. You must make all preparations as soon as
possible." Will got an incredulous look.

"We're stuck in a jungle miles from any help," Will said. "What
do you expect us to do?" Will couldn't be certain, but he saw a
twinkle in Raeta's eyes and a smile playing at the corner of her lips.

"You can start by activating the complex you're now in," Raeta
replied. "It was built as a planetary defense complex." Will walked
around looking over the panels and gauges with strange symbols on
them. He stopped in front of the screen.

"We can't read this language," he said.

"That problem is easily solved," Raeta said. All of you step in
front of the screen. I'll transmit neurobits to your minds and you'll
know what must be done to activate the complex."

"Where's the afsa'lia tse'pi?" Janis asked, stepping beside Will.

"You now stand in it," Raeta replied.

Aubrey was with the ambassador, who had just authorized the
release of two ATVs for his use.

The ambassador was a tall, solid built man with brown eyes and dark brown hair. He wore a worried expression.

"Have you any idea how long the search might take, Mr. Blaine?"

"No, Mr. Ambassador. To tell the truth, I don't even know if those people are alive, but I have to search for them. Vaughn is one of my top people." The ambassador nodded.

"You understand I have to give the Mexican government some idea of how long you'll be in Yucatan." Aubrey didn't like time limits but understood the ambassador's situation.

"The hurricane should have moved away by the time we get there, Mr. Ambassador. They could have washed ashore anywhere. I'm trying to get a focal point to start from. Once I have that, it shouldn't take more than a couple of days to find them, dead or alive."

"Merida will be the best place to operate from, Mr. Blaine. But it's a nine hundred mile drive." Aubrey gave a slight nod.

"We won't be driving, Mr. Ambassador. I've hired two heavy lift helicopters to transport the ATVs and search teams to Merida." The ambassador regarded Aubrey with respect.

"I see you plan for every contingency, Mr. Blaine. I hope you find your people alive. Good luck." He extended his hand to Aubrey who firmly gripped it.

"Thank you, Mr. Ambassador. I appreciate the help you've provided."

Aubrey came out of the embassy to the car where Crist and Moore waited.

"Are the helicopters ready?" Aubrey asked.

"Yes, sir," Crist replied. "We can leave as soon as they load the vehicles."

"Then let's get the show on the road. Have you received that projection yet?"

"Yes, sir," Moore replied. "The boat never came anywhere near the Yucatan. It was kept heading north by the storm."

"Goddamnit! Will and Miss Randall had to wash ashore in Yucatan," Aubrey said, hoping against hope Will was still alive. "That's where they were heading, and that's where we'll find them." Crist and Moore exchanged glances beginning to believe their boss was cracking up.

SIX

The weapons system of the complex was awesome and with Raeta's help they were mastered. She informed them where the food stores were and they alone couldn't defend the Earth against the Kraken. The complex also contained a very sophisticated communications center whose technology seemed beyond human capacity to duplicate. The three of them listened to broadcasts from around the world. Yet with all this high tech equipment they could do nothing but wait for seven days.

Will was trying to get a line on Aubrey from broadcasts hoping to locate him and confirm the possibility of an invasion. It puzzled him as to how Aubrey suspected the truth. Something he hadn't given any thought to until Raeta asked. Janis stepped beside him interrupting his thoughts. The only way he could tell Janis from Ophelia had been the clothes they wore, but now they were dressed in khaki jumpsuits. He saw she looked concerned.

"You've been awful quiet since we arrived, Will." He didn't want to voice his concern about Aubrey.

"Guess I'm in shock from being shot and that storm." He gave her a bewildered look.

"I don't know how we survived, Janis." She put her hand over his and regarded him with a somber expression.

"We made it." She pressed against him and he cocked an eyebrow.

"What?" She got a coy smile.

"On the boat, when I kissed you, I knew you wanted what I did." She looked around the communications room stopping them on him.

"We're practically alone and have time on our hands." Will stared at her, unsure what to say. He had a strong feeling to make love to her but realized they had pressing business that had to be dealt with before any personal wants could be considered. He put his hands on her arms and looked into her eyes.

"I've wanted to make love to you from the moment I saw you, but…"

"But first, we have to do what has to be done," she finished, with a frown. He nodded.

"We've got to put our –" She had her arms around him, pressing her lips to his.

She ignited a passion in him that was difficult to control. He responded by pulling her tight against him. When their lips parted, she put her hands on his cheeks and looked at him.

"Still want to wait, Will?" She wasn't making it easy. If she persisted, he had no idea how long he could contain himself. He pulled her into an embrace.

"No, I don't want to wait. But we must. If we get involved now it will affect our performance when we'll need concentration. Instead of focusing on what has to be done, we'll be worrying about each other. She pulled away from him and his hands dropped to her waist. He saw her disappointment.

"I don't want to wait, Will. If something should happen…" He put a finger on her lips.

"It has to be this way, Janis, if we're to have any chance for success."

Ophelia remained out of sight and surprised to hear her sister. She had always shunned advances by men, now she was insisting this one make love to her. Ophelia sensed just how much Janis wanted that. It made Will Vaughn someone special. They parted when they heard her coming. She stopped in front of them.

"Where do you think Blaine is?" Ophelia asked. It wasn't an easy question for Will. His brow furrowed and he frowned.

"Looking for Janis and me," he replied. "He must know we took a boat from New Orleans."

"Where would he have thought we were going?" Janis asked.

"I know him, and he's here in Mexico or on his way. This would be the logical place to search." Janis noted the odd look she was getting from her sister, and ignored it.

"How would he know where to look for us?" Janis asked. Will bit his lip as he thought.

"I'm not sure. If we can contact him, we may have a chance against the Kraken."

"Ask Raeta how to use the communications system," Janis said. Will glanced at her and nodded.

"Why not?" Will said. "It's the only way to get help." This was the reason Ophelia wanted her sister with her. She always came up with practical solutions.

"Then let's do it," Ophelia said. As they went to contact Raeta, Will thought it best to let the sisters know what Earth was up against.

"Our weapons are inferior to the Kraken. We've got nothing I know of to use against them." Ophelia looked at him.

"You better inform Raeta," Ophelia said.

They stopped before the screen and Ophelia activated it.

"Yes?" Raeta asked, after her image clarified. Ophelia told her what they needed and their concerns. She listened with a growing look of bewilderment. Janis noted Raeta turning her eyes to Will.

"You need to speak with Zeus," she said. "I'll call him. Please wait." She rose and moved off the screen. Will looked at the sisters with an amused smile.

"Zeus?" he asked. A man took Raeta's seat. He had dark blue eyes, jet-black hair, and a neatly trimmed beard. When he looked at the trio, he got a satisfied expression.

"You can change the frequency of the communications unit by adjusting the oscillator on the main panel," he said, in a cultured baritone. "It's a red LED readout that shows the frequency. You should be able to contact whoever you like. As for Earth weapons, we have technicians working on adapting your weapons to be effective against Kraken ships."

"I'll contact Aubrey," Will said. "Once you send us those modifications, he can get them pressed through quicker than anyone." Zeus regarded him with an expression of pride. It puzzled will until he saw the amazed expressions of Janis and Ophelia looking at him.

"You're decisive, Will Vaughn. I'm placing you in command of Earth's defenses as I know you'll do a satisfactory job." Will was surprised at his statement.

"Me? What can I do?" Zeus got a slight smile.

"You'll know what to do," Zeus replied. "I know you'll carry out your task efficiently. You're capable of getting it done correctly." Will shook his head in disbelief.

"I wish I had your confidence," Will said.

"You do. Listen to your companions, they'll give you the best advice, and act on it." The screen went blank and will turned to Ophelia and Janis.

"What the hell did he mean?" Will asked. The sisters exchanged astonished glances, and Ophelia had a suspicion, almost verified by Zeus, concerning Will.

"Let's go," Aubrey said, and patted the pilot's shoulder as he stepped into the rear compartment. The helicopter rose slowly until the ropes became taught and lifted the ATV from the ground. Aubrey looked out the port hatch and saw the other helicopter with an ATV dangling below it.

Soon they were over lush jungle. It was noisy in the chopper and they done no talking. After some time, their problems began. The chopper began to buck and sway. Aubrey saw the pilot having difficulty maintaining control. He stood, gripped the side and stuck his head in the cockpit.

"What's wrong?" Aubrey shouted. The pilot was concentrating on flying and didn't look at him.

"I don't know. All the instruments are fluctuating and the compass is in a spin. This damn beast wants to fly itself. You better have your people strap in. Looks like it's going to be a bumpy ride." Aubrey turned to Crist and Moore and saw they were apprehensive.

"Strap in." They pulled the belts around them as the engine began to sputter and cut out. Aubrey looked out below them and saw a solid canopy of trees. A flash caught his eyes and he looked to where it had been, but it was darting around so fast it was hard to keep track of it. Aubrey now knew what was causing the chopper to act in such erratic fashion. He looked at the men beside him, a cold dread filling him.

"Brace yourselves," Aubrey shouted. "We're going down." The pilot kept the chopper airborne for a few more minutes until the engine gave a final cough and stopped. The weight of the ATV drug it down.

They were braced for the impact, but when it came it seemed much sooner than expected. They were jerked violently, the straps biting painfully. Everything was still and upside down with branches sticking through the skin. They hung in silence for a few minutes. The crash had caused a silent pause in the jungle. Aubrey loosened the strap and used it to lower himself to the roof of the chopper. He quickly learned that each movement disturbed the precarious balance of the craft being supported by trees. He carefully made his way to the cockpit and saw the pilot was dead from a broken neck.

"Poor bastard," Aubrey mumbled and looked up at Moore and Crist.

"Get loose and climb down. We're on our own."

"What about the other chopper, sir?" Moore asked.

"I don't know. We can't risk staying here and having this thing fall," Aubrey replied. "We don't want to be in it when it does so move it." They loosened the straps cautiously and climbed down beside Aubrey. He stepped to the hatch, took hold of a branch mangled by the impact and disappeared into the tree below. Crist and Moore followed. It wasn't an easy climb to the ground and they could hear strains as the chopper fought gravity to pull it from its dangerous position. A loud snapping caused them to think the chopper was coming down on them, but its rear settled against a thick branch with a thud. On the ground, they looked up at the slowly settling chopper.

"Let's get the hell out from under it," Aubrey said. They moved away from the tree holding it up. They found the ATV on its side and pushed it upright but had no tools to cut it loose. Aubrey looked around and knew it would be impossible to drive in such terrain.

"Shit!" Aubrey exclaimed. "We're going to have to walk."

"Walk where, sir?" Crist asked. Aubrey looked around, having a good idea of what direction they had to go.

"To the coast."

They were listening to the helicopters' transmissions when one of the pilots spoke in a grim tone.

"Where's Booker? I don't see his chopper. Base, this is Romeo-Zulu Nine. We don't see Romeo-Zulu Three. Do you have him on radar? Over."

"Negative, Romeo-Zulu Nine. We saw him losing altitude a few minutes ago. Fly back over the area. Over."

"I'm turning back now. I hope Mr. Blaine is all right. Over." There followed minutes of silence before they heard the pilot again.

"Base, this is Romeo-Zulu Nine. Romeo-Zulu Three is down on the trees. I'll standby, Over."

"Romeo-Zulu Nine, do you see any sign of life?" Over."

"Negative. But I can't see the ground. They could have gotten out and I wouldn't be able to tell. Over."

"Return to base, Romeo-Zulu Nine. We'll send in a party on foot. Over and out." The words were a shock to Will. Aubrey was down in the jungle. He had come searching for them.
But what had led him to believe he could find them? There wasn't time to dwell on that. He turned to Ophelia.

"Is there some way we can locate that downed chopper?" Ophelia thought for a moment then nodded.

"I can activate a scanner that should locate it."

"If it does, we'll go out and see if Aubrey's alive. Without him, we don't stand a chance against the Kraken." Ophelia thought of something more relievable.

"There's no need for you to go, Will," Ophelia said. "We've got a guide that can't get lost."

"The little cart?" Janis asked. Ophelia nodded.

"We can send Blaine a message to follow it back here," Ophelia said. "It can do it faster than you, Will." He wasn't so sure.

"You mean if he's able to follow it back," Will said. Janis laid her hand on his arm and gave him a confident look.

"We have to believe he is," Janis said. Will glanced at her and nodded.

"I'll write a message while you program the cart."

Ophelia located the downed chopper on the scanner and fed the coordinates to the cart. Will slipped a note on it and saw Janis shaking her head.

"That won't do," Janis said. "As humid as the jungle is, you need something to protect the note." Will took out his wallet, pulled off one of the plastic photo compartments, and stuck the note in it and placed it on the cart.

"Get this to Aubrey," Will said. Now Ophelia had doubt.

"Don't get your hopes up," she said. "We can't be certain there were any survivors." Will suddenly felt confident of Aubrey's survival.

"Hell, nothing as minor as a plane crash could stop him," Will said. "I know Aubrey's alive, well, and mean as hell."

"I believe you," Janis said, with a slight smile. He got a cynical smile.

"I know the son of a bitch. He's alive."

It didn't take long for the heat and humidity to express their effects on them as Aubrey led the way. Their shirts were wet from perspiration and sticking to them. After an hour, they stopped for a rest. As they sat wiping sweat from their faces, Crist heard a whirring noise and glanced at his companions.
They hadn't heard it and he stood and looked in the direction it was coming from. Aubrey looked at him wondering what he was doing.

"What is it?" Aubrey asked. Crist glanced over his shoulder.

"Don't you hear that noise, sir?" Aubrey cocked his head and listened.

"What the hell is that?" Aubrey asked, getting to his feet. He stepped beside Crist and stared into the jungle. The sound was coming toward them, deviating to circle trees. Moore joined them.

"What can it be?" Moore asked.

"It's certainly no animal," Aubrey said. "That's a mechanical sound." The cart abruptly stopped in front of them and they stared in amazement. Aubrey saw the plastic on it and took it from the cart. He pulled out the note and unfolded it. He read it and looked at Crist and Moore.

"It's a note from Will," Aubrey said. "This little machine will lead us to where he is." A frown came to Aubrey.

"Goddamnit! I should have known better than to think he was dead."

"Do we follow it, sir?" Crist asked.

"If this machine can get us out of this hot fucking jungle, your damn right we follow it." Almost as if it understood Aubrey, the cart turned and started back through the jungle, the men following. Aubrey was astonished at how agile it was as it maneuvered through the dense undergrowth. It let nothing block its path, but simply went around any obstruction encountered.

It took almost two grueling hours of walking before they halted before the jungle shrouded temple. Crist and Moore didn't care much for entering and turned to Aubrey.

"Will can't possibly be there, sir," Crist said. Aubrey gave him an annoyed look.

"Why not?" Crist had no answer except it didn't seem possible.

"This looks like a place no one would want to go into, sir," Moore said. Aubrey glanced at their stationary guide.

"We'll let our little friend show us the way in," Aubrey said. The cart started around the temple It stopped and began beeping. As they watched, they didn't see the floor of the jungle open behind them. A different sound caused them to turn as a metal circular platform stopped.

"An elevator!" Aubrey exclaimed. He walked over, gave it a once over as the cart moved onto it.

"Are we going to get on, sir?" Moore asked, uneasily. Aubrey stepped on and turned to them.

"We got an invitation. I need to talk with Will about running off with that woman. How would that look in his file?"

"Shouldn't one of us remain up here as a guard, sir?" Crist asked.

"Hell no! Who's there to guard against? Let's get below and cool off." Crist and Moore moved onto the platform and it descended into the jungle floor.

When the cover closed over their heads, lights showing the shaft came on. It was comfortably cool and made them glad to be away from the jungle. What would they face when this elevator stopped? Moore wondered. Aubrey wasn't worried. If Will was here, he would have things under control. He had faith in his abilities. His most burning question was, who had built such a structure in an unconventional place? He knew enough to have already guessed the truth. And he knew he was right.

SEVEN

Raeta stood behind Zeus on the bridge. He was lost in thought and she didn't dare disturb him, but there were things she needed to know. She was intrigued at the attraction she had immediately felt for Will Vaughn. It was a feeling she had never experienced before and couldn't decide if she liked it or not. Zeus turned and almost collided with her, causing her to take a startled step back. He cocked an eyebrow as he regarded her.

"What is it, Raeta?" She was hesitant and started slowly.

"I need to know why we've been sent to Earth at this particular time. If I know more about the mission, the less I'll have to bother you with details." Zeus folded his arms and got solemn look. It was difficult for him to accept that he had people among his crew who hadn't been briefed on the early Earth colonies.

"The Kraken have had millennia to infiltrate the human race," he replied. "They developed the unstable economic system of Earth. Through a secret organization, known as The Brotherhood, they've influenced human history in ways I never thought possible. So, Raeta, we're going to Earth to put an end to The Brotherhood, if possible. Is that all you wanted to know?" She felt foolish thinking about her strong feeling toward Vaughn, but had to know how to deal with it in a logical manner. She stiffened her posture to military erectness.

"I must know about Will Vaughn," she said, trying to sound scientific. Zeus smiled and lowered his arms.

"I detect something more in your voice, Raeta." She quickly averted her eyes, unaware that her emotion was so obvious, but he knew. She returned her eyes to him.

"You're correct, Zeus. For some reason I don't understand, I have a strong physical attraction to him. Can you explain why he has this effect on me?"

"He's a direct descendent of my family line." Surprise exploded on her face as she became aware of the resemblance between Zeus and Will Vaughn.

"That's why you feel such a strong attraction for him," he continued. "Think you can handle such an experience?" She quickly stiffened.

"Of course. But I still wish to meet him in person."

"Very well, Raeta. When we attain orbit, you can go down to the complex with me." She was still curious and puzzled.

"Those women with him, will they have the same effect on men?" Zeus smiled.

"They're direct descendants of Athena. What's your scientific opinion of how the men on the ship will react to them?" Raeta was bewildered knowing there wasn't any scientific explanation for sexual feelings above that of mating. It's a biological thing, she thought.

"Emotions are difficult to define in a scientific manner," Raeta replied. "How were they able to find their way to the complex?" Zeus didn't press his point but got a patient smile, respecting Raeta's reputation for logic.

"The Kraken showed them the way," he said, grimly. "They hoped the twins might get them into the complex without being destroyed. But the machines – the watchers of the complex – are alert for any alien form from getting inside."

"Are the people of Earth to be warned about the Kraken?"

"No, Raeta. Nor can we disclose ourselves to the general population. They must continue believing us mythological. Only a select few will know of our existence." She was satisfied with what she heard, although her attraction for will made her uncomfortable. She had never allowed her feelings free rein, then along comes this man and draws them out easily. She must get control of herself. Zeus knew what she was feeling.

"Don't worry, Raeta, we've all given in to romantic urges. Suppressing them only makes it harder to come to terms with them." She regarded him with a hesitant look.

"I'll consider your advice, Zeus. But I've prided myself on learning to control my emotions. I'll deal with Will Vaughn without losing self-control." He got a patient look and shook his head.

"We don't control our emotions, Raeta, they control us. I doubt you'll find yourself an exception to that rule." A frown and stubborn look came to her.

"I've striven most of my life to be an exception. I won't allow myself to fail now. Thank you for the briefing, Zeus. I must return to my station." He put a hand on her arm and gave it a gentle squeeze.

"We'll see who wins in the end, Raeta, your logic or your emotions."

When the elevator stopped, Will and the sisters stood facing Aubrey, Moore, and Crist. Aubrey looked around unable to conceal an expression of awe that made Will smile.

"Welcome to Earth Complex, Aubrey," Will said. "Impressive, huh?" Crist and Moore stared in amazement at the construction they saw around them. The gate opened and the cart whirred, rolled off, and shot off down the corridor.

"What the hell is this place?" Aubrey asked, stepping off the elevator.

"It's a planetary defense complex, Mr. Blaine," Ophelia said. "You seem to have been correct about those visiting Janis and me. It seems they aren't such good friends after all." Aubrey's mouth fell open as he looked from Ophelia to Janis and back. He closed his eyes and shook his head. He opened them and looked at the sisters again.

"They're identical twins, Aubrey," Will said.

"Shall we go to the control room?" Janis asked. They started for the control room with Moore and Crist following.

"What did she mean, I guessed right?"

"They just learned that their visitors was using them to try to gain access to this complex," Will replied. "It seems only humans can come in without being vaporized." Aubrey glanced at the sisters.

"Did they ever perform medical experiments on either of you?" Aubrey asked. Ophelia and Janis exchanged glances and Janis shook her head.

"They seemed to want to gain our trust more than anything," Janis said.

"You're both damned lucky," Aubrey said. "The reason for the abductions is, those little Gray bastards are searching for some special genetic traits. If they had found them in you, they might have been able to manipulate you and gain access here."

"How the hell do you know that?" Will asked, curious. Aubrey smiled as he regarded him.

"I've known about them for quite sometime, Will. It was one of their ships that downed the chopper we were in." Crist glanced at Moore who shrugged. Neither had seen anything.

"Are you certain?" Ophelia asked.

"Damned right! And it isn't the first time they've knocked down an aircraft I was in."

"Why did you come after us?" Janis asked, looking at him with a curious expression. Aubrey smiled.

"To protect you," Aubrey replied. "I had to make a show for Will to get his ass in gear and help, and he's done a damn good job."

"What about those papers I gave you?" Ophelia asked. Aubrey shook his head.

"No one's been able to crack the alphabet. When they do, I don't think we'll find any surprises." Will was suddenly enlightened.

"You've been investigating UFOs for years," Will said. "That's how you know what they're planning." Aubrey nodded with a grim look.

"I've been to a dozen crash sites, Will, three in the Soviet Union. I've worked with a secret Russian group for over ten years."

"But the failure of the experiments of identical twins –" Aubrey interrupted Ophelia, emphatically shaking his head.

"That wasn't my doing. The aliens couldn't afford to let those experiments succeed and expose their secret."

"But the Grays seemed eager to share information with us," Janis said.

"Only so they could find that genetic strain," Aubrey said. "I can't understand why they never tested you two medically."

"Maybe because we cooperated with them," Janis suggested. Aubrey glanced at Will and nodded.

"That could be the answer," Aubrey said. "Everyone they've tested didn't want to be touched by them." He gave the sisters a look of respect.

"You both saved yourselves traumatic experiences by cooperating," Aubrey said, glancing at Will. "Certain artifacts have been found that proves the people the ancient Greeks called gods were a scientifically advanced race."

"What? Gods?" Will asked.

"Enough evidence has been uncovered to convince skeptical scientists that Earth has been visited by an advanced race," Aubrey said. "And they established a base here."

"Is there any connection between them and the Grays?" Janis asked. Ophelia had been thinking about Raeta and decided to tell Aubrey about her.

"A woman, Raeta, told us she was transmitting from a ship on its way to Earth," Ophelia said. "She called the leader Zeus."

"A ship coming here?" Aubrey asked, surprised.

"Yes," Ophelia replied. "It will come into orbit in six days."

"She also said the Kraken were their enemies," Janis added. "Could she have been referring to the Grays?" Aubrey looked relieved.

"So we have help on the way," Aubrey said, pleased. "As for the Grays, we'll just have to wait until we can talk to those people. What can we do in the meantime?"

"I don't know," Will said. "We were told we couldn't defend Earth from this complex only. The man, Zeus, told us he had technicians working on ways to improve our weapons so they would be effective against the Kraken ships." Aubrey's expression turned urgent.

"I've got to find a way back to Washington. Is there anyway you can communicate those modifications to me when you receive them?" Will smiled.

"Wait until you see the communications center," Will said. Crist and Moore were bewildered, uncertain what the others were talking about.

Aubrey was impressed with the communications technology he saw and turned to Will.

"If I can get back to Washington, I'll go directly to the president and get the ball rolling on those modifications."

"Radio for help," Will said. "Your chopper crashed and the other pilot couldn't tell if there were survivors." Aubrey nodded.

"I'll put the call through and head back to the crash site."

"Why not have them pick you up here," Ophelia said. No one can see the complex from the surface." Aubrey frowned.

"How the hell do I explain my radio call?" Will smiled.

"Should anyone ask," Will said. "Tell them it's classified."

The helicopter picked up Aubrey, Moore, and Crist in a clearing not far from the temple. On the flight back to Mexico City, Aubrey regarded Crist and Moore with a somber expression.

"Not a word about that complex to anyone." Both nodded. They weren't sure what they could say if they chose to. Both were perplexed by what they had seen and heard. Aubrey knew he had to get to the president and be convincing. Everything depended on communication from that ship and how soon the invasion would take place. Hopefully the latter wouldn't occur until after the ship arrived, he thought. But he knew better than to count on that.

The fact that a ship was coming might force the Grays to advance their timetable. So much was unknown! Aubrey knew he had a daunting task before him.

Aubrey got an uneasy feeling when he saw the ambassador hurrying to the helicopter as it landed. He was pale as he handed Aubrey a sheet of paper. Aubrey recognized it as an executive order and read it.

"What the hell is the president doing, Blaine?" the ambassador asked. Aubrey looked from the paper stunned.

"I have no idea, Mr. Ambassador. I'll contact General Schiffer on the flight back. As soon as I know anything, I'll contact you."

When the jet was airborne, Aubrey told the communications officer to contact General Schiffer's office. In a couple of minutes, he was speaking with the Chairman of the Joint Chiefs.

"The government's gone nuts, Aubrey," Schiffer said.

"What about the executive order activating Project HAARP, Chet?"

"Damned if I know! The president wants HAARP activated as soon as possible." Aubrey's gut feeling told him he was too late to prevent the invasion.

"What's the foreign reaction to this?" Aubrey heard a loud snort from the phone.

"Every foreign leader, or the ones that count, have agreed with the president. I tell you, Aubrey, they've all gone mad."

"When's the activation to take place, Chet?"

"Day after tomorrow. And there's not a goddamn thing I can do to stop it." Aubrey couldn't believe the president would have acted in such a manner without sufficient reason.

"What reason was given for the activation?" Aubrey asked. There was a silence before Schiffer replied.

"I asked the president that. He told me and I quote, mind my own fucking business and carry out the order. That was the president speaking, Aubrey."

"What do you think is going on there, Chet?"

"It's not just here, Aubrey." He could hear bewilderment in Schiffer's tone.

"It's in all the capitals, Moscow, London, Paris, Berlin, Tokyo. They all seem to be infected with a sort of insanity. I can't explain it."

Aubrey believed he could, but wouldn't say anything until he was alone with Schiffer. The Grays appeared to be working to a plan that already had them controlling the governments. That left the question begging, what the hell could he do?

"Let me know if anymore craziness shows up, Chet. I'll see what I can find out."

"If you know anything about this, Aubrey, for Christ sakes tell me."

"I'll be in my office in four hours, Chet. We can talk then." He heard the rush of air as Schiffer exhaled impatiently.

"All right. I hope you have an explanation for this insanity." As Aubrey replaced the phone, he knew he had to contact Will and have him inform the ship what was happening. Things were moving faster than he cared for, and activation of Project HAARP meant someone wanted to use it to control people. Aubrey could think of only one group who would want population control. He picked up a notepad and wrote the frequency of the complex on it and handed it to the communications officer.

"Contact Will on this frequency." The officer looked at the frequency and glanced at Aubrey with a confused look.

"Goddamnit! I don't have time for explanations. Just get Will on that frequency." The woman set the frequency and began calling. Will responded quickly.

"This is EC, go ahead," Will said. Aubrey took the mike from the panel.

"Will, contact our friends. What we discussed seems to have already began." Aubrey used his voice to express urgency. It took a moment for Will to think of what Aubrey meant.

"You mean it's already started?" Will asked, in a shocked tone.

"Yes. They control some national leaders. Get hold of our friends and tell them we need help in a hurry."

"I'll get right on it, Aubrey. When can I expect your next communication?"

"After I talk with Schiffer. I'll know more then. I never expected this to be a clandestine operation."

"EC out." Aubrey went back to the cabin knowing there was nothing to be done until he was back in Washington. Will would do what he could to call in the cavalry.

"That's what I was just told," Will said. Ophelia and Janis were alarmed by the sudden development.

"We have to contact Raeta," Janis said. "The longer we wait the worse it's going to be." They activated the screen and when she appeared her eyes went to Will. Janis noted it with a frown.

"What is it?" Raetea asked. Will related what Aubrey had told him, and seen Raeta was unable to conceal her surprise.

"I'll inform Zeus. He'll probably want to speak with you." As they waited for Zeus, Janis moved beside Will and he glanced at her. Zeus was quickly on the screen and Will didn't have time to wonder about her action.

"What's going on?" Zeus asked, in a strong, calm voice. Will repeated what he had told Raeta. Zeus frowned and rubbed his beard.

"Is that all the data you have?" Zeus asked.

"I'll have more after my next communication with Aubrey," Will replied, and glanced at his watch. "That should be in about three hours." Zeus nodded.

"Raeta and I will leave in a small ship," Zeus said. "We should land at the complex in about six hours. No matter what you hear, take no action until we arrive." Will nodded.

"I'll inform Aubrey," Will said. The screen went blank and Will looked at the sisters noting the odd expression Janis had. She didn't want Raeta anywhere near Will.

"Looks like we're too late," Will said.

Aubrey was edgy not knowing how much control the aliens had over the president. He knew HAARP could be used to shield the planet from incoming missiles, and ships from space. Things didn't look promising, but he had confidence Will and the sisters would make things work to their advantage. He had to count on those people for help, but their modifications for Earth's weapons was a moot point. What did those little Gray sons of bitches want? He wondered. He wasn't aware that far above the jet one of their ships was pacing his craft.

The president tried fighting the influence in his mind, but it was overwhelming. He knew his cabinet and congress were experiencing the same influence, and no one had the power to overcome it. They all believed what they were doing was the only action they could take.

They knew a ship was approaching Earth; a ship that could not be permitted to land. Project HAARP was the only way to prevent that from happening. The president felt there was something more behind the activating of HAARP, but he couldn't remember what it was that filled him with dread.

The people who led the nations of Earth had sent their approval to Washington for the Activation of Project HAARP. Why had they done so? The question was banished from their minds. They couldn't think like that. It was wrong to question what had to be done, and knew it had to be done. They had no choice. The ship coming toward Earth represented a grave threat to humanity and had to be stopped. All of the leaders knew this, but had no inclination it wasn't their thoughts.

Those who fought for independence of mind were suppressed with great anxiety as behind them stood an alien invisible to them. Their high-domed heads and almond shaped eyes planted their thoughts in the leaders' minds. Each person had the strong impression they were not alone and the aliens considered that dangerous. They could manipulate these people more easily if they didn't know they were being controlled. But controlling human minds was much simpler than had been anticipated.

EIGHT

General Schiffer was tall with dark gray hair and blue eyes. He paced in Aubrey's office, waiting for him to return. As soon as he did, Aubrey called in his top people to brief them with Schiffer. Most of the people, including Schiffer, held incredulous looks as they listened to what Aubrey told them what was occurring.

"We expected an overt invasion," Aubrey said. "Instead, they're working clandestinely. A secret invasion."

"Do you actually believe we've been invaded?" Schiffer asked, skeptically. Aubrey regarded him with a grim expression.

"Can you explain the president's behavior? His executive order to activate Project HAARP? If you can, Chet, I'm willing to listen." Schiffer frowned and shook his head.

"You know I can't, Aubrey," Schiffer replied.

"Sir," Moore said. "Don't you think we should inform Will about Project HAARP's activation?" Aubrey considered the effects HAARP could produce and knew a warning had to be sent to the ship. He nodded.

"Yes," Aubrey said. "Contact him and make sure he understands what HAARP's activation means." Aubrey glanced at the others.

"Let's try to see what we can learn about the enemy," Aubrey said. "That's all people." They filed out of the room leaving Aubrey and Schiffer alone. Aubrey regarded him with a glum look.

"We've got to find someway to stall the activation order, Chet. Any ideas?" Schiffer rubbed the back of his neck and glanced at Aubrey with a defeated look.

"No. The order was sent to all major commands on a need to know basis."

"Looks like we're up shit creek. What the hell can we do?" Schiffer regarded him grimly.

"There are two possibilities. We can try placing the president under arrest or get the hell out of Dodge pronto." Aubrey didn't care for either option and determined on a third.

Only Moore's warning interrupted the wait for Zeus' arrival. Time seemed to drag, and Janis had to keep her feelings for Will hidden, not wanting Ophelia to know.

Will was kept busy checking the instrumentation of the complex and familiarizing himself with its functions. He kept side glancing Janis wanting to forget what he was doing and going somewhere to be alone with her. He forced himself to concentrate on the intricate electronic devices around him.

Ophelia was deep in thought, trying to recall every meeting she and Janis had had with the Grays. There was something about one particular meeting that nagged at her mind. She couldn't define exactly what it was that bothered her. It had been a vague thought she had sensed from the ship's commander, but concentrating wasn't helping her to recall it.

"Look at this," Will said, leaning over an instrument similar to a radarscope. Janis and Ophelia came beside him and looked at the screen.

"What is that?" Will asked. "It's almost in low Earth orbit." Janis glanced at him.

"Could it be one of the Gray's ships?" Janis asked. Ophelia took a closer look and shook her head.

"No," Ophelia said. "It doesn't fit the profile of the ships we've been on." Will pointed to the shape on the screen.

"It's something coming from outside Earth's orbit," he said. "From the direction of Mars, I think."

"How far away is it?" Janis asked. Will glanced at her and felt his urge for her stir.

"It should be in orbit in a matter of minutes," Ophelia said. Janis and Will looked at her with surprise.

"How can you be sure, Ophelia?" Janis asked. Ophelia's eyes widened as she realized she didn't know.

"I just know." It was the only answer she could give along with a perplexed look. Will considered an idea.

"Suppose we're here because this is where we're meant to be at this time?"

"What do you mean?" Janis asked.

"It's just a hunch, you understand. I think we have some connection with Zeus and his people."

"That might explain how Ophelia can read the screen," Janis said. A bewildered look came to Will.

"Why have the Grays waited until now to begin an invasion?" Will asked.

"Why did the Grays defer medically checking us?" Ophelia asked. "They must have some idea about Janis and me or they wouldn't have chosen us for contact." This sparked Will's curiosity.

"What do you mean, the way they chose you?" he asked. Ophelia took a moment to recall, then looked at her sister.

"Do you recall our first visitation, Janis?" Janis expressed puzzlement as she recalled the memory.

"Yes. We knew a week before they came that we had been selected as special contactees. But they never revealed how we were special. Most of what they told us, I don't remember." An annoyed look came to Ophelia.

"I don't recall much now," Ophelia said, puzzled. "They gave us those files and told us to keep them because we were the only ones they could trust. They seemed almost desperate that we trust them." Will frowned as he thought.

"They also knew neither of you could understand what was in those files," he said.

"Then what was behind it?" Ophelia asked. He considered her question and shook his head.

"Perhaps Zeus can tell us when he arrives," Will replied.

Raeta brought the ship into the atmosphere at a steep angle then pulled up in an abrupt braking maneuver. It put heavy g-force on the craft but slowed it to where she could fly it like an aircraft. She came in low over the Pacific making for the homing beacon in Yucatan.

The flight took less than five minutes, and Raeta put the ship down gently in the clearing not far from the temple. She and Zeus unstrapped and started for the hatch when Zeus took hold of her arm and she turned to face him.

"You're about to meet Will Vaughn. How do you feel?" She knew she couldn't lie to him.

"Somewhat excited," she replied. Zeus nodded and smiled.

"Then let's meet the descendants of the gods."

They came around the temple as the elevator stopped and Ophelia greeted them. Zeus felt his attraction for her surge.

"I'm glad you're here," Ophelia said. "I'm afraid I have bad news." They stepped on the elevator beside her and it began to descend. Ophelia had a hard time keeping her eyes from Zeus.

"The president is about to activate something called Project HAARP," Ophelia said. "All I know is that it can prevent your ship from entering the atmosphere. Will can tell you more about it." The elevator came to a soft stop and Zeus smiled as he regarded Ophelia.

"We'll go directly to the command center," he said, stepping off the elevator. Ophelia felt like she was with old friends, but didn't understand why. Raeta was feeling an excitement she had never experienced. The idea of meeting Will face to face was a feeling she was beginning to enjoy. They walked quickly along the corridor and Zeus glanced at Raeta.

"You've got to contact the ship, Raeta, and inform them about this HAARP," he said. She nodded.

When they came into the command center, Will and Janis greeted them and Zeus got down to business.

"What's this HAARP Ophelia mentioned?" Zeus asked.

"I'm not certain how it works," Will replied. "But it destroys anything coming into the atmosphere from space. It's been rumored it can be used to control the population. It's never been tested, but I guess we'll soon know if it works." The sound of his voice gave Raeta chills. Zeus' expression had turned grim.

"We can't man this complex alone," Zeus said. "It takes a minimum of fifty technicians to control everything here."

"I don't think this complex would do any good if it were fully manned," Janis said. "They've moved against Earth governments in a clandestine way and seem to be in control." Ophelia looked at Zeus.

"What can we do?" Ophelia asked. Before he could reply, the complex was rocked by a tremendous blast. They ducked their heads and Will glanced at Zeus.

"What the hell was that?" Will asked.

"Sonic pressure wave," Raeta replied, in a tense voice. "One of the Kraken ships must have tracked us here." Two more blasts followed in rapid succession and the ceiling began to buckle.

"We better get out of here," Zeus said. "It seems the Kraken are determined to destroy this complex." Another blast caused the ceiling to fracture and rocks and dirt showered down on them.
Raeta grabbed Will's hand and pulled him from under the cascading dirt.

A roar filled the corridor and Raeta and Will saw the way blocked. Zeus and the sisters watched the corridor fill with a mass of falling rocks and soil.

"We're cut off," Raeta said. "We must get to the surface. Do you know another way out?" Will wasn't certain there was another way out, but they couldn't stay where they were. Another blast ruptured more of the ceiling sending them scrambling along the corridor, Raeta still holding his hand. The next blast began to make the lights dim, but brightened as they hurried along. As they passed a door, Raeta stopped.

"In here," she said, pulling him through the door. She closed it and leaned against it. She was out of breath, and without realizing what she was doing, she leaned against Will. He put an arm around her wondering if they were going to make it out of this subterranean maze. He hoped Zeus and the sisters were all right.
When Raeta became aware of standing against Will, she found herself reluctant to pull away.

"There has to be a way out of here," Will said, as she turned her face up to him.

"Don't you know?" she asked. He turned a grim look on her.

"I only know about the elevator. But there has to be emergency exits from this place."

"How are we going to find it, Will?"

"I don't know. But we better find it before they pound this place to dust."

After the cave in, Janis thought Will and Raeta had been buried and started to dig with her hands. Zeus took hold of her arm and she turned her face to him.

"They're not in there," he said. "I saw Raeta pull Will out of the way. We've got to get out of here and they'll be doing the same."

"The only way out I know of is the elevator, and we can't get to it," Ophelia said, looking at Zeus. "Don't you know the layout of this place?"

"No," he replied. "The plans for the complex are in the ship's computer and I saw no need to study them before we came here. I wasn't expecting anything like this." He turned, looking around.

"There has to be more than one way out," he said.

"Which way do we go?" Janis asked. Zeus was looking along the corridor when the little cart came whirring up and stopped in front of them.

"This will show us the way out," Ophelia said. Another blast caused the ceiling to sag dangerously.

"Let's go before this place comes down on our heads," Zeus said. Ophelia looked at the cart and thought of what they had to do. The cart turned and sped off along the corridor with the three following.

The next blast dimmed the lights almost to darkness, but they didn't slacken pace. The cart seemed to know exactly where it was going; leading them along a corridor that sloped upward Ophelia and Zeus just started up when a violet sheet of light fell between them and Janis. The sudden flash blinded Ophelia for some seconds and Zeus had covered his eyes. Ophelia, still seeing spots, turned a panicked expression to Zeus.

"They've taken your sister," Zeus said. Ophelia shook her head in disbelief.

"How could they do it from down here. And why only her?" she asked, unable to believe Janis was gone. He had a grim look as he took hold of her arm.

"Matter transfer is how. Why I don't know."

"They wouldn't need her now. Not with the destruction of the complex almost complete." His grip on her arm became a pull.

"We can't worry about that now, Ophelia. We must catch up with that machine and get to the surface." He let go of her arm and took her hand and hurried them along until they saw the cart. It had stopped in front of a door like the one Ophelia had first encountered. She looked for the yellow switch, saw none, and spun the wheel to the left.

As the door began to open, a much closer blast hit above them. Zeus grabbed the cart and pushed Ophelia through as tons of rubble fell into the corridor behind them. Without thinking, she tried pushing the door shut, but it was blocked by rubble. She and Zeus hurried along a narrow corridor until they saw another door ahead. Ophelia stepped ahead of him and turned the wheel. When she pushed the door open, they had to cover their faces against the heat that rushed in. Slowly lowering their arms, they looked out at ground burned black with streamers of white smoke rising from the charred plants. Ophelia turned a frightened look to Zeus.

"Let's hope they didn't see your ship," she said. Zeus nodded.

"We'll have to make a run for it. The ground is going to be uncomfortably hot." Zeus shifted the cart to his other arm, took her hand, and looked at her.

"Ready?" She nodded.

"Let's go."

Crist came bursting into Aubrey's office carrying a photograph.

"What the hell's wrong with you?" Aubrey asked, annoyed by the intrusion.

"Sir, we just got this thermal image from a weather satellite," Crist said, his voice tight with tension. "An area of the Yucatan has been hit by some sort of energy beam. There's a large area radiating a very high temperature." A sad look came to Crist as he handed Aubrey the photo.

"It's the location of the complex, sir."

"What!" Aubrey exclaimed, standing and taking the photo. He looked at it and back to Crist.

"Try to contact Will. We've got to find out what the hell happened down there."

"I already told someone to try to establish communications as soon as I saw the location, sir." Aubrey looked shocked and nodded.

"Good thinking, Crist. Let's go to communications and hope Will and the women got out of there safely."

When they came into communications, Moore turned to face them with a grave look and shook his head.

"We can't raise the complex, sir," Moore said.

"Son of a bitch! How did the Grays know about the complex?" Aubrey asked, unable to keep his anger from escaping.

"What do we do, sir?" Crist asked. Aubrey was frustrated, and it showed.

"Hope they got out all right."

"If they did, sir, they might literally have went from the frying pan into the fire," Crist said.

"The satellite reading gave a surface temperature of 150 degrees Fahrenheit, sir," Moore said.

"And if they stayed inside, they're buried alive. Get a recon plane over the area. I want a damn good look at the area."

"Right away, sir," Moore said.

Schiffer looked over the photos the plane had taken and the thermal image. Aubrey sat before his desk regarding him with a glum look.

"Any idea what caused this, Aubrey?" Aubrey shook his head.

"No, but I'll bet it was the goddamn Grays who are behind it."

"Only a battlefield nuke could cause this sort of damage over that wide an area. What do you suggest we do?" Aubrey looked grim.

"Bring the military to full alert, Chet." Schiffer got a hopeless look.

"I can't do that without presidential authorization, you know that, Aubrey. He's refusing to speak to me on the phone." Aubrey leaned toward the desk with a determined look.

"Then we'll go and see the president." Schiffer got a skeptical look.

"Do you think we'll be allowed to see him?" Aubrey shrugged.

"Why not, Chet? After all, we're his top men in the military and intelligence. He asked us, no insisted, we keep our jobs."

Neither Aubrey nor Schiffer had seen Secret Service and MPs standing guard outside the Oval Office before. A desk was set near the door manned by a presidential assistant Aubrey knew. They stopped before the desk and the man looked up. He was thin with brown eyes and sandy hair. He didn't look pleased to see them.

"What do you want?" he asked, in a bored tone.

"We want to see the president, Sam," Aubrey said. Sam's eyes narrowed with suspicion and he brushed nervously at his eyebrow.

"Why?" Aubrey glanced at Schiffer.

"We think one of our planes crashed in Yucatan," Schiffer replied. "We want the president to get permission from the Mexican authorities for us to check out the site." Sam swiveled slowly in his chair twirling a pencil in his fingers. He got up, gave them an overtly suspicious look, and nodded.

"I'll see what he says. Wait here." They glanced at each other, then the guards. They could only watch as Sam entered the Oval Office.

"These people are fucking paranoid," Aubrey whispered, glancing at the men standing around regarding them with cold expressions. Shiffer looked at him and nodded.

"I told you they were all crazy."

"I've got a good idea what's made them this way. The president never had an intermediary between us and him before."

"I wish we knew more, Aubrey. We need facts before we can make a move." Sam returned and faced them with a cynical smile.

"The president wants you both to get your asses down there and personally check it out. He's on the phone with the Mexican president now."

"He wants us to go?" Schiffer asked, surprised. Sam nodded and jabbed the pencil in their direction.

"That's what he said," Sam replied, holding his cynical smile. Aubrey quickly bumped Schiffer to get his attention.

"We better get the crash team assembled," Aubrey said. Sam leaned forward, his palms flattening on the desk, his expression now cold.

"Do that!" he exclaimed, in a hard tone. "The president wants you to investigate and report back here when you return." Aubrey nodded.

"Of course," Aubrey said.

"I'll authorize transport for the crash team through Andrews," Schiffer said. Sam nodded.

"Just remember to report when you return," Sam said.

As the car pulled away from the White House, Schiffer gave Aubrey a puzzled look.

"What do you suppose this is about, Aubrey?"

"Unless I miss my guess, the president will have a reception committee waiting for us, to make us like the assholes we just saw." Schiffer looked embarrassed.

"Until now, Aubrey, I doubted that story about an invasion. But I'll be goddamned if I can see any other reason for those people to behave as they did." Aubrey patted his shoulder.

"Have that transport loaded with armed troops, Chet. We may get lucky and capture us an alien." Schiffer frowned and got a sad look.

"I'll settle for finding those people you left down there alive." He turned a worried look to Schiffer, his mind now filled with concern for the sisters and Will.

"So would I, Chet. But if we can get a prisoner in the same bag, I'm sure as hell not about to pass up such an opportunity." Schiffer shook his head with a bewildered look.

"I don't think I'll be able to authorize the use of troops," Schiffer said. "Besides, how the hell would you communicate with it?" Aubrey was silent for a moment then looked at Schiffer.

"That remains to be seen, Chet."

NINE

This wasn't the first time Janis had been taken onboard one of the Grays' ships, but never in such an abrupt manner. She was surprised at how tall the Gray she faced was. He also seemed heavier built than others. They regarded each other until Janis felt a thought from the Gray.

"What were you doing in the complex?"

"We were examining it to see how it functioned," she thought back.

"That place built by – enemy. How did you find it?" Janis pictured the storm in her mind, being washed onto the beach, finding Ophelia there and taking Will into the complex.

"Why did you destroy it?" At first, she got no impression from the Gray, and that was puzzling. She sensed hesitation, confusion as to how to answer her.

"Who is this enemy?" she asked. She sensed more wavering as though the Gray was unsure as to what she meant.

"They are the enemy," the Gray thought. Janis sensed it had no conception of what an enemy was.

"Have you seen this enemy?" she thought. "Communicated with it?" The Gray's mind became muddled, confused by her questions. It was clear this particular Gray had never seen the enemy, and couldn't define what an enemy was.

"Why did you bring me onboard?" Its thought was clear.

"To keep you from harm."

"Why did you leave my sister?"

"We couldn't get a firm lock on her. We do not want harm to come to either of you. You two are the only ones who understand what we want." This puzzled her more.

"Neither of us would have been in danger if you hadn't attacked the complex." Again, she sensed confusion.

"We had no choice. It was ordered that we destroy enemy." Janis sensed futility from the Gray and didn't understand what was going on.

"Who ordered the complex destroyed?" Less confusion and something almost like hate from the Gray.

"The Brotherhood. They said the complex must be destroyed." It was clear to Janis this Gray had no idea who had ordered the destruction.

"Will you return me to my sister?"

"If that is what you wish." She bowed her head.

Zeus and Ophelia were being toasted as they crossed the ground to the ship. They halted by the hatch and looked back at the blackened rock pile that had been the temple. Ophelia looked at Zeus bewildered.

"Why did they do this?" she asked. That question was foremost in his mind also. He regarded Ophelia and shook his head.

"I don't know. It was like they weren't certain anything was here."

"Are you sure the Grays are the Kraken you know of?" she asked, not yet ready to concede those she considered friends could become enemies so quickly. Zeus looked at her, confused.

"Gray aliens?" he asked, uncertain what she meant. Ophelia told him about the Grays and her contact with them. She noted from his expression this was new to him.

"We know of no such race, Ophelia. We've never suspected such beings were in the solar system." She stared in silence, feeling relief.

"That's good, Zeus. I've never sensed hostility from a Gray." They entered the ship and stood at the control panel. Zeus pointed out the windscreen.

"Why would the Grays destroy the complex and take Janis?" Ophelia had an answer for the last part of his question, but not the first.

"Why they destroyed the complex is incomprehensible. They took Janis to keep her from harm, I'm certain." She looked toward the elevator and saw a gaping hole where it had been, that reminded her of Will and Raeta.

"We've got to locate Raeta and Will." Zeus nodded, turned, and took an instrument from clamps on the bulkhead. He checked it and stuck it in his belt. He saw Ophelia's quizzical look and patted the instrument.

"It will help us locate them," he said. "They might need help getting to the surface." Ophelia got a wan smile.

They stepped out of the ship just as a flash of violet light appeared to their left and Janis stood there. Ophelia and Zeus went to her.

"Why did the Grays take you?" Ophelia asked.

"To save my life." Ophelia looked at Zeus who gave her a nod. She looked back to Janis.

"Did they say why they attacked the complex?" Ophelia asked.

"They were ordered to by a group called The Brotherhood," Janis replied.

"The Brotherhood!" Zeus exclaimed. Janis nodded.

"The Grays have no conception of what an enemy is," Janis said. "They were obeying an order they were compelled to obey. The Gray I communicated with had no idea why the complex was being destroyed." Zeus frowned and rubbed his beard.

"The Kraken were behind the attack," he said. "I don't understand how they're able to control these Grays."

"What I sensed from the Gray was confusion," Janis said.

"This is most strange," Zeus said. "I never thought The Brotherhood capable of controlling telepathic aliens."

"Save that for later," Ophelia said. "We've got to locate Will and Raeta."

The last blast knocked the lights out. Raeta felt an unbounded excitement at having Will's arm around her in the dark.

"What can we do?" she asked, sounding panicked. He was using a small penlight, but wasn't certain how long the battery would last. He moved it around stopping on her face and held it there. He was suddenly aware of how lovely she was, but thought about where they were and moved the light on stopping it on a locker. She moved away from him and opened the locker to find weapons inside. She picked up one and handed it to Will who turned the light on it.

"What sort of weapon is this?"

"A plasma rifle," Raeta replied. "We may be able to use them to get out of here."

"We both better take two," he said. Raeta handed him another one and slipped a small weapon into her pocket.

"Let's try to find a way out before we do any blasting," Will said. "We might bring what's left of this place down on us. And whoever did this could be waiting outside."

They came to a door and Will opened it onto a corridor filled with the scent of freshly dug earth. He turned the penlight to the left and realized they were headed in the direction of the elevator. Rocks and dirt was strewn across the floor, and caused them to slip on rocks. Will took hold of Raeta's hand and saw she was looking at him with an uneasy expression and gripped his hand. He didn't have to ask the question.

"I don't want to get lost," she said. "I just want out of this place." They moved along the corridor in the feeble glow from the penlight but encountered no door. When it seemed they couldn't find the end of the corridor, Will began thinking he had been mistaken about their direction.

"How big is this place?" he asked.

"I'm not certain," Raeta replied. "But it was a major installation when our people were here. I looked over the plans before we left the ship, but didn't study them closely. I had no idea I would be trapped down here."

"Is there any branch from this corridor?" She began visualizing the plans she had seen. They were vague, but she recalled they should be near a door.

"There should be a door on the left, but I don't know where it leads." Will nodded.

"We better find it. With the circulating system out, the air will become foul quickly." He caught the door in his light.

"There it is," he said. Going to it, Raeta held tightly to his hand. It was as if she was frightened of the dark, but Will felt sexually aroused.

Stopping at the door, he let go of her hand and turned the wheel and the door swung inward. Will moved his light around, recognizing most of the equipment.

"This is a genetics lab." Raeta was familiar with what it was. He was suddenly regarding her with a puzzled expression.

"Why the hell would they put a genetics lab in a defense complex?" Will asked, his gaze locked on her. He expected an answer, but she was unsure as to how much she was allowed to say. He took her arm and pulled her close to him. The excitement this caused was almost too much for her.

"What went on here, Raeta?" She couldn't control herself, and decided to tell him everything.

76

"We created the human race, Will. If we hadn't intervened, there would be no humans on this planet. You're a genetic descendant of Zeus' family, the twins of Athena's." He was astounded and had no idea what to say. He released her arm and stepped away from her, missing the disappointment she showed.

Standing silent, she wanted him to touch her again, but Will stepped out the door and she followed.

"We've got to find a way out of here," he said, moving off down the corridor. Raeta stepped beside him and took hold of his hand.

Ophelia and Janis walked on opposite sides of Zeus as he moved the instrument over the cooling ground. He caught a faint trace of life energy on the instrument.

"They're below us," he said. "We've got to find a way down." Janis wasn't happy that Will was down in the dark with Raeta. It didn't occur to her that she was jealous, just wished she was the one down there with him.

"How can we get them out?" Janis asked, keeping her voice even. Ophelia sensed how Janis felt and had a hard time suppressing a smile.

"Can't we dig down to them?" Ophelia asked.

"No," Zeus replied. "There's too much earth between us, and we have to take into consideration the construction of the complex. There has to be another way."

"Too bad we can't just blast a way down," Janis remarked. Zeus cocked an eyebrow and thought for a moment.

"That might be possible," he said. "I don't know how long our weapons can last under sustained firing, but it might work."

"Anything's better than just standing here," Ophelia said.

"I'll get a weapon," Zeus said.

Will hadn't looked at her since she had taken his hand, nor said a word since leaving the lab. She wondered what he was thinking.

"I believe there's another door just ahead," she said. He turned the light on the wall and saw a door only a few feet from them. If Raeta had waited, they would have passed it in the dark. Will stepped to it, turned the wheel, and pushed it open. What he saw was more to his liking. Narrow spiral stairs went up from the room, yet he said nothing. They went to the stairs and Will motioned for her to start up.

Following her, their steps made a metallic drumming in the darkness. They stopped at the next level and he noted the light growing dim. At the end of the bare room was another spiral staircase beckoning to them. Going to it, he again motioned for her to start up.

At the next level, the light was almost gone, but Will saw the elevator shaft with sunlight streaming in. They hurried toward it. Will turned the dying light up and saw the remnants of the cover twenty feet above them. He turned to Raeta.

"How good are you at climbing?" Raeta bent her head back and looked up the shaft.

"I can make it," she replied, looking at him. "But what do we do when we get up there? That opening isn't wide enough for us to get through." He took the rifles from his shoulders and lay one down and hefted it.

"I'll blast the cover, climb up, and get out. That way I can help you out." She couldn't see his expression, but his voice gave nothing away.

Will leaned into the shaft, aimed the rifle, and fired. He was rewarded with a blinding flash above and a shower of falling sparks and shards of metal. Sunlight blazed down the shaft hurting their eyes. As their eyes became adjusted, Raeta saw a cable that had been blown loose. She took hold of it and began climbing. Will stared, impressed by a woman who took such initiative. When he saw her climb through the opening, he took hold of the cable and started up.

Zeus, Janis, and Ophelia were startled by the blast that tore through the metal cover. As they went to it, Raeta emerged. Zeus took hold of her arm and helped her out.

"I had no doubt you would find a way out, Raeta," Zeus said. Raeta leaned close to Zeus and spoke in a low voice.

"Will found the lab. He knew what it was so I told him the truth." Zeus gave her a stern look but said nothing. He knelt down and extended his hand to Will who was grateful for the help.

"Thanks," he said, getting to his feet. Raeta was surprised when he didn't say anything about the lab. He looked at the black scar surrounding the temple.

"They done a thorough job," Will commented.

"Janis has something to tell you, Will," Ophelia said. Janis glanced at Raeta then to Will.

"The Grays aren't the Kraken." He couldn't conceal his surprise.

"The Grays are being used by the Kraken," Janis continued. "I found out when one took me aboard during the attack."

"Let's go to the ship," Zeus said. "It's more comfortable than standing here in this heat."

The president was satisfied with his decision. With Blaine and Schiffer out of the way there would be no one to question any action he took. He felt it was ingenious sending them to the crash site, but he also felt a strange disquiet, something he couldn't clearly define. He wasn't the first to feel like this, but none wanted to speak about such a vague feeling. The president had the activation of HAARP on his mind and how close it was to becoming operational. Now he wondered why he had ordered it activated. Of course, he thought, to shield the planet against that ship. He had to protect the people of Earth and the other leaders had agreed. They concurred that Earth had to be protected. But against whom? None of them had a satisfactory answer. They only knew Earth had to be shielded, never mind against whom.

With each passing day, the leaders' disquiet grew. It was like they had committed some heinous crime they couldn't remember. Whatever was troubling them didn't last long. Every time the feeling came to mind, it was replaced by a feeling of satisfaction. They had no recollection of the disquiet, until it struck again. Each recurrence lasted longer, and a foreboding grew in them. The president had just experienced his first such feeling, it wouldn't be his last.

Russian president, Kirov was first to have the disquiet reach a crescendo, clearing his mind. He saw the Gray and began to understand what was happening. He recognized the threat, and suffered a fatal heart attack. There would be no chance for anyone to speak of what they thought might be happening. Everything was going well and it was determined to keep it that way, no matter who had to die.

Once HAARP was activated, they could ignore the ship from space. It wouldn't be able to land, and would be helpless to prevent the take over.

The Brotherhood had worked millennia controlling Earth, but faced a crisis. A crisis so unimaginable that it had forced them into the takeover. After Kirov's death, the Grays were instructed to maintain tighter control over their charges' minds. If they didn't, it would be them who faced an indefinable threat to their existence. They obeyed the commands that came from someplace unknown to them from a strong mind that had cleverly gotten control over them.

TEN

The office was quiet as each man tried to understand the significance of what was happening. Knowing the president wanted them out of Washington, neither could comprehend the change in the man who was their boss and close friend.

"What the hell are we going to do, Aubrey?"

"I haven't a clue, Chet. I don't like this situation at all." Schiffer leaned forward and ran his hand over his chin.

"We can't risk walking into a trap," Aubrey said. "They could be waiting at the airport." He wasn't used to failure, yet that was what Aubrey faced.

"We have to get to Yucatan, Chet. I've got to know what happened to Will and the twins." Schiffer was silent as his eyes widened at the idea he had.

"Have you ever done any parachuting, Aubrey?" That got him a puzzled look.

"No, I leave that to people like yourself."

"It's a way into Yucatan." Aubrey didn't take long to consider the idea.

"And the only safe option open to us. By God, Chet, I'm going to parachute out of a plane." Schiffer stood with a determined look.

"Let's get our asses to the airport and get our gear. Can you trust the crew of your jet?"

"No problem, Chet. What's happened to the president bothers the hell out of me. I don't like things I can't explain. Moreso when it happens to someone I like and respect." Schiffer understood how Aubrey felt as he felt the same. He also knew there was nothing they could do by remaining in Washington.

As they came out of the office, Aubrey motioned for Crist and Moore to come with them. Nothing was said until they stepped outside the building. Aubrey looked casually up and down the street. Everything seemed normal, but he was certain someone would be waiting to follow them.

"What is it?" Schiffer asked. Aubrey glanced at him.

"I'm trying to spot our tail." It hadn't occurred to Schiffer the Secret Service might have a tail on them.

"Would they do that?" Aubrey gave him an annoyed look.

"Christ, Chet, you saw how paranoid they are at the White House. Of course they have a tail on us." Moore narrowed his eyes as he looked down the street.

"Sir," Moore said. "That brown Ford Taurus halfway down the block is Secret Service. I know the guy in the passenger seat." Aubrey cocked an eyebrow and nodded.

"Good," Aubrey said. "Let's get to the parking garage."

As they walked, Aubrey glanced over his shoulder. The car Moore had spotted hadn't moved, and wouldn't until they came out in a car. What was needed Aubrey thought, was a ploy to draw them away. He was certain the other exit from the garage would be covered too. As they entered the garage, a thought struck Schiffer.

"We better get the hell out of town before they decide to lock us up, Aubrey."

"I've got an idea," Aubrey said. "Crist, I want you to drive away from here and lead them on a grand tour of the Potomac." Aubrey emphasized his next words.

"Lose them! Ditch the car and bring a cab to Andrews."

"Excuse me, sir, but how are we going to convince them to follow without four of us in the car?" Crist asked.

"Yeah, Aubrey," Schiffer said. "How do we convince them?" Aubrey left the garage without saying a word. The men exchanged puzzled glances, wondering what he had in mind.

Aubrey returned shortly accompanied by three unkempt men in ragged clothes and reeking of alcohol. Aubrey raised his hand to them.

"This is us," Aubrey said. "That car's too far away to see who's in the car, but they'll know it's four men." Aubrey turned to Crist.

"I promised these gentlemen an enjoyable ride and gave them each twenty dollars." They looked at him with pleased expressions.

"They won't get close enough to see who's in the car, sir," Crist said. Aubrey nodded.

"We'll give you five minutes, then leave." Crist hurried to the car and pulled it to a stop in front of his guests. Aubrey helped them in and Crist drove down the ramp.

Moore had returned to the entrance to watch and saw the Secret Service car pull out and follow Crist. He waved to Aubrey who looked satisfied.

"We can now go to the airport without them being the wiser," Aubrey said. Moore got another car and they were on their way. As they drove, the sky grew overcast as a thunderstorm rolled over the capital and they were moving through a blinding downpour. The thunder sounded like artillery fire and the lightning was white and sharp.

Moore pulled to a stop beside a hangar rather than risk being seen in the parking lot. Aubrey now faced a dilemma and looked at Schiffer in an odd way.

"Now what?" Schiffer asked.

"I'm going to have to do the flying, Chet. I can't call in the crew without letting them know where we are." Schiffer got an annoyed frown.

"How can you pilot the plane and jump?" Schiffer asked. Moore turned in the front seat to face them.

"I can fly it, sir. I'm qualified on the Lear jet."

"I didn't know that," Aubrey said, impressed.

"Good," Schiffer said. Aubrey looked at him feeling things were going well.

"We may as well get started, Chet. The parachutes are on the plane." Schiffer wasn't satisfied with the turn of events, but there was no backing out. He regarded Moore for a moment.

"Can you take off in this sort of weather?" Schiffer asked. Moore nodded.

"Sure can, General. Nothing for you to worry about except jumping when the time comes." Schiffer looked at Aubrey who had a smug look. Schiffer exhaled loudly.

"Why the hell are we sitting here, Aubrey?"

"Damned if I know." They got out of the car and were soaked before they got inside the hangar. Schiffer spotted the guard standing inside the front of the hangar and stopped. Aubrey bumped into him and Schiffer pointed. Aubrey looked surprised.

"It's standard procedure to have a guard at a government hangar. I thought you knew, Aubrey?" He did! It seemed their situation had caused a lapse of memory. Aubrey nodded to Schiffer's shoulder.

"Think those four stars will convince him to allow us to take off?" Schiffer cocked an eyebrow and frowned.

"He's a private! Privates don't argue with generals, Aubrey." Schiffer went quickly to the guard who snapped to rigid attention and saluted.

"You're relieved. Report to the officer of the day."

"Yes, sir." He turned and started from the hangar, stopped, and came back to Schiffer. The young man looked nervous, but spoke concisely.

"Sir, would you mind if I waited for the rain to slacken. The officer of the day's post is two miles from here, and I have to walk." Schiffer smiled.

"It's more comfortable at the rear of the hangar, Private. And help yourself to the coffee." He gave Schiffer a pleased smile and nodded.

"Thank you, sir." He headed for the rear without giving them a second look.

Schiffer boarded the plane to check the chutes while Aubrey and Moore waited for Crist. He finally came into the hangar, stopped in front of Aubrey, and wiped the rain from his face.

"Have any trouble losing your tail?" Aubrey asked. Crist smiled.

"Those Secret Service people aren't as sharp as they would like to believe, sir." Aubrey looked pleased and patted him on the back.

"Okay. Let's get ready for takeoff." Moore done a walk-around inspection as Aubrey went through the preflight check. Moore came onboard and pulled the hatch closed.

"Everything's ready, sir," Moore said, slipping into the pilot's seat.

"And we're checked out here," Aubrey said. Schiffer and Crist were strapping themselves in. Moore looked over the instruments and glanced at Aubrey.

"All ready to go, sir." Aubrey nodded and pulled the strap around him.

"Let's get the hell out of here." Moore started the engines and checked their rpm. After another cursory glance at the instruments he pushed the throttle forward and released the brakes. The jet rolled out of the hangar into the pouring rain.

"Make certain your straps are secure, sir," Moore said pulling his tight. "This takeoff might prove a little tricky." Moore slipped the headset on and contacted the tower for clearance.

At first, there was concern about them taking off in such adverse weather, but Aubrey told them they were under presidential order. Reluctantly, they cleared them.

Moore pushed the throttles forward until they could hear the muffled roar of the engines. He let off the brakes and the plane began rolling down the runway. It was quick to lift from the wet concrete and begin its climb. Moore took the plane up until they were out of the clouds and rain and turned southwest. All onboard felt relieved to be away from Washington.

"How long till we're over Yucatan?" Aubrey asked. Moore done some quick mental math.

"Five, five and a half hours, sir."

"Once we jump, Moore, I want you to head for the airport at Mexico City. I know you'll be low on fuel, but you should make it safely."

"Yes, sir. What do I tell them when we land?"

"The truth. That the general and I jumped over Yucatan and I ordered you to Mexico City." Moore looked at his boss and smiled.

"I don't know anymore than that, sir." Aubrey patted his shoulder as the plane continued through the clear sky.

Will paced like a cat in the confines of the ship. What Janis had told him, what he had learned from Raeta, had him wondering what this whole thing was about. He stopped and faced Zeus.

"Who are these Kraken?" Will asked. Raeta was puzzled as to why he hadn't mentioned the lab to Zeus. Zeus gave Raeta an uneasy look, knowing most of the younger generation hadn't been told about the Kraken. Now she was about to learn the truth. He looked back at Will.

"We believe the Kraken are our people," Zeus said, calmly. Raeta's eyes widened and her mouth fell slowly open. Will was really confused.

"Could you please explain that?" Ophelia asked. Zeus decided to tell them all of it. He needed their help and deserved to know the whole story.

"Millennia ago," Zeus began. "Our home world was wracked by a terrible war. We, the losers, were banished. We traveled through space until we discovered this solar system and began exploring the planets. We found Earth inhabited by primitive humanoids, and genetically altered them into the human race. We didn't want to be alone, so we became the gods of your ancient civilizations.

"We thought we had Kraken spies among us.

When they saw what We had done, they formed what is known as The Brotherhood. Since the first civilizations, The Brotherhood has subverted human history without your being aware of it. Certain people knew about The Brotherhood, but only ones who could be controlled were permitted to alter history." Zeus paused for a moment, his audience waiting to hear more.

"The Brotherhood developed the unstable economic system that's plagued all civilizations. They gave you rudimentary weapons, and your history developed into a well-designed program. They guided you into the nuclear age, and I never thought it would prevent you from turning your world into a nuclear wasteland. I was wrong. It was those very weapons that prevented another world war.

"Seeing how they guided you, and your desire for peace, I believe they want to take control and use the population as slaves." They stood silent, their eyes locked on Zeus. Raeta was stunned by what she had just learned.

"You said you adapted a planet for yourselves," Will said. "Was it Mars?"

"No," Zeus replied. "Our planet lies in the outer reaches of the solar system. It has an orbit of 3600 years, and never comes closer to the sun than the asteroid belt."

"What caused your war?" Janis asked. Zeus got a sad look.

"The same thing that caused wars on your planet. Hatred, greed, someone believing he's better than his neighbor. Our war happened so long ago that the records have deteriorated beyond recall. We know of The Brotherhood from watching how civilizations on Earth rose and fell."

"What about Janis and me?" Ophelia asked. Zeus glanced at Will with a proud look.

"Will is, genetically, of my family line," Zeus replied. "You sisters are of the family of Athena. What makes you three so special is you're the only ones with an unbroken genetic line." Raeta looked at Zeus and swallowed hard.

"Tell me more of the Kraken," Raeta said. Zeus looked at her with a frown.

"Not much more to tell, Raeta. Some of them followed us for years, trying to keep the conflict alive."

"What are they doing now?" Will asked. Zeus shook his head.

"I can't be certain," Zeus said. "But they somehow got control of the telepathic Grays. My guess is, they're using them in their takeover of Earth." He got a grim look.

"They already seem to have began doing so." Will frowned and rubbed his chin.

"How can we stop them?" Will asked.

"They have to be destroyed – unless we can make peace with them," Zeus replied. "I see no hope for the latter. They're much too arrogant."

"Isn't there someway we can open a dialogue with them?" Janis asked. Zeus turned to her.

"We don't know who their leader is," Zeus replied. "We have to be cautious. If they discover our planet, it could be an invitation to destruction."

"Why have they been interfering in our history?" Ophelia asked.

"Control," Zeus replied. "And to let us know they're here. It might even be some reason we can't guess."

"We've got to find a solution," Will said. "Or the Earth will be lost."

"Listen!" Raeta exclaimed. They heard the sound of a jet coming low and slow.

They hurried out of the ship and saw parachutes open as the plane turned to the north. The men in the chutes were too distant for identification. One wasn't able to control his descent, and Will knew who it was.

"Aubrey!" Will exclaimed. "Maybe we have help in solving this mess." They walked to where the men would land. Aubrey hit with an impact Will knew had to be painful, and the chute covered him.

"Get this fucking thing off me," Aubrey shouted. Will began uncovering him and Janis laughed. To her, it looked funny to see him struggle from under the canopy. Will released the harness as Schiffer came over smiling.

"We made it, Aubrey," Schiffer said. Aubrey scowled.

"I can see that!" he snapped. It was clear Aubrey didn't like parachuting, and quickly got to what had brought them here.

"What the hell happened, Will?" Aubrey demanded. Will glanced at Zeus and back to Aubrey.

"That's what we've been trying to figure out," Will replied. "These are friends from the ship, Zeus and Raeta." Will looked at Aubrey with a grin.

"How do you plan on leaving?" Will asked, and got a cold glare from Aubrey.

"You don't know what's happening in Washington, Will," Schiffer said. His words erased Will's grin and gave him a bad feeling.

"Then you don't bring good news," Zeus said. Schiffer got an annoyed look.

"We had to get away from there," Aubrey said. "The president has —"

"Someone, or something, controlling him," Zeus finished. Aubrey's eyes narrowed.

"How did you know?" Aubrey asked. "And how did you get here so quickly? I thought you wasn't due for days."

"Let's go to the ship, Aubrey," Will said. "We'll fill you and the general in. We've got to determine how to deal with this crisis."

When everything was pieced together, the picture wasn't bright and the situation seemed hopeless.

"I don't see anything we can do," Schiffer said. "These Kraken have ingeniously out maneuvered us."

"The hell they did," Aubrey said. "We didn't know what was going on. Now we're going to have to do some maneuvering."

"What can we do?" Will asked. Aubrey got a frown and clasped his hands in front of him.

"I'll think of something." But Aubrey could conceive of nothing that would stand a chance of success. They were stranded, without resources, and not a friend left. Aubrey wasn't the sort to buckle under such circumstances.

"I suggest we return to the ship," Zeus said. "We'll have time to devise a plan."

"Are you crazy?" Schiffer asked. "Once HAARP is activated, nothing will be able to come down from space."

"What would you suggest, General?" Ophelia asked. Schiffer regarded her with a lost expression.

"There may be a way around this HAARP," Raeta said. "It's only a possibility, but I don't see why it wouldn't work."

"What do you mean, Raeta?" Zeus asked. She thought for a moment.

"We could convert a probe to explode a pulse generated plasma field," Raeta replied. "If it comes down on top of the device, it should burn out most of its circuits." Will was impressed.

"Sounds good to me," Will said. Aubrey looked from Will To Zeus and nodded.

"If Will thinks it's a good idea, I'm willing to give it a try," Aubrey said. "Can you think of anything better, Chet?" Schiffer got an irritated look.

"Only sit on my ass and wonder what might be done."

"Then you agree we return to the ship?" Zeus asked. Janis and Ophelia nodded.

"We're in this together, Zeus," Janis said. "We've got to try to get something done." As Zeus glanced at Will, Aubrey, and Schiffer, each nodded. Zeus turned to Raeta.

"Prepare the ship for departure, Raeta. I'll make certain our guests are secured." Raeta went to the flight controls and Zeus showed the others to a seat."

"The trip won't take long," Zeus said, as he tightened the straps around Ophelia and Aubrey. "We'll take off in a few minutes, so relax." Zeus took the seat next to Raeta and pulled the straps around him. Janis reached out to Will.

"Hold my hand," she said. "I've never taken off in a space ship like this before." He took her hand and gave it a reassuring squeeze.

"There's a first time for everything," Will said. "This is my first time being on a space ship." Janis got a weak smile as they felt the low hum and she tensed.

ELEVEN

Raeta took the ship away from Earth and set it on autoguidence. She turned the seat and listened to what was being said.

"We've got to be on Earth to be effective against the Kraken," Janis said. She had stated the problem bluntly, and they all knew it.

"Janis is correct," Zeus said. "The Kraken must be forced into the open to be defeated." Schiffer gave Zeus a grim look.

"Once HAARP is operational, it's going to be dangerous, if not impossible, to return to Earth," Schiffer said.

"Not impossible," Aubrey said. Zeus nodded.

"We must consider that if we knock out HAARP with a plasma burst," Zeus said, grimly. "The Kraken will know where the technology came from, and they'll be waiting for us."

"He's right," Will said. "We've got to find a way that won't alert them to our presence. Anything in mind, Aubrey?" Aubrey cocked an eyebrow and glanced around.

"I'm working on something," Aubrey replied.

"Suppose we get back to Earth," Ophelia said. "Then what? Where do we look for the Kraken? Or The Brotherhood?" Schiffer gave Zeus a questioning look.

"Just where would we look for them?" Schiffer asked. Zeus had been considering that, but had come to no conclusion.

"They won't be easy to find," Zeus admitted. "Their base must be in a strategic location, and not obvious to their activity."

"The Yucatan?" Janis asked.

"No," Zeus replied. "It would give them screening but isn't located near enough to a center of military and political power." Will considered that and thought of something.

"Would their base have to be on land?" Will asked.

"No," Zeus said. "What are you thinking, Will?" Will looked at Schiffer and Aubrey.

"Chesapeake Bay," Will replied. Schiffer and Aubrey glanced at each other knowing that would cover a multitude of problems.

"Wouldn't that be obvious?" Ophelia asked.

"Not if they travel by boat," Will said. Aubrey gave him a quizzical look.

"Would you clarify that?" Aubrey asked. Will thought, putting his thought in cohesive form.

"Suppose they use modified boats," Will explained. "A boat goes out in the bay, one of their craft comes up, passengers transferred, and the boat returns to shore. No one would be the wiser because there hadn't been a thing for them to see."

"That would place them in a strategic location," Schiffer agreed.

"How would you get to a place like that?" Raeta asked. That question posed a difficult problem.

"We may have to destroy such a base, if our ship is to be safe in orbit," Zeus said.

"That won't protect you against HAARP," Schiffer said.

"If such a base exists, how do we detect it?" Janis asked. "We have to be certain of its location if further action is required."

"A sensible suggestion, Miss Randall," Schiffer said, looking to Zeus. "How can we do it?"

"What about satellite imagining?" Will suggested. Aubrey now looked to Zeus.

"If your instruments can penetrate the HAARP field, we have a chance," Aubrey said.

"HAARP was designed to stop projectiles," Schiffer said. "Not counter electromagnetic waves." That settled it for Will and he turned to Raeta.

"Can you receive satellite transmissions?" Will asked.

"Certainly," Raeta replied.

"It could prove a source of information," Schiffer said. "We may learn more than the location of their base."

"Of course!" Aubrey exclaimed. "They've got to transmit instructions to units. We may be able to learn what their plan is."

"I'll have someone monitor the satellites as soon as we return to the ship," Zeus said. They also discussed the possibility of interfacing their technologies. As human technology had been checked in ways by The Brotherhood, it was felt it wouldn't be easy. Overcoming that could prove to be a problem, Raeta explained. It was Janis who came up with a solution.

"Why not replace what's in our satellites with your technology?" Janis asked. Zeus was impressed.

"That would save time," Zeus said. "And we can fit them with more sophisticated sensors." Raeta was interested in the discussion, and Will could tell she loved her work.

"I'll work on the basics," Raeta said.

"What do we do in the meantime?" Aubrey asked.

"Try to discover a way to break the telepathic control on the Earth leaders," Zeus replied. "If we succeed, we'll have more aid in combating the Kraken."

"I wonder if we could get the Grays to help?" Janis asked. "Maybe they could transport the president to one of their ships."

"How can you contact them?" Aubrey asked, curious.

"Telepathy," Ophelia replied. "They know when we want to see them."

"You can do that?" Raeta asked, amazed.

"Yes," Janis said. "When I was taken from the complex, they knew Ophelia and I were in danger. I got a sense of disgust from the Gray when I communicated with it. I sensed its displeasure at destroying the complex."

"When can you contact them?" Zeus asked. Ophelia and Janis exchanged glances and Ophelia looked at Zeus.

"Let's wait until we have a plan," Ophelia said.

"How do we know we can trust them?" Will asked.

"We don't have a choice, Will," Janis replied, with a frown.

The people from Earth were impressed as Raeta maneuvered toward a ship that dwarfed them. It seemed larger as they moved through the airlock into the hangar. Leaving the small ship, they followed Zeus and Raeta along corridors and up lifts to other decks. Ophelia felt certain it wouldn't take long for her to get lost on such a large ship.

They met with Zeus' staff, who was then briefed by Zeus on recent developments. The existence of the Grays shocked them, more so that they were in contact with Ophelia and Janis.

"Where do these beings come from?" Vecia asked. The exobiologist had light blonde hair and kept her dark brown eyes on the sisters.

"We don't know," Ophelia replied. "We haven't picked up a clue about their origin."

"They must be blocking your minds," Raeta said.

"That's what we believe," Janis said. "They sense our curiosity."

"They're cautious," Aubrey said. ""Probably don't want any intrusion on their planet." Schiffer got an annoyed look.

"Then why the hell are they intruding on Earth?" Schiffer asked.

"Could it be their planet of origin?" Janis asked. The question brought a moment of silence. Vecia grasped what she meant.

"Are you suggesting this race evolved before humans?" Vecia asked. Janis nodded.

"It's possible," Janis replied. "They breathe our air and aren't uncomfortable in Earth gravity or temperature range."

"If that's true, they may know more about The Brotherhood than we do," Zeus said. "But that makes it inexplicable as to why they're involved instead of preventing the takeover."

"That's puzzled me since Janis told us The Brotherhood ordered the Grays to destroy the complex," Ophelia said. "Who is using who? And for what purpose?" Castor, chief science officer, kept his gray eyes on Ophelia as he rubbed his light brown hair.

"I suggest caution until the situation is clarified," Castor said, with a perplexed look. "We don't want to find ourselves caught between two warring factions." No one disagreed with that.

Raeta took them on a tour of the ship and walked close to Will. This wasn't appreciated by Janis, whose frown grew each time Raeta's hand brushed Will's. Ophelia had been watching her sister, and didn't need telepathy to know she was jealous.

"What's the power source of this ship?" Schiffer asked. Raeta glanced over her shoulder.

"We use the negative, or dark, gravitational force to push or pull the ship," Raeta replied. "Since it's constant throughout space, it's easy to control the ship. There's no waste of interior space for fuel tanks and engines."

"How does your plasma weapons function?" Aubrey asked.

"A vacuum conduit is surrounded by extreme cold," Raeta explained. "Gas is compressed by magnetic pressure, and an electromagnetic charge ignites it as it's fired by a magnetic surge." Raeta gave Will a sidelong glance, bewildered that he had said nothing about what he had learned from her and Zeus. His silence was disconcerting, but Raeta realized none of the Earth people had mentioned the project.

"How did The Brotherhood come about?" Ophelia asked. Raeta turned to the sisters.

"We believe they were spies," she replied. "They wanted to disrupt what we started on Earth."

"Why?" Schiffer asked. Raeta shook her head.

"I haven't an answer, General," Raeta replied. "Your race has been at their mercy almost from its inception." Schiffer and Aubrey exchanged puzzled looks.

"Since the earliest civilizations, The Brotherhood has manipulated mankind's advancement and meddled in your history," Zeus said, rejoining them.

"You've nothing to counter it?" Janis asked. Zeus frowned and nodded.

"We considered it," Zeus said. "But discovered you humans were intelligent enough to get along on your own." Zeus glanced at each of them.

"That's probably why they're taking over," Zeus continued. "They want subject people, not innovators."

"Our ignorance of them provided the means for them to take over," Schiffer said, angrily. "Not a shot fired in a secret invasion." Will shook his head.

"We may be able to stop them," Will said, looking to Zeus. "What's their greatest strength?"

"Anonymity," Zeus replied. "They prefer to let people they control do their work for them. If exposed, your planet might become safe." Will sucked in a deep breath considering what had to be done.

"We have to get back to Earth," Will said. "Let the people know what's going on and who is doing it."

"We can't go blundering around without knowing who we're looking for," Aubrey said.

"I feel our best ally is the Grays," Janis said.

"Then why are they allowing The Brotherhood use them?" Will asked.

"We damn well better find out," Schiffer said.

As the ship neared Earth, Zeus decided to keep it hidden behind the moon until it could safely move into orbit. It was learned that HAARP had been activated, and this forced them to decide on a course of action. Raeta found Will alone on the observation deck staring at the moon. She stepped beside him, her arm against his, but he appeared not to notice.

"If you're going to Earth, I want to go with you." He looked at her, still uncertain about her reaction in the complex.

"Why would you take such a risk?" Raeta shrugged, looking uncertain.

"I wish to help." He looked into her eyes and she averted them.

"Want to tell me about it, Raeta?" She avoided looking at him.

"There's nothing more to tell." Will knew from her rapid speech, and body language, it was something more. If Raeta was feeling the same about him Janis was, Will knew he had trouble. He felt attraction to Janis and Raeta, but wasn't certain how to handle it.

"All right, Raeta, I'll relay your request to Zeus." She looked back at him with a slight smile.

"Whenever you're ready, Will, I'll be available." She walked away as Will scratched his head wondering what she meant.

A small probe was used to retrieve the first satellite. It was brought aboard, modified, and put back in orbit. Another was put in a synchronous orbit above the moon to receive the satellite's signal without exposing the ship. After a week, it was known The Brotherhood still hadn't ventured into the open. It was assumed they were having difficulty controlling the population. Will knew they had to move against The Brotherhood, and decided to press the issue.

"Correct me if I'm wrong," Will said, glancing around the table. "But I've learned HAARP isn't effective in polar regions."

"That's true," Schiffer said. "Earth's magnetic field at the poles breaks up its waves." Aubrey regarded Will with an uneasy expression.

"What are you thinking, Will?" Aubrey asked. Will looked at Zeus.

"I saw small ships in the hangar," Will said. "How many can fly in one, Zeus?"

"Two, why?" Will glanced around at the people.

"I propose to take one of those ships to Earth over the Arctic," Will replied. Once in the atmosphere, HAARP won't be activated and I'll be able to land."

"We can't be certain of that, Will," Aubrey said, alarmed. Will's expression turned hard.

"Since the rats haven't come out of their holes, it's time to find a way to plug the holes, Aubrey."

"You don't know where to look for them," Schiffer said. "We don't know where their base is."

"We don't have to worry about that, General," Will said, determined to have his way. "If we let the population know about them, they're beaten." Zeus glanced around and nodded.

"Will has a valid point," Zeus said. "What he proposes is less complicated than openly challenging them." Will gave him a nod.

"I have to go with him," Janis said. "I can contact the Grays should we need help." Raeta gave her a hard look.

"He must have a pilot," Raeta said. "I can do that." The look she got in return from Janis, Zeus saw was trouble.

"You'll both be needed," Zeus said. "We'll modify the ship." Aubrey looked at Will and grinned.

"What's the plan, Will?" Schiffer asked. He hadn't worked out details, just a general idea of what he wanted to do.

"I've got to find out if my contacts are still reliable. Then get subliminal messages broadcast over the major networks informing the people of The Brotherhood. It's the quickest way I can think of to destroy their control. If Janis can contact the Grays, maybe we can convince them to join us."

"You're making assumptions, Will," Ophelia said. He nodded.

"This may be the only way we have to avoid conflict," Will said. Zeus got a grim look.

"To battle the Kraken would devastate the Earth," Zeus said. Aubrey looked at Schiffer.

"What do you think, Chet?" Schiffer frowned and shrugged.

"What have we got to lose," Schiffer countered.

"We have to move," Will said. "The longer we wait the more time The Brotherhood has to consolidate its hold over the people." He glanced at Raeta and Janis, not liking being caught between their rivalry with him being the prize.

The modification completed, the three met with Zeus.

"You understand there's no way we can help if you get into difficulty," Zeus said. Will nodded.

"We'll handle it," Will said. "We'll use Janis' house as a base. I'm hoping she and Raeta will be safe there while I'm gone." Janis started to say something, but Will quickly raised his hand.

"I don't want any argument. I've got to work alone if I'm to get help from my contacts." Janis got a hurt look and nodded. Zeus was glad he wasn't in Will's shoes.

"You have the ship's weapons," Zeus said. "Once you use them, The Brotherhood will know the technology, so use discretion." Will looked at the women with an unwavering expression.

"If I'm not back in twenty-four hours, I want you both to return to the ship," Will said, in a no-nonsense tone. "Is that clear?" They glanced at him and nodded.

"All right, let's go."

As Raeta checked the instruments, she glanced over her shoulder at the passengers.

"Make sure your straps are snug," Raeta said. "We're going to hit magnetic turbulence over the pole." Janis and Will checked the straps. Raeta lifted the ship and took it out the hatch and down toward the moon's surface. Will didn't know what to expect when they landed, but knew it was up to him to disrupt the takeover of Earth. He was more uncertain of the women, but would worry about that later.

The turbulence felt like a hammer blow, and will saw Raeta struggling to control the ship. It was rocked and tossed in violent maneuvers that put them through heavy g-forces, but Raeta leveled out over the icecap and turned south.

"Is there someplace close to the house we can land, Janis?" Will asked.

"There's a clearing in the woods about a mile from the house."

"Show Raeta where to land," he said, loosening her straps. He released his straps and leaned forward.

"Can you set down in a wooded clearing, Raeta?" She nodded, keeping her eyes straight ahead.

"I'm staying low to avoid radar," she said. Will reached up and patted her shoulder causing her to shiver. Janis stood beside Raeta looking out the windscreen and saw the area she was familiar with.

"Over there," Janis said, pointing.

TWELVE

Raeta brought the ship in from the west, using the setting sun as a shield. She approached the woods, maneuvered, and set the ship down. They headed for the house moving among the trees. Movement caught Will's eye and he extended his arms stopping the women. He pointed to a man who stood by a tree with a clear view of the house.

"Are there more around?" Janis whispered. Will was wondering that as he looked the man over, noting he had no night vision equipment. He turned to the women.

"There might be one or two more around," Will whispered. Raeta felt alarmed.

"What are you going to do?" Raeta asked, softly. Will cocked an eyebrow in the growing darkness.

"You two are going to wait here. I'm going to quietly take that out." He didn't give them a chance to say anything, just slipped off among the trees.

He made his way behind the man, whose attention was lax. Will felt he had made too much noise in his approach, but the man was unaware he was behind him. Will stepped forward and chopped him at the base of the skull. He dropped without a sound. Will used the man's' belt to bind his hands behind him. He stood him against the tree so to anyone watching it would appear he was at his post. Will took his handkerchief and stuffed it in the man's mouth. Will was satisfied, and hurried back to the women.

"We can't stay here," he said, stopping in front of them. "We're going to have to take that guy with us."

"Where can we go?" Janis asked. He considered, and chose where to go.

"I've got a friend who lives just outside Washington. We'll be safe at his place."

"We can't fly there," Raeta said. Another problem, Will thought. There wasn't much chance of finding transportation, so he decide they would have to walk.

"Mr. Jacobs lives just a couple of miles from here," Janis said. "He's a friend of ours. Maybe we can get a ride from him."

"We've got to risk it," Will said. "We can't stay around here." He saw how Raeta was dressed, and silently moaned. They would have to chance going to the house.

"Raeta has got to change clothes," Will said. Janis nodded.

"She's about my size," Janis said. "Do you think it's safe to go to the house?"

"I don't know," Will replied. "But we've got to chance it."

Will lifted the unconscious man over his shoulder and turned to the women.

"Make certain none of his equipment is left," he said, in a low voice. Janis picked up the rifle and Raeta his pack. It was almost dark as they started across the open field. Will hoped another watcher didn't have night vision gear. The man proved no light burden, but leaving him would alert any of his friends if they came looking for him.

After a few minutes, they stood at the back door and Janis opened it as Raeta held the screen door. Will hurried in and put the man down and turned to the women.

"Get Raeta changed, but don't use any light. Then we'll go see that man." The women looked like shadows moving through the dim twilight. Will took the man into the basement knowing that after he regained consciousness he would be able to work his hands free.

Only a few minutes had passed, but he wished Janis and Raeta would hurry. When they returned, he smelled perfume but couldn't see either woman clearly.

"Let's go," Will said, and they went out the back door. The low light of a crescent moon gave the dark landscape form.

"Lead the way, Janis," he said. They followed her away from the house into a field overgrown with high weeds. As they moved, there was no indication anyone else had been watching the house. Will felt relieved they had gotten this far with little trouble, but hoped their luck would hold once they were on the road.

There was no traffic as they stepped onto the road and moved along at a brisk pace. Janis pointed to a small cottage.

"That's Mr. Jacob's place," Janis said. They walked toward the lighted windows and stopped before the porch. Janis turned to Will.

"Let me do the talking," she said. "They may have been around looking for Ophelia and me." Will nodded as she went up on the porch and knocked. A man with white hair, blue eyes, and a kindly expression opened the door.

"Janis," he said, surprised. "Where have you and Ophelia been? There have been people asking question about you both." She glanced over her shoulder at Will then back to Jacobs.

"I thought there might be, Mr. Jacobs. This is Will and Raeta. They've helped Ophelia and me avoid those people. We need your help to get into the city." Jacobs looked at Will and Raeta and made an odd request.

"Please hold out your hands." Janis got a puzzled look. Will and Raeta held their hands out, Jacobs looked closely at them and nodded.

"What were you looking for?" Will asked, curious.

"The people asking about the girls have peculiar hands," Jacobs replied. "The little finger on the right hand is crooked and the ring finger of the left hand is bent down and can't be leveled with the other fingers. All of those people had the same sort of hands, and I'll be damned if I believe it's a family trait."

"Those people pose a threat to your world," Raeta said, drawing a puzzled look from Jacobs.

"Don't you mean the country?" Jacobs asked. "They spoke with foreign accents. I thought they might be terrorists until they showed CIA identification."

"Shit! That's bad news," Will said. "It means they run the show. How long ago were they here?"

"Three days," Jacobs replied. "But there were a lot of them."

"Can you give us a ride, Mr. Jacobs?" Janis asked. He smiled and took keys from his pocket.

"Take the Camry, Janis. I've my pickup if I need to go into town. I never did like that damn car." Janis took the keys with a smile and kissed him on the cheek.

"Thank you very much, Mr. Jacobs," Janis said, squeezing his hand.

"If you want to thank me, get those damn foreigners out of the country." Will smiled.

"That's exactly what we hope to do, Mr. Jacobs," Will said. She handed Will the keys.

"You know where we're going," Janis said. Getting behind the wheel, he slipped the key into the ignition as the women crowded in beside him. Janis sat next to him as he backed the car into the road and turned the car toward the city.

"What did he mean, they had CIA identification?" Raeta asked. Will kept his eyes on the road.

"It means they control the intelligence gathering apparatus." He gave Raeta a curious look.

"What about the deformed hands, Raeta?" he asked. She gave him a worried look.

"It's the first I've heard about it."

"There might be an advantage in it."

"What sort of advantage, Will?" Janis asked.

"If the Kraken have deformed hands, we have a sure way to identify them," he replied. "I'm damn curious as to why they have such an interest in you and Ophelia."

"They probably learned about us from the Grays. Maybe they believe we pose a threat to them."

"Then they know you cooperated with the Grays, and that they didn't check you medically. If I came across information like that, I would want to know what makes you two special."

"What's the plan, Will?" Raeta asked.

"What we came here for – to break the power of the Kraken. I don't want to involve the Grays until we're certain of success."

"How certain can you be about your friend?" Janis asked. Will glanced at her and smiled.

"Damn certain. He's in charge of R&D at Georgetown University. Very few people know his department exists."

"Could he be under the influence of the Kraken?" Raeta asked. Will shook his head.

"Not Zachary! He's not influenced by anyone, even a president. And he's not easily fooled. He probably knows more about what's going on than we do."

"How do you know that?" Janis asked.

"He has contact with the top scientists in every field. If anyone had an overview of what's happening it's Zachary."

As they drove into the suburbs, the traffic became heavier causing them to slow down.

"It looks so damn normal!" Will exclaimed. "If I didn't know what was going on, I would have no suspicion."

"It's the way The Brotherhood works," Raeta said. "I used the ship's library to learn what I could.

It wasn't much, but deception is how they prefer to operate." Will looked on a street that looked like any weeknight.

"I've got to hand it to them, they're doing a damn good job," he said, glancing at the women.

"We're going to have to operate the same way. If we're lucky, the people will never know it happened."

"You sound so confident," Janis said. Will laughed.

"It keeps my morale up when I'm scared. Believe me, this is one time I'm really scared."

"Of what?" Raeta asked, looking baffled. He glanced at her and his expression became grim.

"Failure. It's the only thing that spooks me."

"You've never failed?" Raeta asked. He stopped for a light and looked at her.

"I've screwed up a lot. I get over it, but the idea bothers me."

"That doesn't make sense, Will," Janis said.

"I know. But it's part of being human – feeling irrational."

Will pulled the car to the curb and shut off the engine. He sat looking over the street. There were a few cars parked along the street and he saw a couple walking hand in hand.

"What's wrong, Will?" Raeta asked, uneasy. He waved his hand at the scene before them.

"Nothing! Everything's just as you would expect it to be. Unbelievable!"

"Where's your friend's house?" Janis asked. He pointed to a two-story house down from where they had parked.

"The gray one. Let's go." They got out of the car and walked leisurely along and went up on the porch and Will pressed the doorbell. The door opened and a man with jet-black hair and brown eyes that widened in surprise.

"Jesus! Where have you been, Will?" Will's suspicion kicked in.

"Has someone been looking for me?"

"Yes, really weird people with awkward hands. What the hell are you involved in?" Will glanced up and down the street.

"Can we come in, Zachary? I don't feel comfortable standing out here."

"Sure," Zachary said, stepping aside and opening the door wider. When he closed the door and turned to Raeta, he reached out and took her hand.

"Where did you find this lovely lady, Will? And don't tell me she's an intelligence operative, I won't believe it." Will hadn't noticed before, but the tight lemon colored miniskirt made every curve of Raeta's body stand out. Will stared at what Janis had accomplished. Janis stared too, envious.

"It's a long story," Will said. "Her name is Raeta, and this is Janis Randall." Zachery gave a pleased nod as he looked at Janis.

"Two! How selfish, Will, to keep them for yourself. I can't blame you though. Now tell me how you came to be in such charming company?"

"We need your help," Will said. Zachary's expression turned serious. This was the first time Will had ever asked him for help.

"Let's go in the living room," Zachary said. "I'll fix us a drink and you can tell me what's going on. I'm curious by some unusual occurrences lately."

It took almost an hour to relate what had been happening. When Will finished, Zachary looked at him and puckered his lips.

"So that's it. I knew something odd was going on, but had no idea it was anything like this." Zachary looked at them.

"How can I help?" Will quickly explained what he had in mind.

"Do you think it could work, Zachary?"

"I believe so. But if they control the president, there's a good chance he won't see the message. What do we do about that?" Will rubbed the back of his neck.

"I'll try to contact the Grays," Janis said. "See if they can take him onboard one of their ships." Zachary tugged on his ear as he turned his eyes to Raeta.

"You're certain the people on your ship can do nothing?" Zachary asked. Raeta looked at Will.

"Their ship can't come into orbit because HAARP has been activated," Will said. Zachary frowned.

"I wondered why it was being activated a year early," Zachary said, with an odd look. "Then we're on our own?" Will nodded.

"But we have to operate covertly, Zachary. We've got to keep this as quiet as possible," Will explained. Zachary shook his head.

"That's going to make it difficult, Will. If we ask others for help they're going to have to be told what they're up against."

"I know. But we can't say anything more than necessary to secure anyone's help.

If it were up to me, I would broadcast the goddamn story and let the people take care of the bastards. But this is an invasion by stealth, and we have to fight it as such."

"We can't reveal our presence because of our past contact with your people," Raeta said. "The Brotherhood suspects we might come to your aid, so they activated HAARP."

"You say they're the same as you?" Zachary asked.

"That's what we think," Raeta replied. "We don't know for certain. They make it seem humans are making the decisions, while the Kraken remain in the shadows and control events." Zachary glanced at her smooth hands and slender fingers.

"Your hands aren't deformed," Zachary said.

"I can't explain the deformity," Raeta said. Zachary gave her a nod.

"That's not important," Zachary said. "We need to contact someone who works at the network relay to help with the plan. Colin Wherter may be that man. He has the say so over all broadcasts from satellites. We may be able to beam your message to a satellite and get it beamed back to Earth in network programming."

"Is there anyone else who might help?" Janis asked.

"I think we should see Dr. Klast," Zachary said. "He's a psychologist and might know the best wording for maximum effect."

"It's been awhile since I seen him," Will said. "Can we talk to him now?"

"I'll give him a call," Zachary said, getting to his feet.

"Wait a minute, Zachary. Those people were here asking about me. It's possible your phone is tapped. Better call from a public phone." Zachary looked shocked and nodded.

"You're the expert in cloak and dagger operations, Will, I'll take your advice."

Stopping at a nearby pay phone, Zachary came back to the car. As Will pulled out, he noticed a dark sedan pull out half a block away. They had a tail. Will didn't say anything, just kept a watch on the rearview mirror and saw the car's lights come on.
It made no move to close with them and that puzzled Will. He was determined to lose them and made an abrupt turn down a residential street and parked.

"Everybody down."

"What the hell's going on?" Zachary whispered, from the backseat.

"We picked up a tail. I'm hoping we can lose them." They stayed down for some minutes, but no car came past. Will knew they had seen him turn, yet no car had followed. Was he becoming paranoid? No! Will didn't believe that, but where had the tail gone?

Will raised his head above the seat and looked out the rear window and saw an empty street. He didn't believe his luck. At least, not this sort of luck. They had to have seen him turn! Where the hell were they?

"I don't like this," Will said.

"What is it?" Raeta asked, from beside Zachary.

"We were being followed," Will replied. "I turned, they didn't."

"So we were lucky," Janis said, beside him. He shook his head as he looked over the street again.

"I don't think so, Janis. They're waiting for us to move."

"What the hell can we do, Will?" Zachary asked, uneasy. There was only one thing to do – they had to leave the car and get to Dr. Klast's on foot. The street was shadowed where the car set, so it could be done. They would have to move cautiously, and one at a time.

"Zachary, slip out the curbside door and got behind that hedge. Raeta, you follow, then Janis. Do it easy. Open the door only wide enough to slip out." Zachary was opening the door before Will finished speaking. He kept to a crouch and slipped across the sidewalk and behind the hedge. Raeta followed emulating his movements. Janis had wide eyes locked on Will.

"What are you going to do?" she asked, alarmed.

"Never mind. Just get out of the car."

"You can't go up against them alone, Will." He looked at her, their faces close together.

"I'm not planning to. I'm going to draw them away from you three. I'll meet you later at Klast's house. Now get out." She gave his hand a squeeze turned on the seat, pushed the door open and slipped out. Will heard the latch click as the door was pushed shut.

He waited a few minutes, sat up, started the car and pulled away. He kept glancing in the rearview mirror and saw the car pull out behind him, this time without lights. Will sped to an intersection, made a right turn, and burned rubber down the empty street. He had slowed enough for them to see his turn. Something wasn't right. They still weren't trying to gain on him, but held their distance. He had to do something to give himself time to get away on foot. He saw his opportunity beside a dark house.

Will turned into the alley before the tailing car seen him. He got out slipped along the side of the garage and waited. Squatting in the shadows, he saw the car turn the corner, slow down, and come along the street. They were looking for him, but went past the alley without stopping. Will was surprised. How the hell could they miss seeing the car? He shivered involuntarily realizing something was going on he didn't understand. After watching the car pass the alley three times without stopping, he decided it was time to get to Klast's house where he hoped the others would be waiting for him.

THIRTEEN

"I tell you, Chet, this lack of action and not knowing what's going on with Will is driving me up a wall."

"What can I say, Aubrey? There's not a damn thing we can do. Will and the girls will do their best." Aubrey got a disgusted look.

"That's just it," Aubrey said, waving an arm. "They might need help. Where can they find it? How do they know who they can trust?" Schiffer put a hand on Aubrey's shoulder.

"Quit worrying. You know Will can handle the situation." Aubrey looked at Schiffer.

"There's got to be something I can do? I'm going to see Zeus."

"He's just as helpless."

"Damnit, Chet, I need something to keep me occupied." Schiffer nodded.

"Let's see if he has some work we can do."

They found Zeus helping reassemble another satellite. Schiffer and Aubrey stopped behind him and he turned to them.

"What can I do for you, gentlemen?"

"We need work," Aubrey said. "Lack of action isn't my style, Zeus."

"He's worried about Will and the women," Schiffer added. Zeus nodded with an understanding look.

"I'm worried about them too," Zeus said. "I can use you two to monitor satellite transmissions. The people I have doing it now will be more useful examining the components. It may give us a clue as to how The Brotherhood manipulated your scientific progress." Aubrey spread his hands with a grateful look.

"Just so I'm distracted," Aubrey said. Zeus nodded.

"You might learn about them from transmissions," Zeus said, in a grim tone." "If Will starts anything, you'll probably be the first to hear about it." Schiffer got an agreeable look and tilted his head.

"Sounds interesting," Schiffer said. "Who knows, we may even get a clue as to what they plan for Earth and its inhabitants." Aubrey nodded.

"Okay, Zeus," Aubrey said. "We'll monitor satellites for you."

Will made it to Klast's home. He had watched for some time as the car had circled the block. Their action was confusing and unsettling for Will. He knew they had to have seen his car.

So why their lack of interest? Maybe Klast could shed light on it. Will had to learn something soon so he would know what had to be done after the broadcast.

He stopped on the corner across from Klast's house and watched the lighted windows. Nothing seemed out of the ordinary, Will thought. Like hell! Everything seemed out of place. He walked up on the porch, taking a look up and down the street. A tall man with salt and pepper hair and hazel eyes opened the door.

"We've been expecting you, Mr. Vaughn. Your companions have been most concerned about you."

"They made it all right?"

"Yes, Mr. Vaughn. Please come in." Coming into the living room, Janis and Raeta came to him.

"What happened, Will?" Janis asked. Will shrugged.

"Damn if I know! They just kept going past the car. I know they had to see it, but they didn't stop."

"Is that unusual?" Raeta asked. Will got a puzzled look.

"Unusual, no. It's screwy as hell. I don't understand what's happening."

"We better find out, Will," Zachary said. Will noted his odd expression.

"How do we do that?" Will asked. Klast glanced at Zachary and stepped in front of Will.

"You better have a drink, Mr. Vaughn," Klast said. "And a seat. I'll tell you as much as some colleagues and myself have been able to piece together.." He sat down between Janis and Raeta. Klast handed him the drink and sat down facing them.

"Your companions have filled in quite a few blanks," Klast began. "I've a more complete picture, but a lot I'm going to tell you is speculation."

"You have to know more than me, Doctor," Will said. Klast leaned back and draped his arms over his legs.

"I've learned there's a base in the southwest," Klast said. "Acquaintances in different specialties have been sent there by the government. As one of them told me before she left, she had been drafted. If they refused to go, their families were threatened. I haven't been able to glean a clue as to what's going on at the base."

"Whatever is, you can believe it's not for the benefit of Earth's people," Raeta said. Klast nodded with a solemn look.

"Some scientists sent there were particle physicists and nuclear engineers," Klast said. "Chemists, space engineers, and, most oddly, biologists. I think they might be constructing space ships. If they are, what are they to be used for? If they control Earth, who are they going to use those ships against?" A heady feeling of insight flashed in Will's mind and he looked at Raeta.

"They must know about your world," Will said. "They could be preparing an assault."

"We must warn Zeus," Raeta said. Janis looked at Will and nodded.

"I don't know how you can," Zachary said. "The Brotherhood controls all communication. I called the station and found that Wherter's been replaced."

"At Area C there's a transmitter," Will said. "We should be able to send a signal to a satellite the ship's monitoring."

"What's Area C?" Klast asked. Will glanced at Janis and felt she might not like going there, but it was the only chance he could see. Will explained what Area C was used for. Zachary leaned forward with a grim look.

"It's possible The Brotherhood is using it for the same purposes," Zachary said. "If they control the guards, it's very likely we can get our asses shot off, Will."

"I'll be the only one taking any risk. I know secrets about Area C even Aubrey doesn't know."

Ophelia had been pacing in her cabin trying to recall that strong, odd impression she had gotten from the tall Gray. What had the impression been about? Why was it so tenaciously bothering her? In light of what had happened, she felt it had been about The Brotherhood. As she could recall it was the uneasy, confused sense she had picked up from it. But why was it sticking so stubbornly in her mind? It hadn't been fear, more like anxiety about exposure. But exposure of what?

"Damnit!" she exclaimed. She couldn't clarify it and that was frustrating. The more she considered it, the more uncertain she became as to how much she was reading into it. Yet there had been the odd feeling from the Gray. That she was certain of. Ophelia wondered if the people on the ship might have a method to enhance memory. She went to see Zeus.

On the bridge, Ophelia was told Zeus was in his cabin. She had the bridge controller ask if she would be able to see him. She was told to come, and on arriving at the cabin, found him waiting and gestured for her to come in. After being seated, Ophelia faced Zeus hoping he held the answer to her vexing problem.

"Why did you want to see me?" She explained, and asked if there was a way to stimulate her memory. Zeus regarded her in silence for a moment after she finished.

"I'm not certain, Ophelia. We can ask Dr. Medina, and see if he can think of anything."

"Can we see him right away?" Zeus cocked an eyebrow, nodded, and went to the intercom.

"Can you come to my cabin, Dr. Medina?"

"I'll be there in a few minutes," A bass voice answered. He turned back to Ophelia with a puzzled look.

"What do you think the Gray was trying to conceal?" Ophelia frowned and shook her head.

"That's what I want to find out. I've got to be certain I'm not seeing more than the original memory." Zeus folded his arms and thought for a moment.

"If you can clarify it, we might get a fuller picture of what's going on with them." As Zeus spoke, Ophelia saw surprise grow on his face.

"What is it, Zeus?" He glanced at her, looking uncertain.

"Nothing I want to say anything about at present."

Medina came into the cabin and regarded Zeus.

"Why did you want to see me?" Zeus nodded to Ophelia.

"I'll let Ophelia explain. If anyone can help her you can." Zeus looked at Ophelia as she began telling Medina what she hoped to achieve. Medina stood rubbing his chin.

"Memory enhancement," Medina said. "There's an experimental drug that stimulates the nervous system."

"What about hypnosis?" Ophelia asked. Medina shook his head.

"It isn't a reliable memory enhancer," Medina replied. Ophelia glanced at Zeus as she got a determined look.

"I'll try the drug, Doctor." Medina looked at Zeus who nodded.

"It's her choice, Doctor." Medina looked back at Ophelia.

"We'll see if you can learn what you want from your cerebral neurons." Zeus took hold of her hand as she stood and faced him.

"You must have something important in your memory, Ophelia," Zeus said. "I don't think you would feel so strongly if you didn't." She got a weak smile and squeezed his hand.

"There's only one way to find out," she said. "Ready, Doctor?"

Schiffer was first to catch the strange message coming from a satellite.

"Listen to this, Aubrey." He switched the speaker on and the signal that seemed random quickly fell into a pattern Aubrey recognized as a code.

"Get Zeus, Chet. He may have a way of decoding this." Schiffer turned to the communications officer to see if she knew anything about decryption. The word was unknown to her and she gave him a baffled look. He glanced at Aubrey and smiled.

"Guess they're not as advanced as we thought," Schiffer said, and turned back to the woman. "Please ask Zeus if he can come and see us." She nodded and turned to the intercom. When Zeus responded, she told him the Earthmen wanted him in communications. He acknowledged he would be there quickly. Schiffer looked at Aubrey.

"I hope to hell he'll know what we're talking about," Schiffer said.

A few minutes later, Zeus came in and faced Aubrey and Schiffer.

"What is it?" Zeus asked. Schiffer turned up the volume and they listened for some minutes. Zeus' expression became one of bewilderment.

"It's a code," Aubrey said. "Is there some means to decode it?" Zeus nodded.

"The computer should be able to read it," Zeus said, and turned to the communications officer.

"Record and process this transmission," Zeus said. They watched her delicate fingers move over the communications panel then looked at Zeus.

"The computer's reading it," she said. Zeus nodded.

"How long before the computer can give a readout?" Zeus asked. She puckered her lips and thought for a moment.

"I'm not certain," she replied. "I'll put it on visual." She adjusted a small control under the monitor. Aubrey leaned close to Schiffer.

"You should have asked her if anyone could read it, Chet." Schiffer gave him an annoyed look and looked back at the monitor. What was there appeared as gibberish.

"What the hell is it?" Aubrey asked, puzzled. Zeus remained quiet, staring at the monitor and slowly turned to look at the Earthmen.

"A sophisticated cryptograph," Zeus replied. "One that's not going to be easy to break."

"Is it from your people?" Schiffer asked. Zeus motioned for his brown haired, blue eyed communications officer to make adjustments on the control panel. She quickly turned a surprised look to Zeus.

"It's coming from the vicinity of Mars," she said, amazed. The men were also surprised.

"How can it be coming from Mars?" Schiffer asked. She looked at him shaking her head.

"It's not coming from Mars," she said. "But in that general location. It's a signal from deep space." Aubrey looked at Zeus.

"You're certain your people isn't transmitting this?" Aubrey asked. Zeus looked to his officer who shook her head.

"This is an alien signal," she said. Schiffer got a frustrated look.

"Now who the hell's getting involved?" Schiffer asked. Zeus got a grim look.

"Someone already involved," Zeus replied. "I believe this to be from the Grays."

"What makes you think that?" Aubrey asked. Zeus inhaled slowly, forming his thoughts.

"It's not from our world. The Brotherhood has limited space flight capabilities. That leaves the Grays."

"We need to know what they're saying," Schiffer said. The woman got an uncertain look.

"I'm not certain the computer can cope with this," she said.

"It was programmed to recognize and translate alien languages," Zeus said.

"Languages not too dissimilar from ours," she said. "This is completely alien. It's possible, given time, the computer may be able to translate some of this."

"Begin the program," Zeus said.

They sat in the car looking down on Area C. It looked as it usually did to Will. Guards at the gate, some of the buildings had lighted windows, it was the same as when he had last been here.

"Are you certain there's a safe way in, Will?" Zachary asked.

"Yeah. The guards know me so I might be able to bluff my way out, if I have to."

"You can't go alone, Will," Janis said. He regarded her in the semidarkness.

"I can't take anyone with me. The guards will shoot anyone they don't recognize." She took hold of his hand." I have to go alone," Will said, emphatically.

"Won't they find it odd you showing up without having come through the gate?" Klast asked. All that concerned Will was getting to the transmitter.

"I hope I don't have to explain my presence, Doctor. I want to get in, use the transmitter, and get the hell out. I have no intension of standing around chatting with a guard."

"You want us to wait here?" Zachary asked. Will had already decided what they should do.

"No. Wait by the intersection. If you hear gunfire, get the hell away fast. If I'm able, I'll meet you back at Dr. Klast's house." As Will opened the door, Raeta took hold of his arm. He could see the concern on her pretty face.

"Maybe we should find a different way to contact the ship," she said, her voice filled with anxiety.

"We can't waste time, Raeta." He patted her hand and got out of the car.

"Don't worry. I've got more lives than a cat. But I've used up more of them than I'm entitled to." He was quickly fading into the shadows. Klast started the car and headed toward the intersection. He pulled off the road and began their tense wait for Will to return.

Will stood behind a tree and timed the perimeter guard. When he passed, Will began moving down the slope holding onto trees He dropped to the ground and crawled to the fence and waited for the guard to pass. The dew from the weeds clung to his chin and the air had a hot smell to it. He figured he had about three minutes to get under the fence and across the compound.

If he got hung up on the fence, it would be over real quick. The guard passed and moved slowly to the far end of the compound.

Will lifted the bottom of the fence and used his other hand to scoop out loose soil. He quickly had enough space to crawl through, but the guard was on his way back.

Will kept down, blending into the dark ground as he heard the man's boots crunching on the rock as he passed. The footsteps faded into the distance. Will lifted the fence and wriggled under it, got to his feet, and crouched as he made for the building. He moved using the shadows of the buildings for cover.

He stopped at the door and turned the knob, surprised when it opened. He stepped inside, glad the building was dark. He went to the room with the transmitter, slipped in and leaned against the door listening. Everything remained quiet and Will went to the transmitter. The room had no windows and he turned on the light.

The transmitter was off, and he wondered if anyone would know when he turned it on. He couldn't waste time thinking about that. He switched it on, sat down at the key and began sending a discarded code Aubrey would easily recognize. He finished in less than three minutes and shut the transmitter off. He now had to get out of the compound. He turned the light off and waited for his eyes to adjust to the darkness. This would be the most dangerous part of his endeavor.

Will got out of the building and was about to move toward the fence when he saw the guard. He pressed himself against the side of the building. Its shadow kept the guard from seeing him as he passed. The guard was almost to the fence where Will had come under. His foot slipped and he fell, his leg sliding under the fence. Will's heart leapt into his throat and he began to sweat. The man got to his feet swearing in a low voice and looked down. Will began to consider how to handle the guard, but the man kicked dirt, swore again, and moved on.

Will hurried to the fence and quickly slid under. Keeping close to the ground, he moved back up the slope using the trees to pull himself up to the road. He hurried toward the intersection and abruptly stopped and stared. A highway patrol car was parked behind Klast's car, and Will knew he couldn't approach openly. He went along the opposite side of the road in the ditch planning how to take out the trooper. He moved into high weeds and continued his approach to the car.

FOURTEEN

The drug was beginning to have its effect on Ophelia. It had begun almost immediately after Medina had given her the pressurized injection. An odd tingling had spread down her arm and through her body. It felt like insects crawling on her. She was becoming sensitive to things she had never known. Ophelia recalled things with clarity, noticing things she hadn't when the event occurred. She thought of the meeting with the Gray and felt its odd thoughts. She could see its face in minute detail, but its thoughts were what she wanted to know.

Ophelia concentrated on the thoughts of the Gray. Sensations, pictures began to coalesce in her mind. She saw a blue world, not unlike Earth, but she was aware it wasn't Earth. There were differences she could see. Ophelia didn't understand until she realized these were memories of the Gray. She looked over a vast alien city when the sky suddenly erupted in a blinding flash that slowly faded to a dark, blasted landscape. She felt sorrow and futility.

Earth appeared as if she was approaching it from space and a feeling of elation filled her. She stepped out and felt like she was home, but something was wrong. Just what, Ophelia couldn't grasp. There was a passage of time and Ophelia saw a ship appear in the sky. She knew it was a threat because of the creatures it carried, but she could get no clear image of them. It soon became apparent they were hostile and ruthless. She felt anger, degradation, and enslavement

There came a burst of fire, a loathing for killing, yet a dreadful need to kill. It was confusing for Ophelia until she saw who was doing the killing. It was Grays! Grays with deformed hands now forced other Grays to do their bidding. This was quickly replaced by a strong sense of freedom. The hateful Grays were gone, and the concept of enemy became a distant memory.

"Wake up, Ophelia." She heard the voice from a great distance. She opened her eyes and saw Zeus and Medina standing over her. Alarm filled her.

"I recalled what the Gray knew." Zeus put a hand on her shoulder.

"You told us as you watched," Zeus said, in a gentle tone.

"I don't understand what it means," she said, with a confused look. Zeus and medina exchanged grim expressions.

"We do, Ophelia," Zeus said. "The Grays' home world was destroyed with an asteroid.

After finding Earth, they were followed and enslaved by the Kraken. They rebelled and were punished. The Kraken found they could control the minds of the Grays and is forcing them to aid in taking over Earth. They don't have a choice, or any memory of what happened." Ophelia glanced from Zeus to Medina with a puzzled look.

"But I thought the Kraken were your people," Ophelia said, becoming more confused.

"That's what we believed," Zeus said. "Now we know the truth."

"The Kraken are a race that seek to dominate," Medina said. "We have never had a clear idea of what caused the war on our world. It seems clear the Kraken were behind it. After winning, they controlled the minds of our people who banished us to wander in space."

"What are they doing on Earth?" Ophelia asked.

"I believe they need slaves," Zeus replied. "The probable reason for the clandestine takeover is they don't want another revolt. One by humans wouldn't be as easily overcome as the Grays." She looked frightened.

"We have to find a way to warn Will and the others," she said, feeling a sudden urgency. Zeus shook his head.

"If we reveal ourselves," Zeus said. "It's possible we could be destroyed. Humanity would then have no one to help them."

"How is it you never discovered the Kraken were different from you?"

"Their anonymity, Ophelia," Zeus replied. "They work out of sight, letting others do their dirty work."

"If it was only possible to take one of them prisoner," Medina lamented. The intercom sounded and Zeus went to it.

"Yes?"

"You're wanted in communications," a woman said. "The Earthmen have received a transmission from Earth." Ophelia was quickly on her feet facing Zeus.

"I'm coming with you." Zeus nodded and they left the medical lab together. Ophelia felt it was a message from Will.

"I don't think it's going to be good news," she said, looking at Zeus, who frowned.

"I've not been expecting any," he admitted.

Coming into communications, Aubrey came to them with a dour look.

"The Kraken control all communications," Aubrey said. "And they're sending scientists to a base in the southwest. Will believes they're building spaceships there." Zeus' shoulders slumped. This was worse than he expected.

"We're going to have to leave for our planet," Zeus said. "We can't afford to wait any longer."

"We can't leave Janis, Will, and Raeta," Ophelia said.

"There's no way to recall them," Zeus said, firmly. "The longer we remain the greater the chance of exposure. If the Kraken learn we're here, they'll do everything in their power to destroy us."

"There must be someway to safely contact them," Schiffer said. Zeus flashed him an annoyed look.

"How?" Zeus asked. "We can't send another ship because we don't know where to look for them."

"I'm expendable," Aubrey said. "I can go and try to locate them. If I'm not back in forty-eight hours, leave. Give them that much of a chance, at least, Zeus." Zeus thought about Raeta, Will, and Janis, but it was Ophelia's expression that decided him.

"Very well," Zeus agreed. "But I won't wait any longer than that." The Earth people looked relieved.

Will was close enough to get a good look at the trooper, and what he saw made him shudder. He was the first person with deformed hands Will had seen. The trooper had to be taken out. Once that was done, they would head for the ship and take off.

Will moved silently until he was just across the road and could hear what was being said.

"This is a restricted area, Dr. Klast," the trooper said. "You all have to be taken in for interrogation. Your presence here is suspicious."

"But I told you—" The trooper waved his hand in an impatient gesture.

"I know what you said, Doctor. But the only way you're leaving here is in custody." The trooper went to his car. As he picked up the mike, Will hit him with a stun from the small plasma weapon. He sprawled on the road as Klast came to Will with an alarmed look.

"What do we do now, Mr. Vaughn?"

"Get the hell off this planet, Doctor. We'll take the patrol car back to the ship." Will rolled the trooper on his back and looked at Klast.

"Help me get him to your car." Klast and Will carried the trooper to the car as the others got out. They slid him onto the rear floor.

"What are we going to do, Will?" Janis asked, stepping in front of him with Raeta and Zachary.

"We've got to get to the ship. There's nothing more we can do here."

"The ship's modified for three people only," Raeta said. Will gave that a quick run through.

"It can't be helped, Raeta. We've got to risk all of us going." He saw a flash of uncertainty cross her face and took hold of her arms.

"The ship can lift off with all of us, can't it?" Raeta heard the urgency in his voice and nodded.

"It's going to be a tight squeeze, Will," Raeta said. He patted her shoulder.

"The incontinence won't last long."

"Will, look!" Janis was pointing down the highway as three patrol cars, with flashing lights, was headed their way.

"Shit! He must have opened the mike," Will said. "Get in. We've got to make a run for it." Will climbed behind the wheel and started the car as the others piled in. He wasted no time in swinging it around in a U-turn with tires squealing. Will pressed the accelerator and the tires smoked as they headed away from Area C with the patrol cars gaining on them.

Will kept an eye out for another road to turn onto, but could discern none ahead. Hitting a long stretch of straight highway, he floored the pedal and began pulling away from the pursuing cars. That was when the first bullets hit the car.

"Get down," Will shouted, as he fought to keep the car from sliding. The metallic thumps of the bullets hit the car and filled the interior with flying shards of safety glass. Will spotted a dirt road to the left and knew it might be a dead end, but it went in the direction of the farmhouse. What the hell! He thought, and slewed the car sideways, straightened the wheels and tore down the dirt road. It was a few minutes before their pursuers passed, and those few minutes was their salvation.

Will pulled the car off the road and among the trees as the sound of engines faded.

"Stay where you are," Will said. They wondered why he wanted them to wait. They heard the sound of engines growing louder until the cars roared past them and down the dirt road raising a cloud of dust.

"We're going to have to walk," Will said. "I figure we're a couple of miles from the ship, so let's go." They got out and waited for Will, but he was leaning against the wheel. Zachary went to him.

"What's wrong?" When he looked up, Zachary knew Will was in pain.

"You're going to have to go on without me. I've been hit." They clustered around the door.

"We're not going without you, Will," Raeta said. He turned his eyes up to her, trying to keep from showing pain.

"You have to. I don't know how long it might be before they figure they're chasing the wind and double back. I can hold them off. That should give you time to get to the ship." Zachary looked at the others and turned back to Will with a stubborn look.

"Let's get him out of the car," Zachary said, and looked back at Will. "We're not leaving you to face those bastards." Zachary and Janis helped him out of the car and pulled one of his arms over their shoulders and slipped arms around his waist. They hurried across a dark field as Will lost consciousness.

"How bad is the wound?" Klast asked.

"No way to tell until we get to the ship," Raeta replied. Klast glanced over his shoulder.

"You could be causing him more harm carrying him like that," Klast said.

"We can't worry about that," Janis said, sharply.

They went as fast as they could with Raeta and Klast relieving Janis and Zachary of carrying Will. Raeta saw the vague outline of the ship.

"There's the ship," she said, unable to quicken her pace. They crowded into the little ship. Raeta made a cursory check of the instruments and lifted off. She kept the ship low and avoided population centers. When they were over the icecap, she nosed the ship into space

When Will regained consciousness, he found himself in unfamiliar surroundings. He started to push himself up on his elbows but the pain deterred him. He turned his head and saw a man with dark hair working at a lab bench.

"Where am I?" The man turned and came over beside Will.

"You're on the ship. I'm Dr. Medina."

"Did the others make it?"

"We certainly did," Janis said, stepping beside Medina. "We wouldn't have without you. This is the second time you've been shot saving me, and I wish you would stop it. It's upsetting." Will smiled.

"I'll try to remember that next time people start shooting," Janis laughed, and took his hand.

"Anything new about what's happening on Earth?" Her smile faded.

"We're on our way to Zeus' world," Janis replied. "We need weapons and reinforcements before considering any further action."

"What about the Grays, Janis?"

"Ophelia hasn't been able to contact them. It's almost as if they were never here." Medina put a hand on her arm and she looked at him.

"That's enough for now," Medina said. "He's got to rest to heal properly." Will got a bewildered look.

"What about that beam Raeta used on me in the complex? That healed me immediately." Medina smiled.

"Unfortunately, Mr. Vaughn, we can only use it once. After that, the effects aren't so dramatic." Janis gave his hand a squeeze, bent down and kissed him.

"I'll stop by later, Will." She left and Medina patted his shoulder.

"You were shot through the groin, and lost a lot of blood. Relax, don't let your muscles tighten or you'll take longer convalescing."

"Whatever you say, Doc." Will exhaled feeling just how weak he was. He closed his eyes and consciously relaxed.

Schiffer and Aubrey sat with Zeus at a meeting of his advisors to determine what, if anything could be done for the inhabitants of Earth.

"We must assume they have subjugated the entire population," Raeta said.

"Then we need to find a way to break their control," Aubrey said.

"That won't be easy," Castor said. "Until we devise a way to disrupt the HAARP field."

"It's no use speculating," Zeus said. "Once we're home, we can count on scientists to evaluate and plan for contingencies." Janis and Ophelia sat silent, unable to explain their loss of contact with the Grays. The abrupt lack of communications from them seemed ominous.

"If they're building space ships, your planet can be the only possible target," Schiffer said. "They'll be coming after you – unless we devise someway to stop them."

"I agree," Vicea said. "But how long do we have?"

"Months," Aubrey replied. "Considering the size of the work force. They have to consolidate their hold on Earth and finish construction of their ships."

"They won't act prematurely," Schiffer said.

"We need a way to monitor their progress," Janis said. "Unless we're certain, they could give us a nasty surprise."

"I agree," Schiffer said. "We need recon on Earth that can report on their progress."

"How do you propose we do that?" Castor asked. "We can't put one of our satellites in orbit, it would be detected immediately. And we're moving out of range of the modified satellites. What course is left?"

"You need an agent on Earth," Will said, coming slowly into the room.

"You shouldn't be here, Will," Raeta said. "You should be resting." He gave her an impatient look.

"I've been resting for the past ten days," Will said. "Besides, if the Kraken win, I'll have eternity to rest. You need someone on Earth to keep you informed, and the only way to do that is to send someone to Earth." Aubrey cocked an eyebrow and got a stern frown.

"And you believe you're that person?" Aubrey asked. Will looked at him and nodded.

"Who the hell else is expendable? You Aubrey?" Aubrey scowled.

"You're in no condition to go," Janis said.

"Dr. Medina can patch me up enough to give me a fighting chance," Will said, looking around at the people, most with unreadable expressions.

"There isn't any choice, Zeus," Will said, grimly. "It's me, or remain blind and deaf." Zeus nodded.

"Will's right," Zeus said. "We need someone who won't be influenced by their control." Zeus looked at Will and frowned.

"Will's the only one who stands a chance of success," Zeus added, catching the hard look he got from Raeta.

"He'll need a pilot," Raeta said. Will gave her a hard look and shook his head.

"I'll train to pilot one of the small ships," Will said. "What I'll need most is a form of communication they can't monitor and trace." Will turned his gaze to Castor.

"Can you devise something?" Will asked. Castor puckered his lips, considering an idea.

"I believe so," Castor replied. "I've been working on something I feel will prove successful."

"Good," Will said. "I'll get with you later and you can explain how it works."

"Isn't there someway to talk you out of this, Will?" Ophelia asked.

"No," Will replied. "It's a job that has to be done, and I'm the one who can do it."

"Or die trying?" Janis asked, with a disapproving look. He gave her a weak smile.

"I wouldn't have it any other way, Janis, and you know it."

"We'll start your training immediately, Will," Zeus said. "You have to leave within the next three days or the ship won't make it to Earth." Will nodded.

"Then let's get moving," Will said. "The people of Earth are counting on us – if they can conceive they have a chance."

Zeus assigned Raeta as instructor pilot. She was the best and Will needed to be trained in a short time. Castor devised a miniature microwave transmitter that operated on a narrow band, and taught Will how to align it so it would blend with the communications grid of Earth and remain undetectable. Will knew there was risk of discovery, but accepted the risk as he had on other dangerous assignments.

Raeta's instruction was so complete that Will was able to pilot the ship after only four hours. Once he had the ship's idiosyncrasies in hand, it would be easy to fly.

It was more difficult learning the code Aubrey devised, but Will committed it to memory and was ready to go.

He told Zeus he wanted to leave without anyone knowing his departure time. He knew he would only get further arguments from Janis and Raeta, although neither had said a word since the meeting. Zeus set his departure for when they were sleeping.

"Good luck, Will," Zeus said, extending his hand. Will gripped it firmly.

"You just hurry back with the cavalry, Zeus. No telling when I might need them."

"We'll return as soon as we can. Hopefully with a means of defeating the Kraken." Will nodded and went through the hatch, closing it behind him. He took his place in the pilot's seat and gave Zeus a thumbs up through the windscreen. Zeus hurried from the hangar deck and started the airlock cycling. As soon as the hatch showed stars, Will lifted the craft and moved out of the hangar. He turned the ship toward Earth determined to do the most possible damage to the bastards who had taken his world from him.

FIFTEEN

"Do you know where Will is, Zeus?" Raeta asked, stopping beside him. He glanced at her, knowing she wasn't going to like his answer.

"He left a few hours ago." He saw her pained expression and knew she was losing against her emotions.

"He didn't tell me he was leaving," she said, angrily.

"He told no one but me," Zeus said. "He felt it better this way, Raeta. If he had waited, you and Janis would have tried to dissuade him from going." She looked surprised.

"You were the only one who knew?"

"Yes, Raeta."

"Can I communicate with him?"

"No," he replied, firmly. "He told me he wanted to maintain a communication blackout until he had something to report."

"I'm talking about now, before his ship reaches Earth."

"No, Raeta. There's to be no communication with Will. It will only jeopardize an already dangerous mission. I want you to inform the Earth people that he's gone." She lowered her eyes to hide the turmoil of emotions inside her and nodded.

"Very well, Zeus."

Will let the autoguidance do the navigating for the accelerated three-day journey. He wondered how the Earth had changed in the time he had been away. He didn't want to speculate as it usually turned out wrong. He had to prepare himself for the unexpected. He knew, at least, how to identify the Kraken, and felt that gave him an edge. He was confident the implant Medina had placed behind his right ear would block the Kraken's telepathic control. He slept most of the time, as Medina had instructed.

When Earth appeared as a bright orb, with a smaller orb at its side, he began considering where to land. The place had to be isolated, yet convenient to work from. Will decided on the southwest to see if he could locate the base Klast had told him about, but that was a lot of territory to cover. There were numerous government installations in the area, and he had to find the right one, and decided it would be an air base.

Approaching the polar region Will hoped they wouldn't be as alert since they controlled the population, but he didn't dare assume anything. He knew he had to be cautious or he would be dead – or worse. He knew it would probably be suicide to fly over any base in the area. Will would check out each base on foot. He had been trained in the Mojave, so Will knew the desert. Still caution was the better part of valor. As he began losing altitude, he thought of Janis and Raeta. A difficult problem with no easy solution. He was strongly attracted to them both, but that had to be put off until later. When he got back – if he got back – he would try to work out a relationship with them.

The icecap was coming up rapidly and he took manual control. Will thought of the equipment he had with him. The pulse weapon and the small transceiver. Zeus had insisted he bring a dozen plasma demolition charges, and he might find a use for them. The equipment was fine, but it would be his instinct he was going to depend on for survival. Will recalled times he had far less and had survived. Those had been against human adversaries. Just how different were the Kraken? They seemed to work the same as humans and would look for weaknesses. They preferred subterfuge rather than open conflict. Then there were the Grays. How the hell did they fit into this?

The ship began to shake from magnetic turbulence and he began concentrating on flying above the icecap. Once down, he kept the ship high enough to avoid obstacles.

Like Raeta, he would avoid flying over cities. No use advertising he was here. It was dusk over North America, and he could see the lights of cities and gave them a wide berth. Will became aware of the lack of air traffic, and glanced at the instrument panel and saw nothing was flying, but him. He had to get down as soon as possible to avoid detection.

He began braking and landed east of Holloman Air Force Base in the foothills of the Sacramento Mountains. He found a ravine large enough to conceal his ship, and set it down. He shut everything down, and knew it was decision-making time. Will would have all night to scout and see what he could. The darkness would be advantageous as cover. He went to the hatch, opened it, and stepped into the chill desert air. He closed the hatch and turned to the lights of the air base about two miles away.

Will moved away from the foothills into the desert at a pace where he could cover ground quickly. He came to within three hundred feet of the perimeter fence and saw no guards. He saw nothing but jets lined up along the runways, but there was no activity he could see. This made him very cautious as he moved along the fence.

He had moved about half a mile when he saw a sight that made him stop and stare. Setting on the runway were a dozen sleek craft whose design he didn't recognize, but saw no guards. Will wanted a closer look at one of those craft, but dared not tamper with the fence as he knew it would set off an alarm, and he wanted no company. He went along looking for someway past it and when he came to the end was stopped again at what he saw.

Here were a dozen more of the craft in various stages of construction, and he saw people working on them, people who moved like robots. They carried material to and inside the ships while others done work on the outside of the ships. He saw guards, and every one was a Gray. This is a hell of a surprise, he thought. He took a closer look at the people and saw ones with malformed hands didn't seem to be under any control. That's when the idea blossomed in his mind and made him shiver. The people with the deformed hands must be hybrids of human and Kraken. It was a concept that was overwhelming. It appeared the Grays were part of the invasion, and it must be the Grays who controlled the Kraken. What the hell did this mean? Maybe what Aubrey suspected from the beginning? The Grays had been using Janis and Ophelia.

Will stiffened when he felt the cold metal touch the back of his neck.

"Don't turn around," someone whispered. "Just back away with me." Will backed away from the fence in a crouch until they were away from the lights of the base.

"Now you can turn around." He turned and found a woman in her twenties with chestnut hair and gray eyes. His eyes dropped to the Smith and Wesson Model 59 she held. A 9mm automatic he identified by the straight butt.

"Who are you?" she demanded, the weapon steady in her hand.

"Will Vaughn. I used to be an intelligence agent until these Grays took over." She regarded him with suspicion.

"Hold out your hands." Will did as she wanted and she looked at them closely.

"A person can't be too sure of who is who nowadays," she said.

"Who are you?" Will asked. "And how have you managed to evade their control?"

"I'm Cathy Hilman. As for keeping out of their control, that's something we've been working on."

"We?"

"Yeah. There's a group of us hiding in the mountains. I saw your ship land and followed you. What are you doing here?"

"I told you. I'm an intelligence operative here to spy on these bastards. Try to find out about them. Tell me about the group you're with, especially how you've kept your minds free." She stuck the weapon into the waistband of her camouflaged pants.

"Dr. Martin can explain better than me. I'll take you there." She turned and started toward the mountains, Will beside her.

"Any idea what's been going on in the world? I've been away for awhile." She turned a surprised look on him.

"Are you shitting me? Where have you been, outer space?" Will smiled as he nodded.

"That's right. Couldn't you tell from my ship?" She stopped abruptly and regarded him with uncertainty.

"Are you for real?" He kept his smile but knew he had let an amateur take him easily.

"You're damn right. You saw me land. Didn't you wonder where I came from?" She started walking again, Will matching her pace.

"I didn't get a good look at your ship," she said, glancing at him. "Who were you with?"

"Friends. Hopefully they'll be back with enough reinforcements to kick the Grays off Earth."

"Why didn't they do it when they were here?"

"The invasion caught them as much by surprise as it did those of us who suspected what was happening. They were going to help modify weapons so we could fight."

"That would have been suicide," Cathy said, glancing at him with a twinkle in her eyes. "These bastards control peoples' minds. Why our group hasn't been affected is something Dr. Martin's been trying to discover."

"How many in your group?"

"Twenty-three." Will began thinking and shaking his head.

"There must be other groups like yours around the world. Have you tried to communicate with them?" A sharp, cynical laugh escaped her.

"That would be the quickest way to bring them down on us. Dr. Martin tested that. He set up a remote radio a mile from here, activated it, and a Gray ship was on it at once." She kept her eyes on Will.

"We have no idea how they found it so fast." This gave Will pause for thought.

"Here we are," Cathy said, pointing to a narrow fissure in the rock. "There's a good sized cave on the other side. Go on in." He stepped to the fissure and began wriggling through. He watched Cathy come through and let her lead the way.

He noted the dim light from lanterns placed at intervals along the cave wall.

"This way," she said, taking the lead. Will followed her into a well-lit cave. People looked in apprehension as Cathy took him to a tall, thin bald man whose black eyes never left Will. She stopped and held her hand to him.

"Dr. Martin, this is Will Vaughn. He's an intelligence agent here to spy on the Grays' base." Martin regarded him with open suspicion.

"What makes you so sure of that, Cathy?" Martin asked.

"I saw him watching the base and checked his hands." That didn't satisfy Martin.

"Do you know Dr. Zachary Taylor?" Will asked. "Or Dr. Theodore Klast?" Martin gave him a cold look.

"Only by reputation," Martin replied. Will glanced around at the people that had gathered around him.

"They're on a space ship heading for a planet in the outer solar system," Will said, loudly enough for all to hear. "They know what's going on. The people they're with are determined to return and put an end to this aggression. I came from that ship. I'm here to learn and transmit information to them."

"You can't transmit!" one of them exclaimed. "They'll be on you before you know it." Will pulled the transceiver from his pocket and held it up.

"This is a narrow band microwave transmitter," Will said. "Undetectable." Will offered it to Martin, who took it and looked it over, and handed it back with a less suspicious look.

"I never thought of using microwaves," Martin said. "But who would we broadcast to?" Will gave him a look that was easy to read.

"When are these people coming?" Martin asked.

"It may take as long as six months," Will replied. "Until then, Doctor, we're on our own." Will turned and looked at the people around him then turned back to Martin.

"Why do you think these people are unaffected by the Grays' mind control, Doctor?" Martin regarded him and shook his head.

"It's a mystery. I can find no physiological difference."

"Is it possible they have stronger psychic resistance, Doctor?" Martin rubbed his chin.

"That could be it," Martin said. "It would explain why I've been unable to find a difference." Will smiled and tapped his head.

"This is where you're controlled, this is where you block it."

"What are you talking about?" Cathy asked. Will glanced at her and his audience.

"All of you disrupt the Grays' control, and that keeps your minds free. We need a prisoner to find out how you do it."

"That's a tall order," Martin said.

"Are you crazy?" Cathy asked, incredulous. "If we bring one of those people here, the Grays will know where we are." Will turned a steady gaze on her.

"Are you certain about that?" Will asked. "Have you tried bringing one here?" Martin was looking at Will with interest.

"He's right, Cathy," Martin said. "We must risk it." She stared at Martin in disbelief, then at Will, who was noticing how pretty she was. But she hadn't looked pretty when she had that automatic aimed at him, but he couldn't blame her.

"Will you help me try to get a prisoner, Cathy?" Will asked.

"Where do you intend getting one?" she countered.

"People who don't know what's going on aren't controlled." She got a puzzled look.

"That limits us to where we can get a prisoner," Will said. Her eyes widened and she shook her head.

"You are crazy if you think you can get into Holloman." Will smiled and clasped his hands behind him.

"I haven't had time to look the place over," Will said. "Once I do, I'll have no trouble getting in." Cathy stared in disbelief.

"You're serious," she said. He nodded.

"I sure as hell am," Will said. "We might be all that stands between the Grays and their domination of Earth. I feel it's worth the risk." She gave martin an uncertain look. Everyone seemed frozen. A blonde woman came to Will and held her green eyes on him.

"How can I help?" she asked. Others then began offering to help. Cathy was the last to volunteer.

"You're all crazy," she said, not believing what she had witnessed. She looked at Will.

"I must be too," she said. "Because I believe you." Will looked at these people who were willing to put their asses on the line. Will looked at Martin.

"We start ops tomorrow night," Will said. "I need a clear picture of the layout and security of the base. Once I know that, we're as good as in."

"It's getting out that has me worried," Cathy said.

"That might be difficult but not impossible," Will admitted. "I've got some weapons in my ship our space friends gave me. Once these weapons are used, the Grays will know where the technology came from, and there's no telling how they'll react. They might devastate the planet." The blonde who had come to him took hold of his hand.

"I don't care what they do," she said. "I would rather die than live my life in a cave, or be a slave for them. I don't see any choice but to fight."

"There are few of us," Will said. "We need to find others like ourselves and have them join us. The information we gather, and send to our friends, will quicken the day of retribution." There was loud agreement as Martin stepped in front of Will and extended his hand. Will took it.

"You're what we've been needing – hope. Thank God you finally got here," Martin said.

SIXTEEN

"It's been over a week since Will arrived on Earth," Aubrey said. "And we've heard nothing from him."

"What do you propose we do about it?" Zeus asked.

"Something! Anything!" Janis exclaimed, impatiently. Zeus saw Raeta had the same concern, but kept quiet. Zeus looked back to Aubrey.

"There's nothing we can do," Zeus said. "We're so far from Earth that if he called for help, we couldn't get back in time to do anything for him."

"But it isn't like Will not to report," Aubrey said. Zeus knew how they felt. He, too, had a vague uneasiness at not having heard from him.

"He knows what he's doing," Zeus said. "He's been in this sort of work long enough to know when to report. I'm assuming he has nothing to report. If he had, I know we would have heard from him."

"We don't know how things are on Earth," Janis said. "Maybe –"

"Maybe he's been taken prisoner," Raeta injected. Zeus looked steadily at her, considering what the Kraken might do if they had captured Will.

"In that case we'll have to consider Will dead," Zeus said. "But I don't consider that a plausible option."

"I agree," Aubrey said.

"Then why hasn't he reported?" Raeta asked, sharply. Aubrey had no answer and shrugged.

"I don't know. It's just… well, maybe he has a reason for not reporting," Aubrey said.

"Until we know different, we must assume Will is alive and operating against the enemy," Zeus said. "His transmitter may have malfunctioned or gotten damaged." They sat in awkward silence before Raeta started to speak. Zeus had anticipated her.

"No, Raeta. I'll not permit anyone to try to go from this distance. Once home, we'll have the wisdom of the Pantheon. They may want to take some action to forestall any attack by the Kraken."

"How much longer before we reach your world?" Janis asked.

"About two Earth days," Raeta replied.

"How long to devise a viable plan?" Aubrey asked. "Then return to Earth and carry it out?" Zeus knew they wouldn't care for his estimate.

"At least six months," Zeus replied.

"And what the hell do I do in the meantime?" Aubrey asked. Zeus regarded him for a moment before replying.

"I'm counting on you and General Schiffer to train our people in infiltration and sabotage. You two will have the most important task. I'm sure you realize we just can't go barging back to Earth. We must return by stealth."

"Just like the Kraken," Janis said, sharply. Zeus nodded.

"In somewhat the same manner," Zeus said. "If we wish to keep from fighting a full scale war, that's the only way. The Kraken way." Aubrey was nodding.

"I see your point, Zeus," Aubrey said. "You can count on Chet and me to train your people well." Zeus got a weak smile.

"I'm worried about Will too," Zeus admitted. "But what he chose to do, he did for all of us, Earth as well as our world. I have no doubt he's probably giving the Kraken a hard time." Aubrey laughed.

"I'll be damned if I don't believe it, Zeus," Aubrey said.

Their prisoner was a hybrid with a blank mind. She had yet to be given a personality by the Grays. Will turned from her to Martin.

"The Grays are efficient," Will admitted. Martin nodded.

"Now what?" Martin asked. "We can't sneak around them."

"Any ideas, Doctor?" Will asked. Martin had been considering a plan, but wasn't certain it would work.

"We might be able to hypnotize someone and send them into the base," Martin replied. "What they learn can be revealed by post-hypnotic suggestion."

"What could they see that we haven't already seen?" Cathy asked. Will noted Martin was hesitant to answer.

"If you have any ideas, please share them, Doctor," Will said. Martin looked back at the woman.

"I believe people become this way through a process," Martin said. "Their memory and personality erased. New thoughts and commands are put into the empty mind. It might help if we knew how the process worked." Will agreed.

"If we discover this process, could we duplicate and reverse it?" Will asked.

"I'm not certain about the last, Will," Martin said. Will inhaled deeply.

"I'm your volunteer, Doctor," Will said.

"No," Cathy said. "The Grays would know you from Janis." Martin looked from her to Will and nodded.

"I'll do it," Mitch Blair said. He was an average guy with brown hair and eyes. Will liked Mitch because he was courageous and innovative.

"You understand the risk?" Martin asked. Mitch nodded.

"I know, Doc," Mitch replied. "I'll probably look like the rest of our kind before they change them. It's a challenge."

"It's your show, Doctor," Will said.

After putting Mitch into a hypnotic state, Martin turned to Will.

"I've given him the suggestion that his mind will go blank when he's told the trigger word," Martin said. "Someone will have to go with him to the base and say the trigger word. After that, he'll learn what he can and return here. I'll then bring him out so he remembers what he's seen."

"Sounds simple enough," Will said. "Let's hope it works."

Will and Cathy watched as Mitch walked onto the base without any unusual reaction from the Grays.

"Now we wait," Will said. Cathy leaned over and kissed him. When she pulled away, he stared at her.

"What was that for?" She took hold of his hand and regarded him with a coy smile.

"I want you to make love to me. I've felt this way since I met you, Will."

"Christ, Cathy, look at where we are." Her smile turned seductive.

"We're alone."

"In the desert!"

"I know a cozy place not far from here. We've got the time and I've got the want. Don't you want to make love to me?"

"It isn't that, Cathy. It's just that –" Her smile dropped to a frown.

"Janis? Raeta?"

"No. I've avoided personal relationships. In my line of work, it's too risky."

"Then you have no excuse not to, do you?" He thought about how women had always seemed attracted to him. He had never understood it, and he didn't want to hurt her feelings.

"All right, Cathy, show me this cozy place." The smile she got was most telling.

"This way," she said, pulling him by the hand.

They went to an old miner's shack that contained a wood burning stove, a cot with a blanket and this hard mattress. He saw this when she lit the hurricane lamp on the rickety wooden table. It wasn't what he would call cozy, but would serve their purpose. As Will walked toward the cot, he felt the floor sag under his weight. He stopped and looked down, then knelt and began feeling the boards. Cathy stood watching him, bewildered.

"What are you doing?" He glanced over his shoulder at her.

"How many times have you been here?"

"A couple of times. Why?" Will kept moving his fingers along the open space between the boards.

"You're lucky you haven't fallen through this floor. There's nothing under the center of this place."

"And you want to know what's down there?" she asked, annoyed. Will's curiosity had been sparked. Why would anyone build a shack over a mine entrance? He wondered.

"We have to check it out. It might be a way into the base." Cathy got a frustrated frown.

"That's not why we came here, Will." He stood and put his arms around her.

"I'll make it up to you, Cathy. I think it's important we find out where that hole leads." He gave her a kiss and looked around for something to pry up the boards. He saw a rusted pick head, picked it up, and began prying up the boards. He looked into the black pit but could discern nothing.

"Bring the lamp here." She took it from the table and came beside him. As she knelt, they saw a metal extension ladder vanishing into the darkness. She glanced at Will with wide eyes.

"What could be down there, Will?" He glanced at her, quickly making up his mind.

"I don't know. But I don't think a miner would use a ladder. I'm going down for a look."

"I'm not staying up here alone." Will smiled and nodded.

"Okay. Follow me." Will slipped over the edge of the floor and put his feet on a rung and went down far enough for Cathy to start.

"Hand me the lamp." She bent down from the edge and handed him the lamp. He turned it around looking at the shaft they were going into. Its walls seemed to have a peculiar sheen to them, almost like they were polished. He lowered the lamp to his knees but couldn't see the bottom. The light given by the lamp wasn't strong enough to show very much unless it was close. How far down this shaft went he couldn't guess from the ladder, but Will was determined to find out what was down here. Cathy stopped above him and looked down.

"How far down does it go?" she asked.

"I can't be sure. But from the length of the ladder, I would guess twenty, twenty-five feet." She looked around in the feeble glow.

"Who could have dug this place?"

"That's what I hope to learn, Cathy." He started down the ladder, the sounds of their feet on the rungs made dull metallic rings. It took only a moment before they were standing at the bottom of the ladder.

"Let's go." She was hesitant about moving into the dark tunnel. Will knew she was frightened.

"I feel the same about this place, Cathy, but we've got to find out what's down here." She took a firm hold of his arm and looked at him.

"I'm ready, Will." He slipped his arm around her waist and they walked along the tunnel. The walls had a uniform look like the shaft, and its appearance stopped him in his tracks. He took his arm from her and ran his hand over the wall. He glanced at her with surprise.

"This place is plastic-coated."

"What?"

"Touch it, Cathy. This whole place is covered with plastic." She reached out and ran her finger over the surface and looked back at Will.

"Who could have made this place?" she asked, in a frightened voice.

"Let's see if we can find out." he moved on, she stayed right at his side holding his arm.

They moved for some minutes with no change in the surroundings. When they stepped into a large chamber, they found out why this place was here.

"Oh, my God!" Cathy shouted. Will couldn't believe what he was seeing. Bodies lined the walls of the chamber encased in plastic. He stepped closer and moved the lamp along, seeing they all had the deformed hands.

"This must be their failed experiments," Will said, grimly. "Ones that couldn't adapt to their control were killed and brought here."

"Why would they do such a thing?" He was as mystified as she was.

"I don't know, Cathy. But we've got to get the hell away from here." They hurried back through the tunnel to the ladder.

"Go up, Cathy." She wasted no time climbing the ladder. As Will came out of the shaft, she stared at him with a horrified expression.

"Do you think they still come here, Will?" He got to his feet wondering the same thing.

"I don't know. But we can't risk returning here." He quickly replaced the boards and she blew out the lamp and they left.

Walking through the desert, an idea struck Will.

"I wonder if there are anymore excavations like that in the desert?" She gave him a sickly look.

"You think there are more?" He nodded.

"That one looked pretty full to me. Let's get the hell back and get Mitch."

Mitch sat in his hypnotic trance as Cathy and Will related what they had found.

"How can they be so cruel?" one woman asked. Will shook his head at her lack of understanding.

"They don't think of people the same way we do," Will replied. "I don't know what their reason is, but it sure as hell isn't to our benefit."

"Let's see what Mitch learned," Martin said. They gathered around as Martin brought him out of the trance.

"What did you see at the base?" Martin asked. A look of disquiet came to Mitch and he seemed reluctant to speak.

"We have to know, Mitch," Will said. It seemed hard for him as he appeared struggling for words. A distressed moan escaped him.

"They change people."

"We know that, Mitch," Martin said. "How do they change them?" Mitch grimaced.

"They take their minds by some sort of neuro-electrical process."

"Were you able to learn how the process works?" Cathy asked. Mitch gave her a sad, confused look.

"No. The concept is too alien. I don't think any of us could understand it. The device is to large to be moved."

"So they bring the people to the base?" Will asked. Mitch nodded.

"The worst part is, the people are chosen at random. They intend to convert the whole of humanity into slaves for the construction of their ships." Everyone glanced at their companion with an uneasy feeling. Now they were beginning to understand the scope of the struggle they found themselves locked in.

"How many of those conversion units are there?" Will asked.

"Only the one – for now," Mitch replied. "They're constructing several more at various locations around the world.

"Did you learn their locations?" Martin asked.

"No. They don't seem to know either. For some reason, their leaders aren't telling them what's going on."

"I find that rather odd," Will said. "Maybe there's dissension among the Grays. That would explain why Ophelia and Janis were treated easy. If that's true, then it's imperative we find a way to contact the Grays who are against what's happening here."

"Were any of the Grays opposed to this program?" Martin asked.

"I'm not certain," Mitch replied. "I felt dissatisfaction from a few, but it wasn't clearly defined." Will and Martin exchanged looks.

"We've got to contact the dissident Grays."

"How can we tell one from the other, Will?" Martin asked. He had no solution to that question.

"I don't know. But we've got to find a means of communication without giving ourselves away."

"That won't be easy," Cathy said.

"There has to be a way," Will said, determined to find it. "We need help, and if we can get it from the Grays, then goddamnit we have to find a way to make contact."

They all agreed to put the base under constant surveillance in order to see if they could spot which Grays might throw in their lot with the humans. Only after careful observation would they attempt contact. Contact would be tentative until they were certain of the attitude of the Grays.

Will was aware of the risk this action entailed, but was certain they needed the aid of friendly Grays, if there were any. Now was the time for his first report to Aubrey.

He slipped out of the cave that night and moved away from the mountains into the desert. It wasn't long before he was shivering as it took him some time to transmit in the special code. When he finished, he wondered how long it would take the transmission to reach the ship. He returned the transmitter to his pocket, and turned, bumping into Cathy. He could see her smile in the light of the half moon.

"It's time to keep your promise, Will."

"What promise?"

"The night at the shack, you said you would make it up to me."

"It's too damned cold out here. And there's no privacy in the cave."

"There's a place we can be warm and uninterrupted." Will got a baffled look.

"Where?" She slipped her arms around his neck and kissed him. She pulled back with a smug smile.

"Your ship is the perfect place to make love." Will exhaled in resignation as he realized she had been planning this. He wasn't reluctant about making love to her, so she had him right where she wanted him, and she knew it. He put his arms around her and pulled her against him, kissing her. When they parted, he looked at her with a smile.

"Want to go to my ship?"

SEVENTEEN

Aubrey stood in Zeus' quarters with the other Earth people. Raeta and Castor were also present.

"I finished decoding the message from Will," Aubrey said. "I feel it contains information that concerns your people Zeus." Aubrey watched their reactions. Anticipation was plain in Janis and Raeta's expressions, but the others were harder to read.

"The people you call the Kraken," Aubrey continued. "Are controlled by the Grays."

"How can that be?" Castor asked, surprised.

"Will says humans are being converted into mindless automatons to work for the Grays. He also believes those with the deformed hands are hybrids of humans and Grays."

"I don't believe it," Janis said. "I never sensed hostility from any Gray I encountered."

"Will discovered they are behind the invasion," Aubrey continued. "He found a cave where they put the bodies of the hybrids who couldn't be converted."

"What purpose could possibly be behind such bizarre action?" Klast asked. Aubrey shook his head.

"That remains unknown at present, Doctor," Aubrey replied. "It's apparent they want our world, just as they wanted Zeus' world. The reason is anyone's guess."

"Did he say anything about the conversion process?" Zachary asked.

"He doesn't know how it functions, but he's working on it."

"It seems odd that Grays have been seen for years and never a hint of this," Ophelia said. "Why now? They never harmed Janis or me."

"They must have been the vanguard of the invasion," Schiffer said. "Sent to do medical experiments to see if we were susceptible to their mind control techniques. Once that proved viable, their invasion got underway. You two may have been their ploy to convince others that they were friendly and peaceful."

"I agree," Zachary said. "It's more convenient to check out a race before you attempt contact. If you can take over without conflict, so much the better."

"That's not what I got from a Gray," Ophelia said. "Zeus agrees it was different Grays that enslaved the friendly Grays and gained control over them."

"They never attempted any medical experiments on Ophelia or me," Janis said.

"That doesn't address the question of why they invaded at this time," Klast said. "What made them take this action now?"

"There's one possibility," Raeta said, and drew all the attention. "They may need to overhaul and build new ships. But they're incapable of physical labor and this is their solution." Zeus shook his head.

"Why conquer a planet just to maintain their ships?" Zeus asked. Schiffer nodded.

"They could have built secret bases," Schiffer said. "And used abductees for labor."

"We're getting nowhere with speculation," Ophelia said. "They are quite frail, strong only in telepathic abilities. Their ships are automated. I can't second guess their motives."

"Where do they come from?" Castor asked. "And could they have caused the war on our home world?"

"There's too much we don't know," Aubrey said. "Miss Randall is correct, we're getting nowhere with speculation and conjecture."

"I agree," Zeus said. "They put people they could control in positions of power to prevent conflict. Those too strong to control, they put through conversion to keep from having to face the threat of rebellion."

"What do you suppose the conditions on your home world are like now?" Janis asked. Zeus had avoided thinking about that, but since the question had been asked, he had to respond.

"I can't say," Zeus replied. "But I wouldn't want to return after millennia of alien domination." Raeta and Castor nodded.

"I think we should bring Vicea into this," Janis said. "She's an exobiologist and might provide some insight into the Grays' psychology."

"A valid point," Aubrey agreed.

"It could prove interesting to hear what she thinks of the Grays," Klast said. "Maybe she can deduce their recent action better than we have."

"It's still only guesswork," Schiffer said.

"True," Zeus said. "But an expert guess might prove valuable."

"We may learn something Will could use," Raeta said.

"I'll have Vicea join us," Zeus said, rising and going to the intercom.

Will faced a difficult problem. Since he had made love to Cathy, she became jealous every time another woman spoke to him. He knew this was causing tension in the group and resolved to do something about it at the first opportunity. He knew he would have to be blunt with Cathy, but suspected she wouldn't give up easily.

They lay side by side in the cold desert night observing the base, and in particular a Gray who had seen them but raised no alarm. It seemed a hopeful sign they may have found a cooperative Gray. Cathy snuggled up to Will. He knew what she wanted and it was her way of saying so. He looked at her pretty face in the dim glow from the base.

"We have to talk, Cathy. This relationship has gotten out of hand." She gave him a puzzled look.

"What do you mean, Will?"

"I mean you're too damn jealous. Everyone in the group knows about us from your actions. We've enjoyed a sexual relationship, but that's all it was. There was no commitment from either of us."

"But I love you, Will." He shook his head.

"No you don't. You're infatuated with the relationship. It's not love. I want you to get a grip on yourself and stop this jealousy act. It's bad for you, for me, and for the group and what we're trying to accomplish." He could see the hurt she expressed, but it had to be said.

"I know it doesn't seem that way to you, Cathy, but that's the way it has to be."

"You want one of those other bitches, don't you?"

"Christ! Try to understand that in my line of work, I can't afford any ongoing relationship."

"Why not?" she asked, angrily.

"It's proven dangerous. I was in love just after I came into this work. Somehow the other side found out about her and threatened to kill her if I didn't backoff. I didn't, and they killed her."

"I'm sorry, Will." He looked at her with a soft expression.

"Don't be. Just understand that you're not in love with me."

"Don't you want to go on making love?"

"I feel it best we stop for awhile." As she lay silent beside him, he had some idea of what must be going through her mind, but the situation had to be resolved. She looked at him.

"All right, Will if that's the way you want it."

"It's not what I want, it's a matter of necessity." She flattened herself on the ground. Will followed suit and looked toward the base. They saw two Grays standing by the fence looking in their direction.

"Do you think they know we're here, Will?" Fear was explicit in her tone.

"If they do, they're not doing anything about it." As they watched, the Grays turned away and moved back into the base. It gave them a sense of relief, but also disappointment. Will felt he may have missed an opportunity.

"We better get out of here," he said. "We're not going to see anymore tonight." They crawled back into the desert away from the glow of the base, and got to their feet.

"Why were they watching us, Will?" The question surprised him.

"How do you know they were watching us?"

"It was what I felt they were doing." This was unexpected and not to Will's liking. It could mean the Grays had exerted an influence on her mind. He took hold of her arm and hurried them along.

"What are you doing?" He glanced at her.

"Getting you as far away from here as possible. They may have been trying to control you, so you can't come back here."

"Be sensible, Will. I would have known if they were trying to control me."

"Really? Then how did you know they were watching?" Cathy stopped abruptly causing Will to spin and face her. She had a frightened look.

"I just felt it."

"How many times have you felt you knew what the Grays were doing?"

"Oh, God, Will! If it's true, how can I protect myself?" He pulled her along as they resumed walking.

"Staying the hell away from the base is the only way."

Back in the cave, Will told Martin of Cathy's experience. Martin had her explain how she felt when she knew the Grays were watching.

"Interesting," Martin said. "I believe they used a soft telepathic probe to see if she knew what they were doing."

"They knew what I was thinking?" she asked, alarmed. Martin puckered his lips and rubbed the back of his neck.

"It's possible," Martin replied. "If they were projecting thoughts, then it stands to reason they knew."

"They could know what we're saying right now," she said, a horrified expression coming to her. "They could know where we are." Will put a hand on her shoulder and gave a reassuring squeeze.

"I don't think so," Martin said. Will looked at him.

"I think they were trying to communicate on a low telepathic level," Will said.

"To what end?" Martin asked. Will had given considerable thought to that on the walk back, and came to the only logical conclusion.

"They wanted Cathy to know they were watching, but didn't want others of their kind to know it," Will replied. "I think those two may be the ones we can make contact with."

"That could prove risky, Will," Martin said.

"I know. But if they're trying to communicate with us clandestinely, I think the risk worth taking." Martin couldn't argue with Will's logic. They were in need of help, and the people Will had told them about were too far away.

"How do you plan to make contact?" Martin asked. Will glanced at Cathy and frowned.

"I haven't figured that out yet."

"Let me do it," Cathy said. "It was my mind they touched." Will looked from her to Martin.

"She has a point," Martin agreed. Will was torn between letting Cathy take the risk or doing it himself. He knew having the implant eliminated him from the attempt, so it had to be her. It was a hard decision, but seemed to be the only one. Will nodded.

"We'll return to the base tomorrow night," Will said. "Have any of the others had a similar experience?"

"If they have, they've not mentioned it," Martin replied.

"We better tell them," Will said. "It involves them as much as us."

"Is it possible this might work?" Cathy asked.

"All we can do is try," Martin said, patting her arm.

"We've got to do a recon," Will said, facing the others." I don't want to try this without some possibility of success."

"What have you got in mind?" Mitch asked. It was risky, but Will felt Mitch would agree.

"Are you willing to undergo hypnosis again, return to the base tomorrow and try to locate the two that was communicating with Cathy?" Mitch nodded.

"I'll do what I can," Mitch said, and looked at Martin. "Can it work a second time?"

"I see no reason it shouldn't," Martin said.

"I would prefer to go, Mitch, but with this implant, I doubt I could learn very much."

"It's okay, Will," Mitch said. "We can't have Cathy taking such a risk, can we?" It was then Will realized Mitch was in love with her. He also realized they had tried to communicate with her in the manner they had with Ophelia and Janis. What if the Grays were only able to make a telepathic link with women? He knew of no instance where they had communicated with a man. This put a new perspective on the problem.

"We might have to use Cathy," Will said. Martin looked surprised and Mitch angry.

"In God's name why, Will?" Martin asked. Will glanced at Mitch feeling sympathy since he now knew how he felt about her.

"It's possible these grays contacted the sisters I told you about. For some reason, they seem to be able to communicate more easily with women. If these are the same Grays, then they're friendly."

"And if they aren't?" Mitch asked, his voice edged with anger.

"Let's leave it up to Cathy," Martin said. "She can say whether she wants to do it or not."

"She's going to need a clear mind," Will said.

"You want to try hypnosis?" Martin asked.

"It's the only way to be certain our message gets across," Will replied. Mitch was giving Will a cold look.

"Do you think it will work?" Mitch asked, his tone hard. "I think it's too great a risk for her."

"I don't know if it will or not, Mitch," Will said. "But if Cathy agrees, we've got to try."

Cathy was calm and quiet as she walked with Will through the desert. The hypnosis seemed to have cleared her mind and filled it with the message they wanted the Grays to get. Will was glad she wasn't talking, as he didn't much care for what they were about to try.

As they neared the base, he put his arm around her and they went down on their stomachs. They crawled closer to the fence than they had dared go before. If this was to work Will felt she had to be close to them. He looked along the fence but saw no Gray. They would have to wait until one came along, then have her communicate the message.

Hours passed and no Gray came to the fence. Will was beginning to feel uneasy and decided that if no Gray showed up in the next half hour, they would get away from there. Time passed, and he saw no Grays anywhere. He took hold of her arm, turned her, and they crawled away. Away from the lights, he helped her to her feet.

"We didn't get a hell of a lot accomplished tonight," he said. She nodded. It seemed odd that she hadn't spoken since Martin put her in the trance, but was told that was to be expected.

"Let's get back to the cave." Again, she only nodded and started to walk. Will stood staring at her back, not liking this at all. He hurried up beside her and took hold of her arm stopping her. She turned to face him.

"Is something wrong?" She shook her head. Will suddenly had his warning system blaring in him.

"Have you been in communication with any Gray?" She shook her head. Still holding her arm, he pulled her along with him. Something wasn't right, but he had no idea what it might be.

They continued across the desert with an icy breeze hitting them in the face. There was no complaint from her and no slackening of her pace. Will glanced at her knowing she wasn't right, and hoped Martin could do something for her. His mind was preoccupied when the blow came on the back of his head.

It was after sunrise when Will came to. He sat up rubbing the back of his sore head. He remembered Cathy! He got to his feet and looked around but didn't see her. What the hell happened? he wondered. Will looked at the ground and saw footprints.
Two men had been waiting for them. The tracks showed that she had gone with them willingly. All the prints were evenly spaced showing an unhurried stride.

It seemed to Will that Cathy had been communicating with a Gray or those men wouldn't have known where to be waiting for them. What did they want with her?

Will felt they would have wanted him instead, and hurried back toward the base following the footprints until they vanished. He looked at the fence but saw no activity. The base looked deserted. He thought of going to look for her, but common sense won out. Cathy was in there, but how long would it take to locate her? If he did find her, he couldn't be certain she would come with him willingly. He had to get back to the cave, as there was nothing else he could do. They had set a trap and like a rookie, he had fallen into it. It cost Will a bruise, what was it costing Cathy? Will had to consider the safety of the other people. He began to run even though each step caused a sharp pain in his head. He had to warn the others to evacuate, as the cave was no longer safe.

When he came into the cave, Martin was there to greet him.

"What happened, Will?"

"The bastards set a trap and now have Cathy." Martin's shoulders sagged.

"They got everybody here, except me. Men were on us before we even knew they were in the cave." Will stared at Martin, his pain forgotten.

"How did they miss you, Martin?"

"I was in an accident a few years ago, Will. I've got a plate covering my frontal lobe. That's the only thing I can think of to explain how they missed me."

"We're going to the base and get our people back." Martin stared, incredulous.

"There's two of us, Will! How can we do anything?" Will calmed down and thought for a couple of minutes.

"By being in more than one place at the same time, Martin."

EIGHTEEN

The Earth people were awed as the ship neared Zeus' world. The sun's dim glow gave the golden shell of the atmosphere a magnificent aura against the blackness of space. Zeus had invited them to the bridge just to see the approach.

"I've never seen anything so beautiful," Ophelia said, in a soft tone.

"I thought you would like seeing our world in this way," Zeus said, standing beside her.

"What causes the glow around your world?" Zachary asked.

"We have suspended minute gold particles in the upper atmosphere," Zeus replied. "It insulates against space and retains the planet's natural heat."

"That must have taken tons of gold," Schiffer said. "Where did you get it?"

"On Earth. Your ancient people believed gold to be the metal of the gods and believed it had no value except for us. The Brotherhood stepped in and convinced people that gold was very valuable. This caused the Europeans to decimate the natives of Central and South America and the Caribbean islands, in their lust to possess gold."

"What is this Brotherhood?" Aubrey asked.

"We're not sure," Zeus replied. "It could be renegades from our people, or now that we know about the Grays, your people controlled by them."

"How were they able to remain secretive for such a span of time?" Klast asked.

"They were the people behind the people with power and wealth. No one became aware of them because they were focused on their leaders," Zeus replied. "They distracted people from the real power brokers."

"Someone must have suspected something," Janis said. Zeus wasn't certain of how they may have taken care of a chance discovery.

"If anyone got suspicious, they were probably bought off or killed," Zeus said. "Your most notorious butcher was one of their henchmen."

"And who was that?" Aubrey asked.

"Adolf Hitler," Zeus said, grimly. "He made reference to The Brotherhood in February 1945."

"What reference?" Schiffer asked.

"I know the words well," Zeus said. "It's one of the few vague references in your history about The Brotherhood. Hitler said, 'I must now disastrously accomplish everything with the short span of a human life… where others had an eternity at their disposal, I have only a few miserable years. The others know they will have successors.' The others he was referring to was The Brotherhood."

"They helped him assume power so they could use him?" Janis asked. Zeus nodded.

"Him and countless others. It was their way to control your history's development along paths they wanted."

"To what end?" Klast asked.

"Probably to bring about what's now happening," Raeta replied, coming on the bridge. "The Pantheon wants us to report immediately, Zeus. The Earth people are to be interviewed."

"What status do they want the ship kept on?" Zeus asked.

"Emergency standby," Raeta replied. Zeus nodded.

"I thought that might be the case."

"What does that mean?" Aubrey asked.

"That we could leave for Earth anytime," Zeus said.

"Without knowing what the conditions there are?" Ophelia asked.

"It's the way we must proceed for now," Raeta said. "We could find ourselves in a shooting war sooner than any of us imagine."

"Does that include the Pantheon?" Schiffer asked.

"Yes," Zeus replied. "They want the ship ready for a quick departure, should it become necessary." It was then they felt the first turbulence of the atmosphere as the ship made its descent.

In what seemed a very few minutes, they felt the light impact as the ship came to rest. The people from Earth glanced at each other nervously, not knowing what to expect. Zeus turned to them and stretched his hand to the open hatch.

"Welcome to Olympus," he said. "We must go before the Pantheon. Please follow Raeta. I'll join you shortly."

They followed her off the bridge and out the hatch. They stepped onto a platform that was high above an imposing city. Raeta looked at them with an expression of pride.

"This is Chronus," she said. They felt as if they were indeed looking at a city of the gods.

It had tall, silver and gold needle like spires and massive buildings that glimmered in what appeared to be sunlight.

"How can you have bright sunlight this far out in the solar system?" Zachary asked. Raeta got a proud smile.

"We created an artificial source of light as bright as the sun, but without the radiation hazards the sun emits."

"Astonishing!" Schiffer exclaimed. Even Aubrey was impressed, but he imagined this metropolis in ruin unless they were able to reverse the events that were transpiring on Earth.

"This way," Raeta said, holding open an elevator door. Once in, she followed and pressed the button at the panel bottom. The elevator dropped so swiftly, they thought they were falling until it gently slowed to a stop. They stepped onto a wide platform as a long tubular vehicle stopped and Raeta opened a door on it.

"This will take us to the Pantheon," she said. "Please get in and be seated." They entered and were surprised at its comfort. Raeta sat down facing them.

"What action might the Pantheon take, Raeta?" Aubrey asked.

"I can't guess about what action they may decide on."

"Have you another world you can go to?" Zachary asked. Raeta was puzzled at the question.

"What do you mean?" she asked.

"This one could be destroyed," Aubrey said. She looked at him surprised.

"Make that clear to the Pantheon," Raeta said.

"You're much too practical, Raeta, not to be aware of the danger this world faces," Aubrey said.

"Bring that fact to the Pantheon's attention also," Raeta said. "It will be more plausible coming from someone whose world had been invaded." Aubrey smiled, thinking her quite an extraordinary woman.

The vehicle stopped in front of an imposing building that looked like an ancient Greet temple. Anyone who had seen photos and drawings of Greek temples couldn't have mistaken it for anything else.

"This is most impressive," Klast said, looking at the massive façade. The others were awed by the ornate edifice. Raeta led the way through massive double bronze doors into a marbled, high ceiling corridor lined on both sides by towering columns.

Golden light fixtures along the walls glowed brightly from the globes set in them. She led them into a small anteroom.

"Please wait," Raeta said. "The Pantheon will want to see you." She quickly went through another door. They took seats on the comfortable sofas along the walls.

"What do you think they'll decide, Aubrey?" Schiffer asked.

"I don't know. But I know what I'm going to do." Schiffer got a quizzical look.

"What?"

"Chet, we need their help. I've got to convince them their world will be endangered if they allow Earth to be held by the Grays. I have to convince these people to help us." Schiffer shook his head.

"I wish I was as certain as you, Aubrey. I still haven't a clear idea about what's going on." Aubrey patted his shoulder.

"Don't worry, Chet, we'll get into this fight yet."

Ophelia sat beside Janis regarding her in a serious manner.

"Worried about Will?" Janis looked at her.

"What makes you think I am?"

"I know how you feel, Janis. Emotion that strong can't be concealed. I favor it. You've needed someone and I'm glad you found him." Janis was surprised and couldn't think of any response. Ophelia smiled and put her hand on Janis' arm.

"Believe me, Janis, I understand."

"Why bring it up now, Ophelia?" She averted her eyes from Janis, not wanting to say what she was thinking.

"I want to know." Ophelia looked back at her.

"It's possible we may never see Will again." An expression of shock came to Janis.

"I can't believe that. A hurricane, and being shot twice, didn't kill him." Ophelia gripped her sister's hand.

"You have to face the fact that Will may already be dead." Janis turned her face away, not wanting Ophelia to see the tears that idea caused. Ophelia put an arm around her shoulders and gave a gentle squeeze.

Raeta reentered the room and motioned for them to follow her.

"The Pantheon wants to see you." She led them into a marbled chamber lined with five golden chairs on the left and five on the right. Between them, facing the doors, sat an impressive looking man and most attractive woman.

The man was muscular with gray eyes and white hair and neatly trimmed beard. The woman had black hair and brown eyes. When they stopped before them, Raeta bowed her head as she had done to Ophelia.

"These are the Earth people," Raeta said. The man looked them over carefully with a slight smile as he looked at Ophelia and Janis. He leaned over and whispered to the woman. Her eyes widened as she looked at the sisters.

"You are the descendants of Athena?" she asked, in a soft, firm voice. Ophelia stepped forward and bowed her head as Raeta had done.

"So we have been told," Ophelia replied.

"Seeing you leaves me with no doubt. I am Hera."

"Where is the one of Zeus' lineage?" the man asked.

"He returned to Earth," Raeta said. "He's sent us information that I believe vital to our survival." This brought a noisy stir of words from around the room.

"What is the information?" Hera asked. Aubrey stepped forward with a confident expression.

"Zeus told us of a war long ago that banished you from your home world," Aubrey said.

"That's true," the man said, in a strong baritone. "What has that to do with us now?"

"The Kraken are on Earth, planning an attack against you," Aubrey replied. "This time they will be using Earthmen as their soldiers. Unless you resolve this problem, you may face defeat and banishment again." The murmur around the room became louder as the man regarded Aubrey with a troubled expression.

"How can these creatures make people fight one another?" Hera asked.

"They have the power to take away a person's memory and personality," Aubrey said. "They then use telepathy to control them."

"Are they doing this to your people?" a woman from the side asked. Aubrey looked at her and nodded.

"Those who resist were killed."

"What makes you think they mean to attack us?" Hera asked. That was the question Aubrey had been waiting for.

"The base Will has been watching is the site of construction for ships. There's no reason to build them except for war.

They have no enemies left on Earth. You are the enemy they intend sending Earthmen to fight." The room exploded in an uproar.

"Silence," the man said, loudly. The chamber became instantly quiet.

"Are you certain of this?" he asked. Aubrey knew he had them almost convinced.

"I have no doubt," Aubrey replied. "Abandon Earth and the human race, and you condemn yourselves to another war." Again the room erupted. The man looked at Hera, and she nodded, giving nothing away by her expression.

"Raeta, see that the Earth people are made comfortable," Hera said. "We must discuss this among ourselves." Raeta bowed her head and turned to them.

"Follow me," Raeta said. "I'll show you to your quarters."

Aubrey paced with his hands behind him as Schiffer sat watching him. He felt he knew what was in Aubrey's mind.

"You might as well sit down and relax, Aubrey. There's not a damn thing left for us to do." He turned to Schiffer, took his arms from behind him and folded them.

"Did I leave anything out, Chet?" Schiffer shook his head.

"You told them how it is. There wasn't anymore you could have said." Aubrey's brow furrowed as he got a worried look.

"But did I convince them?"

"You gave them the facts, Aubrey. They have to convince themselves. These people are intelligent and will do what needs to be done."

"I wish I was sure, Chet. Goddamnit! I keep thinking I left something out they should have been told."

"I heard you, Aubrey, and you left nothing out."

"Do you think they'll help?"

"They don't want to be run out of this solar system the way they were before," Schiffer replied. "And especially not by the same enemy that drove them from their home world."

Ophelia and Janis were surprised when Zeus showed up at their apartment. He regarded them with a reluctance that puzzled them.

"You have something to say you would rather not say," Janis said, feeling a cold dread. He looked at her, inhaled deeply, and nodded.

"The Pantheon wants the both of you, Aubrey, Raeta, and me to return to Earth."

"What for?" Ophelia asked.

"They want us to act in any manner that will give them time to get armed," Zeus replied. "We're not prepared for war. We're to gain time for them to prepare."

"Why us?" Janis asked.

"You were in contact with the Grays. Since they never harmed you, the Pantheon believes there may be a diverse group among them, one that doesn't want war. I told them you weren't able to get the conception of enemy from one Gray. That's what led them to the decision to send you."

"You mean, we're expendable," Ophelia said. Zeus nodded.

"I guess that's one way to look at it."

"What about Will?" Janis asked. "Has Aubrey heard anymore from him?"

"The distance we are from Earth, any message would take sometime to reach here," Zeus said. "We might get a message anytime." Janis glanced at Ophelia.

"Do you think he's dead, Zeus?" Janis asked. The question shocked him.

"No, Janis, I don't. Whatever gave you such an idea?" She looked down at the floor and clasped her hands.

"I'm trying to be realistic about his chances," Janis replied. Ophelia looked at Zeus.

"It's my fault," Ophelia said. "I didn't want her to get her hopes up, so I suggested she consider the possibility."

"I believe Will's alive and keeping the Grays in turmoil," Zeus said. There followed an awkward silence that Zeus broke.

"Neither of you have to go on this mission. Do you want to return to Earth?" Janis looked at Ophelia then to Zeus.

"I'll go," Janis said. Ophelia looked at him and nodded.

"That leaves Raeta and Aubrey," Zeus said.

"I don't think either would consider not going," Janis said. "They both care about Will."

"I see you've noticed Raeta's attraction for him," he said, with a sly smile.

"It wasn't easy to miss," Janis replied, testily.

"I'll speak with them and inform the Pantheon that we've agreed to return to Earth."

"What are our chances of surviving once we get to Earth?" Ophelia asked. Zeus gave her a serious look.

"As good as we make them," Zeus replied, turned, and left.

They were apprehensive as they walked into the Pantheon. Janis was curious.

"Who is the man beside Hera?" Janis asked. Zeus looked at her with a proud smile.

"Zeus, my grandfather." Janis quickly looked at the man, and saw they resembled each other. They stopped before Hera and Zeus.

"You are all very brave," Hera said. "We wish to thank you for agreeing to help us. Zeus will be utilizing some of our latest innovations in weapons and communication technology. Raeta will have no problem adapting them to Earth weapons."

"Should we discover Grays who are opposed to war," Janis said. "What message do you wish us to give them?"

"We need some idea what they might expect in return for their cooperation," Ophelia said. Zeus stood and Hera looked up at him.

"Tell them we would welcome friends, that we hold no animosity for what happened ages ago," he said. "We would look forward to combining our technologies and exploring the galaxy together."

"Can the Earth participate?" Aubrey asked. The man gave him a firm nod.

"Our children must share such an adventure with us."

"Then we go with hope," Ophelia said.

"May you be successful," Hera said. "And return safely."

NINETEEN

It had taken a week of sneaking around to find the dynamite and long cold nights placing the charges and rigging them to be detonated, but the task was completed.

"When do we make our move?" Martin asked.

"I hope to hear from Aubrey first," Will replied.

"Why?"

"We're going to be needing help soon. If I don't hear from him in a few days, we'll blast the hell out of those ships."

"What about Cathy and the others on the base?"

"The charges are away from any building. I'm hoping they'll attract attention that will allow us to get in there and try to locate them."

"Do you believe they're all right, Will?"

"There are a lot more people than our group in there, Martin. We're going to have to get as many out as we can, if they seem normal."

"How will we decide that?"

"If they speak normally, they're not under the influence. Cathy must have been under the influence of a Gray when you hypnotized her. She didn't speak on the way to the base, and I assumed it was the hypnosis, but learned better."

"That's awful thin criteria to work on, Will."

"I know, Martin, but what else do we have?" There wasn't an answer to that and both knew it.

"What do we do while we wait?"

"Try to find where the people are being held, Martin."

It didn't take long to discover the people were held in temporary shelter next to what Will assumed was the conversion building, not far from the main entrance of the base. If things went as planned they would get into the building and try to destroy the converter. How long it might take to get the people out was another matter, as neither Will nor Martin had any idea how many people were there. Also, the problem of what to do with them once they were free.

"The more I think about this, Will, the more complicated it becomes. How the hell are we going to handle this alone?"

"I've been considering the same thing and haven't come up with anything useful."

"Let's face it, Will, getting those people out is overly ambitious. We've got to settle for our own people. The rest will have wait until we're reinforced."

"I agree." Martin looked relieved.

"Then we go after our people tonight?" Will nodded. He hadn't heard from Aubrey and saw no alternative.

"Let's check the detonator and make certain it will function, Martin."

The rest of the afternoon was spent in preparation. They worked out the details, rechecked the equipment, and waited.

"Do you think those people on the spaceship will send help, Will?"

"Not hearing from Aubrey, I doubt it. Being on our own, there's not a hell of a lot we can do."

"Is there a possibility of nuking the bastards?" Will got an incredulous look.

"Hell no, Martin. That would poison most of the state, and we wouldn't be able to escape the blast." Martin nodded.

"It was a thought, Will. Any idea how we might make an impression on the Grays?"

"I've been giving that some thought, but so far nothing's come to mind."

"What about taking one of those ships?"

"I doubt I could fly the damn thing." Martin got a cynical look.

"They mean for our people to fly them." Will nodded.

"I'm sure they do, but under the Grays' control." They sat for a few minutes in silence until Will looked at his watch.

"It's time to go, Martin. Let's hope we can pull this off." They got up and left the cave.

Outside, they zipped their jackets against the cold of the desert night. Like shadows, they moved across the landscape toward the base. Will wasn't certain of success, but was committed to trying to free the group. He worried how Cathy might feel toward him, assuming she hadn't been put through the converter. His next thought was whether there was a way to reverse the conversion process. He decided it might be premature to destroy the converter before finding out. Will tried to keep his mind on anything but failure.

He began thinking about Janis and had thought a lot about her lately. He was glad she and Ophelia had gotten away from Earth, and wondered if he would ever see them again. The thought of seeing them was something to look forward to.

They were close to the main gate and saw no Grays. This puzzled Will. Did they know Martin and he were coming? What were they planning? Had the Grays been able to get past the mental blocks that kept Martin and him free? Martin looked at him with an uneasy expression.

"Where are they, Will?" Martin whispered. Will glanced at him and turned his eyes back to the base.

"I don't know, but I'm getting a bad feeling about this."

"Do you want to wait?" Will was about to say yes when he looked over the base and saw no activity. He looked at Martin.

"Let's see if we can stir someone up. Set off the explosives, Martin." Martin quickly adjusted the transmitter frequency and pressed the detonator. They were rewarded with a large flash to the southeast and it took a couple of seconds before the sound reached them. When it did, another flash in the dark not far from the first followed by a third. They looked at the base. Nothing! Still no activity.

"What the hell's going on?" Will asked, more to himself than Martin.

"They must be up to something, Will." Will pulled the automatic from his belt and boldly stood.

"Let's go see what those bastards are doing."

They walked openly through the main gate, keeping alert for any movement. Caution took hold just inside the gate, but it was in vain. They saw no one; Grays or humans.

"Do we go on?" Martin asked. Will bit his lip and looked at him.

"Yeah. I'm awful damn curious now." They moved onto the base looking in each building they came to, but found them devoid of any living creature. They went to the structure where they believed the people had been kept, but it, too, was empty.

"They've abandoned the place!" Will exclaimed.

"How could they have done it without us knowing?" Will looked around. Everything was just as it had been when he first seen the base and shook his head.

"Beats the hell out of me. Where and how could they have taken all those people?" It was a mystery, and neither knew where to begin to look for an answer.

"What doesn't make any damn sense is they left all those ships," Martin said. "What the hell are they up to?"

"We better find out or we might just be screwed."

"How so?" Will considered that as he stuck the automatic back in his belt.

"They might come back and catch us here." Martin gave him an incredulous look.

"You don't think they've gone to all this trouble just to flush the two of us into the open, do you?"

"We can't be certain they didn't, Martin. I'm going to try contacting Aubrey and let him know what's happened." Martin got an annoyed look.

"We don't know what's happened." Will looked at him with a frown.

"We'll go into orbit," Will said. "We may have better luck with transmission."

"Let's go, Will. This damn place gives me the creeps. All the lights on and nobody around makes it spooky." Will nodded.

"Let's head for the ship. The sooner we get off this planet the better I'll feel."

They hurried back across the desert and up into the foothills. It wasn't easy climbing in the dark but they made it to the ship after a couple of bruising falls. As soon as Will was in the pilot's seat, he began bringing the ship's systems on line. When Martin seen how cramped it was, he almost complained. But recalling how he had felt at the base, he held his tongue.

"How long will it take? To get into space, I mean." Will kept his eyes on the instruments as he replied.

"We have to go to the pole before we head into space. I would estimate about half an hour."

"What do we do when we get there, Will?"

"Contact Aubrey. It will take some time due to the distance, but it's essential we get help if we're to find out where the Grays took the people."

"Why do you think they moved them?"

"I wish I knew, Martin. I sure as hell don't believe it was because of us. They must have had this in the works for sometime. Otherwise, how were they able to do it so quietly and quickly?"

"Do you suppose they took them back east?" Will hadn't given much thought as to where they might have been taken, but it crossed his mind that if the Grays had a secret base close to Washington they wouldn't have to worry about concealing their movements. If, as he suspected, HAARP was now keeping the majority of the population complacent, the Grays could move about with impunity.

"That's possible, Martin."

"Think there are other groups like us around?"

"If HAARP wasn't able to affect our group then there has to be others in similar circumstances. Even if they somehow found each other, and banded together, I can't see how they could do much on their own. More than likely they would be sticking together for company and out of fear." Will pressed the controls and the ship lifted silently, turned north, and began gaining altitude. He gave it all the speed he dared in the dark, skimming over the surface just above the treetops. He concentrated on what lie ahead so he could make any maneuver that became necessary.

Passing some cities, the lack of motion caught his eye and he decided to take a chance and fly over a large city. He circled to the west and came in over Denver. The streets were lit up but there wasn't a person to be seen anywhere, it looked deserted. Martin gazed down at the empty streets as an unreasoning fear grew in him.

"Where the hell are the people, Will?" His voice was somewhat high pitched. Will glanced at him.

"Take it easy, Martin." He returned Will's look with a panic stricken expression.

"Tell me where the damn people have gone?"

"They're probably at home in a blissful state. That's what HAARP was supposed to do, make them passive so they would cause no trouble." Martin's expression became one of helplessness.

"Let's get away from here." Will resumed his course north.

They could see the ice cap ahead and Will adjusted the controls for the flight into space. When the instruments showed they were well within the strongest area of the magnetic field, the ship began hitting heavy turbulence. He nosed the ship up and headed away from Earth.

Will took the ship into a geosynchronous orbit above the moon and connected his microwave transmitter into the ship's more powerful communication system and began transmitting. When his short call for help had ended, he quickly shut the system down.

"Now what?"

"We wait, Martin. It's going to take them awhile to receive it."

"Why is it going to take so long?"

"It's the distance, Martin. The signal has millions of miles to travel and it's not going to get there fore about five hours." A small amber light on the instrument panel began blinking steadily.

"Why is that light blinking?" Will turned and saw the steady pulses and knew a ship was nearby. He turned his eyes to the windscreen but could see nothing but stars in the blackness of space.

"What's it mean, Will?"

"A ship's closing with us and I'm looking for it."

"A ship! Ours or theirs?"

"We'll find out soon enough." Will saw a glint off something metallic. He had spotted the unknown ship but couldn't identify it. He couldn't tell if it was closing with them or not, and he lost it.

"Can you see it?"

"I only caught a glimpse of it. I can't be certain they know we're here."

"Where is it now?"

"I lost it. It looked like it was heading away from us."

"What if it's a trick to make us think that, Will?" Will glanced at him and shrugged.

"They'll have us before we know it. If they get us, I don't know what we can expect, but I don't think it will be pleasant." Will continued to search for the elusive ship. The interior was filled with a brilliant burst of violet light. Martin and Will found themselves facing a tall Gray. Neither was aware how it had come to be here so suddenly.

"Friend," the Gray thought. Will felt no threat from it. The men glanced at each other then back to the Gray.

"Why have you brought us onboard?" Will thought.

"I wish to meet with Janis and Ophelia. They understand, know, what we want."

"They're not on Earth," Will thought.

"I know," the Gray replied. "They will return soon. When you meet with them, tell them I must confer with them about the unfortunate situation on your planet. I will be anticipating contact with them." Will nodded.

"I'll give them the message as soon as I see them." The Gray looked at Martin with watery black eyes.

"Your friends are well and have not been subjected to conversion," the Gray thought. "I hope they can rejoin you soon."

"Where have they been taken?" Martin thought.

"To a secret place to undergo testing we do not understand. Those of us who opposed this mad action are too few to make any protest."

"This secret place, where is it?" Will thought. The Gray formed a confused picture in Will's mind that was a familiar shape, but too out of focus for him to define.

"Can you make it clearer?" The Gray nodded.

"It is in your capital, underground. I have not seen the place. That is why I cannot define it more clearly, but will try." The Gray seemed to concentrate, and the picture became clear enough for Will to recognize.

"Jesus Christ!" he exclaimed, aloud. "Why are they there?"

"It is a place where the strange ones meet with your people, and have done so for many Earth years," the Gray thought. "It is known as the secret place because your population has not been told of the contact your leaders established with the strange ones." Martin's thought was of rescue. If Will knew where the place was, they could go there. The Gray turned its eyes back to Martin.

"It would be foolish for you to try," the Gray thought. "The secret place is too well guarded by your people. They will not allow you to enter and might even destroy you if you tried."

"What were you thinking, Martin?"

"About getting our people out of there."

"Forget it. We wouldn't stand a chance in hell of getting in there, let alone getting back out alive."

"Ophelia and Janis will know how to get your friends out," the Gray thought. "Tell them of this place. Tell them not to try entering until they have communicated with me. We will be able to help."

"Do you trust this creature, Will?"

"I believe what its told us and intend to cooperate. I want to see those people freed alive, too. But I also want to go on living." Martin's shoulders slumped in helplessness.

"All right, Will. But how long are we going to wait before doing something?"

"The sisters are on their way back to Earth," the Gray thought. "But too far away for me to contact them. You will meet with their ship soon. I will now return you to your vessel." There was a brilliant flash of violet light and they found themselves back in the cramped ship. Martin glanced quickly around, stopping his eyes on Will.

"Did that really happen?"

"Sure did, Martin. We better try contacting the ship heading for Earth." He reached over and powered up and set the frequency. A few minutes later, the speaker started sounding out the code Aubrey had devised. Will listened, trying to decode it as he listened. He was only able to make out part of it and not enough to make sense from it.

"What was the message?" Will shook his head.

"I didn't get enough to understand what Aubrey meant. We're going out and meet their ship, Martin. We have a lot to tell them, and I hope they have good news for us and Earth.

"By the way, Will, where is that secret place the Gray told us about?" Will got an angry look.

"Under the goddamn Pentagon."

TWENTY

Aubrey had deciphered Will's message and was taking it to Zeus in the control center with Raeta. He didn't like the news and spoke as he stopped behind them.

"Will's left Earth. He'll rendezvous with us in two days." Raeta's brow furrowed.

"Why did he leave?" she asked. Aubrey shook his head.

"He didn't say, just asked for coordinates."

"It must be important," Zeus said. "But how does he know we're coming?"

"We'll find out when we see him," Aubrey replied. "He's not acknowledging any communication."

"He must not want the Grays to get a lock on him," Raeta said. Will's action was a mystery to Aubrey; he had never abandoned a mission before.

"Whatever the reason, it's unlike Will to take such action. Can we possibly rendezvous with his ship sooner?"

"I'll check our position," Raeta said. "I should be able to get enough speed to meet with his ship in twelve hours." She made her check and handed the coordinates to Aubrey.

"Inform him of the new rendezvous time," Zeus said. "We don't want to miss him." Aubrey went back to the transmitter knowing Will might not be acknowledging transmissions but he would be listening. He quickly encoded the new rendezvous time and coordinates and began to transmit. There was no way to know if Will was the only one receiving the transmission, so Aubrey kept it short. The ship's sensors had detected no other ships nearby, but that didn't mean they weren't there. Aubrey's concern was getting Will back safely and learn what he knew. Ophelia came in while Aubrey was lost in thought.

"Is something wrong?" she asked. Aubrey turned to her.

"I'm not sure. I got a message from Will. He's left Earth and meeting us soon." Ophelia got a relieved smile.

"Janis will be glad to hear that," Ophelia said. "Why did he leave?" Aubrey shook his head..

"Reata's going to rendezvous with him in twelve hours." Ophelia turned a puzzled look on Aubrey.

"I don't like this, Mr. Blaine. If Will left Earth, it can only mean bad news."

"That's what I've been thinking, Miss Randall, and I've conceived some terrible ideas."

"Speculating won't do any good," Ophelia said. Aubrey nodded.

"I know, but can't help it. That's why I've kept them to myself."

"There probably wasn't anymore he could do," Ophelia said. "And thought he better let us know." Aubrey had thought of that too.

"Let your sister know Will's on his way."

Will decoded the message quickly as it was too short to miss any of it. He now knew they would meet in approximately twelve hours. He was glad but couldn't get over what the Gray had called the secret place. No one knew all the Pentagon's little nooks and crannies, so it was possible for subterranean rooms to exist without their being general knowledge. But what were they used for? Who were the strange ones? That was the poser for Will. He felt certain neither Aubrey nor Schiffer had any knowledge about it. That beggared the question, who the hell did? How long had it been there? He was determined that when they returned to Earth, he would find out about the secret place.

"Good news, Martin, we'll be meeting the ship in about twelve hours." Martin looked relieved.

"I'm glad. I was beginning to think we were out here all alone." Will was puzzled.

"Back on Earth I felt the same way, even deserted by the enemy. It's a hell of a feeling."

"What can we do after we meet the others, Will?"

"We'll have to figure that out. Right now, I haven't a clue as to what's going on. Why did they take our people and not put them through conversion?"

"That Gray said they had been taken for testing. I wonder what it meant?"

"I don't know, Martin, but I sure as hell don't like it."

The ships were on a converging course. Once together, they could analyze what they knew and make some plan, but what would be remained to be seen. They knew that no matter what they decided, they could count on no help for at least four months.

Unless they took action, Earth might be lost.

If that happened, they would have a long fight to get it back, and that was the last thing they wanted. They had to defeat The Brotherhood and Grays in a way so no one on Earth would suspect what had happened. How they were going to explain the missing persons was something Will didn't even think about. He would leave that up to Aubrey and Zeus.

"There's the ship," Raeta said, pointing to the scanner on the instrument panel.

"Prepare to come along side and dock," Zeus said.

"What do we do with that ship?" Raeta asked. Zeus felt it prudent to keep it.

"Put a magnetic lock on it," Zeus replied. The ships moved along side each other as Raeta done some delicate piloting. They were then joined and the airlocks open. Will and Martin were waiting to enter the larger ship, and all were there to greet them and Will introduced Martin.

"What the hell happened, Will?" Aubrey asked. Will frowned and shrugged.

"All the people are gone, vanished along with the Grays. I flew over Denver and there were no people to be seen." They stood in a shocked silence. Will told of their meeting with the Gray and informed the sisters of its message.

"The Gray said you knew what they wanted, Janis," Will said. "Any idea what it meant?" She stared at him with a puzzled expression, then looked to Ophelia.

"What could it have meant?" Janis asked. Ophelia looked perplexed.

"I don't know," Ophelia replied, looking at Will

"It specified Janis?" Ophelia asked.

"It specified you both," Martin said. "But named Janis as the one who knew."

"I don't understand," Janis said, shaking her head. "I never recalled much from any meeting with them. How could I know what they want?" Will put a hand on her shoulder.

"Why don't you try contacting them now we're closer to Earth?"

"Wouldn't that be dangerous?" Raeta asked. "Some of those Grays might pick up on it."

"She has a point," Martin said. "Is there someway you might be able to contact the one Will and me saw?"

Janis and Ophelia stood silent for a moment.

"I may know a way," Martin said.

"What is it?" Janis asked.

"We could try hypnosis. It might be possible to focus your mind on that one Gray."

"It's worth a try," Janis agreed.

"At least here she won't be close enough to be influenced like Cathy," Will said. The name Cathy loosed jealousy in Janis.

"Who is Cathy?" Janis asked, in a tight tone. Opelia smiled. It was so unlike Janis it seemed amusing. Will's eyebrows rose and he noted Raeta giving him a sour look.

"She was one of our people," Martin replied. "We hypnotized her, trying to contact what we thought was a friendly Gray. Instead, it influenced her. That's how I think they learned where we were hiding."

"And you want my sister to risk that?" Ophelia asked, in an indignant tone.

"This Gray knows she's going to contact it," Will said. "If she focuses on that particular Gray, I see no danger for her."

"It's up to you, Miss Randall," Aubrey said.

"How do I know which Gray I'm supposed to communicate with?" Janis asked.

"It's a tall Gray," Will replied. "About a head taller than most."

"That's the one who took me from the complex," Janis said. "I know the one you're talking about, and I'll be glad to communicate." Ophelia put her hand on Janis' arm with a hesitant look.

"Are you certain?" Ophelia asked. Janis patted her sister's hand and smiled.

"I'll be fine," Janis said. "It told me then that I knew what they wanted, but I still don't know what it meant."

"We can go to my quarters," Raeta said. "She'll be more comfortable there."

Martin quickly had Janis in a trance and Ophelia guided her mind to the Gray and it sensed her presence.

"I've been waiting for your communication, Janis. But you are still far away."

"I'm getting closer. You've said I know what you want, but I'm not aware of it. Can you tell me what it is?"

"The Brotherhood is the enemy of your people and mine. It was created by the strange ones, the ancient ones."

"How are they able to control you?" Janis thought. The Gray seemed determined to answer, but felt it couldn't.

"I cannot disclose that. They control many worlds, many races. They use people to fight against one another while they control the battle."

"Can you be more specific?"

"It used the ones who wanted power on the world of the one you call Zeus. The Brotherhood determined to hunt them down and destroy them. They fear them because they have no means of control over them. In creating your race, they created more beings that cannot be controlled easily. Most people of Earth are beyond their control, but they plan something different to gain control."

"I have been unable to learn what it is, Janis. They are going to attempt it in the secret place. You must stop them or the galaxy is doomed to their dominance."

"What can we do?"

"You must return to Earth and find the secret place. Once there, you'll know what must be done. The one called Will Vaughn knows the location of the secret place."

"You haven't answered my question. What is it you want that I know about?"

"The destruction of The Brotherhood, Janis. Our freedom! You have been aware of this all along, but not consciously. Now that you are aware, please do your best to free us."

"I'll tell my friends, and we'll do all we can."

"I ask no more than that, Janis." Contact was broken and Janis was wide awake and recalling the conversation. She related what the Gray had told her.

"This Brotherhood is alien to all of our worlds," Raeta said.

"That's the way I understood it," Janis said. "They have some control over the Grays it wouldn't tell me about." Aubrey turned to Will.

"This secret place, where did it show you it was?" Aubrey asked. Will inhaled audibly drawing everyone's attention.

"The Gray showed me the Pentagon, Aubrey."

"The Pentagon!" Aubrey exclaimed. Now he was beginning to put some of the puzzle together.

"A secret base," Aubrey said. "Zeus, a secret base where The Brotherhood would have access to military and political power. You couldn't ask for a more perfect location."

"But how long has it been there, Aubrey?" Will asked. "What was its original purpose?"

"We'll have to get to Earth before we can find those answers," Ophelia said.

"The Gray said they were going to try something different to be able to control humans," Janis said. "But it didn't know what." Will and Martin exchanged glances.

"It told us they were going to be testing humans in a way they didn't understand," Will said.

"We must find and destroy that place before they start their experiments," Janis said.

This was all happening too fast for Zeus. He held up a hand and everyone became quiet.

"We can't go rushing to Earth," Zeus said. "We must have a plan that can give us a chance for success." Raeta stepped beside him.

"Zeus is right," she said. "We must do this in a way we can win. If not, and these experiments are successful, the galaxy will be controlled by The Brotherhood."

"That's a hell of a lot to rest on our shoulders," Martin said. His words were answered silence, each thinking of the awesome responsibility that had been thrust upon them.

"That leaves one question," Ophelia said.

"What's that?" Aubrey asked. She looked at him with a grim set to her lips.

"How are we going to do it?"

They would use the time it would take to reach Earth to devise a viable plan. Everything each of them came up with had flaws, and they needed as near perfect a plan as they could come up with. Each planning session ended in frustration as someone pointed out some aspect that would prove difficult, if not impossible to overcome.

"Goddamnit! There's got to be something simple, yet effective. Something they wouldn't be anticipating," Will said, fed up with all the talking. Raeta had an idea.

"Why not the direct approach?" she asked. "It's the last thing they would be expecting."

"What do you mean?" Aubrey asked, interested. Raeta took a minute to clarify her thoughts before replying.

"We have the other ship," she began. "This one is too large to attempt the magnetic turbulence without sustaining damage. We could go down in its wake at a safe distance. When it's destroyed, we'll just be a piece of it falling. That should get us through the HAARP field." No one could find any snag in the plan, until Janis came up with the most terrifying one.

"Once down, how will we protect our minds against The Brotherhood and the Grays?" There was a moment of silence.

"Martin and I are protected," Will said.

"There must be a way to protect ourselves," Aubrey said, frustration clear in his tone. Ophelia and Janis looked at each other sharing an idea.

"There just might be a way," Ophelia said.

"Let's hear it," Aubrey said.

"It may be possible for Janis and me to put mental blocks in each of your minds," Ophelia said. Will looked at Aubrey as his face lit up.

"Do you really think that would work?" Raeta asked.

"I don't see why not," Ophelia replied. "We've never tried it before, but my Ophelia and I believe it would provide a minimum of protection."

"Then we better start," Zeus said. "We'll be passing Luna in twenty-seven hours."

Ophelia had the stronger telepathic power and Janis acted as a booster. Janis held Ophelia's hand while she held Aubrey's. The sisters sweated from the intense concentration. Janis had to put her emotions aside when it came to Raeta. When she found that Raeta was experiencing the same sort of attraction to Will that she was, it surprised her. In that moment of joining, the two women understood each other more clearly than any of the others. Zeus was last to get the mental block. His mind was touched by Ophelia's and both felt the attraction between them. Ophelia was more than a little flattered that he should feel this way about her, but it was something to be discussed later – if any of them even survived what they were about to undertake.

After closing with Earth, Raeta released the small ship and guided it out ahead. If the plan worked the way she had calculated, they would drop in its wake without detection. Aubrey had no idea at what altitude HAARP waves would become strong enough to destroy the ship, so they were counting on it being a moderate altitude.

When they felt the turbulence of the ship entering the atmosphere, tension began to mount. They dropped through the sky, Raeta keeping them directly behind the small ship. They continued down so long with nothing happening, they began to believe that maybe HAARP wasn't as destructive as they had believed. They watched the small ship guide lower and lower when suddenly they were blinded by a bright flash. When it faded, a mass of fragments were burning as they fell. They continued down with no indication they were being tracked. Raeta leveled off above the Atlantic and turned west.

"By God, it worked!" Aubrey exclaimed. No one said anything as the tension drained from them. Making it down without mishap was more than they thought possible with such a large ship.

"Where do you want me to land, Will?" Raeta asked.

"Pick an open spot in a woods close to Washington," he replied. "We can walk from there." Raeta saw woodland in the distance by a river, but no clearing large enough to set down in. She saw a dirt road running through the woods and felt it was just big enough to accommodate the ship. She deftly maneuvered around and set down on the road.

"Now that we're here, what's our first move?" Aubrey asked. Will had the answer ready.

"You try to see if the president's still here. I'll head for the Pentagon and see if I can find a way underground."

"What about us, Will?" Zeus asked.

"Wait here," Will relied. "If we're not back in six hours, get the hell out. That should be more than enough time for us to do what has to be done."

"I'm going with you, Will," Martin said. "Those people are my friends too."

"All right, Martin, let's go."

TWENTY-ONE

Martin and Will headed away from the ship at a quick pace, and simultaneously saw a path and stopped. It proved to be a shortcut to a paved road. He glanced at Martin.

"This is new territory for me, Will." Will nodded.

"We'll go this way." As they went along the path, Will began to feel they were being watched, slowed his pace, and kept alert for any movement. When the tingling of his spine reached a peak Will put out his arm and stopped Martin.

"Someone's watching us." Martin looked around, but all he saw was trees.

"You sure?"

"I've been in this business long enough to know when I'm being watched." Again, Martin glanced around.

"I don't see anyone."

"If they don't want to be seen, you're not going to see them."

"What do we do?" Will took a long, slow look around.

"We move on, Martin. If they want to talk, let them come to us."

"That doesn't sound smart." Will glanced at him.

"It's not. But right now, they have the advantage. So let's move."

They went along the path for ten minutes before Will heard someone coming through the woods. He and Martin stopped. Whoever it was made certain they knew where they would appear. A young girl, Will estimated to be about twelve, stepped in front of them. Her light brown hair was stringy and matted; her soft blue eyes seemed vacant. Both men were surprised, as they had been expecting an adult.

"Who are you?" she asked, in a monotone. Dirt smudges covered her face, the blouse she wore was torn in several places, and her jeans were caked with dirt. It looked as if she hadn't taken a bath in sometime.

"We're friends," Will replied, gently. "Are there more people in the woods?" She was openly alternating between fright and suspicion, and regarded them with an uncertain look.

"It's all right," Martin said, bending down to her. "We're here looking for friends." It took her some minutes to make up her mind as the men waited patiently.

"Follow me," she said, abruptly. They followed her off the path into the woods that gave scents indicating autumn would soon be along. There had been a steady rain recently as they walked across the soft ground. The girl moved among the trees, certain of where she was going. She stopped and turned to them.

"Wait here. I need to know one of your names."

"I'm Will Vaughn." She nodded, turned in among the trees, and was out of sight.

"How do you suppose she wound up out here, Will?" He shook his head looking in the direction the girl had gone.

"I don't know, Martin. Whatever we've missed about the disappearance of people, she might provide the answer."

"I hope you're right."

A few minutes passed, and they heard the approach of more than one person. The girl reappeared with a man whose clothes were ragged. His face had a heavy growth of beard that was unkempt like his black hair; his brown eyes showed exhaustion. Surprise for the two men was becoming common. After Denver and the girl, they hadn't expected to see anyone.

"Who are you?" the man asked, his expression one of hope.

"This is Dr. Martin and I'm Will Vaughn. What happened here? Why are you out here in the woods?" The girl and man exchanged puzzled glances before looking back at them.

"Don't you know?" the man asked, bewildered.

"Know what?" Martin asked. The man's lip began to quiver and Martin thought he was going to break down.

"The people disappeared. Vanished!" the man replied, distraught.

"When did it happen?" Will asked, surprised.

"I don't remember," the girl replied. "I woke up and found myself alone in our house. My father, mother, and two sisters were gone."

"Everyone disappeared?" Martin asked, finding it hard to believe.

"We're the only ones who didn't, as far as we know," the man said.

"How many are with you?" Will asked.

"Five others," the girl said. "We found each other by accident and remained together. Do you know what happened to the people?"

"No," Will replied. "You can come with us. We'll take you to where you can be cared for."

Back at the ship, Zeus, Raeta, and the sisters were having a hard time believing the entire population of Washington, except for seven people, had simply vanished.

"If it happened here and Denver, what about the rest of the country?" Ophelia asked. "For that matter, the world?"

"How the population of a city, possibly the planet, with a few exceptions, could vanish is something beyond my ken," Martin said, looking baffled.

"Has Aubrey been back?" Will asked.

"No," Raeta replied. Will got an impatient look..

"I'll find him," Will said. "He was going to the White House, so that's where I'll head." He took a small hand-held radio from his pocket.

"I'll contact you every half-hour," Will said. "Keep you informed of what I find." Zeus nodded.

He left the ship and went the way Aubrey had taken. Will knew the disappearance must have occurred while he was at the Arizona base, but it was difficult to conceive of so many people vanishing at the same time. What was even more puzzling was that it happened to the Grays too. Questions with no answers. Seven people here, Martin and he all survived whatever had happened. But what was the explanation?

"To hell with it," Will said. It was too damned frustrating to speculate.

As he neared the city, he became aware of how quiet it was. There were no natural sounds like wind, birds, insects, and no man-made sounds. Will stepped up his pace and came to a car that had crashed into a utility pole. He looked in and saw no bodies or blood. He didn't waste time but moved on. He checked his watch and called the ship, telling them he had nothing to report.

The closer he got to the city, the more profound the silence. Will shuddered at the stillness. It was something he had never experienced and it was rattling him. He saw movement on the road and quickly slipped into a ditch for cover. The man was too far away for recognition, but he decided it had to be Aubrey. He climbed back on the road and hurried toward him. They stopped facing each other.

"What the hell happened here, Will?" Aubrey's speech was rapid and high pitched.

"Beats the shit out of me," Will replied. "We're wondering if the whole planet's been depopulated. Did you make it to the White House?"

"Hell no!" Aubrey exclaimed. "The city is too damn spooky. I didn't go in far." Aubrey turned, looking around.

"This damn quiet is unnerving, Will."

"Martin and I came across seven people in the woods. They weren't affected by whatever happened, and that means more people have survived."

"We can't take time to search for survivors, Will. Let's get back to the ship and get off this ghost planet. We've got to get someplace where we can try to figure out what's happened."

"Damnit, Aubrey, none of us have any idea what's happened. How the hell are we going to find answers in space?"

"I don't know," Aubrey replied, his voice calm. "But we aren't doing any good wandering around here." Will conceded he was right.

"Okay, let's go to the ship."

Janis had news when they returned.

"The girl knows something, Will. I sense a deep fear in her, but she won't face it."

"Any idea what it might be?" Aubrey asked. Janis shook her head.

"She's been traumatized so badly she refuses to acknowledge it consciously," Janis replied.

"Isn't there someway to find out?" Raeta asked.

"We can help her if we take her back to our world," Zeus said.

"How?" Ophelia asked. "She needs to face what happened to her and her family."

"What could a child possibly know?" Aubrey asked. "We have no idea of what's happened."

"I'm not certain what it is she's aware of," Janis said. "I do know we have to try and find out, and help her at the same time." All stood silent trying to determine their next move.

"I'm for getting the hell away from Earth," Aubrey said. "There's nothing more we can do here."

"I agree," Martin said.

"They're right," Zeus said. "We need scientific evaluation to determine what's occurred." Will glanced at each of them.

"Whatever it was took the Grays too," Will said, grimly.

174

Raeta lifted the ship through the atmosphere and headed for the pole. She was aware they had to risk the turbulence and knew there was no one below to see their flight. Without saying anything to Zeus, Raeta made an orbit of Earth before leaving for Olympus. She recorded as many scientific readings as she could and transferred them to a disc she could use in her lab.

The discussion about what might have happened to Earth's population had to address the fact that it had also happened to the Grays. They couldn't even guess at what the cause might be, and discussion ceased. They found no radio or TV broadcasts from Earth, although they picked up the functioning satellites.

"You're the logical one, Raeta," Zeus said, when they were alone. "What's your opinion?" She shook her head.

"I can only speculate, Zeus." He nodded.

"I value your opinion, Raeta, because of the way you think. So speculate."

"Will said no ships left the Arizona base, so I would be inclined to look for a temporal or interdimensional shift." Raeta got a bewildered look.

"But how this was accomplished on a planet-wide scale is beyond my comprehension." She paused holding a slightly alarmed look.

"Unless it was a naturally occurring phenomena." Her words gave Zeus a chill.

"Could such a natural phenomena exist without our detecting it?"

"That remains to be seen, Zeus. I hope our scientists can discover it. Because it occurred in this solar system, that puts it close to home." He regarded her grim, baffled expression.

"Have the sisters had any success with the girl?" Raeta shook her head as a sad expression came to her.

"No. I've never known anyone so young who experienced such fear. As for the others, they're only bewildered by their experience." Zeus cocked an eyebrow.

"Why is the girl the only one who seems to know something?"

"You'll have to ask Ophelia or Janis, Zeus."

"What do we tell the Pantheon and the scientists?"

"Only what we know," Raeta replied. "I'm going to recommend that automated probes be placed in orbit around Earth to monitor conditions.

If it was caused by something on Earth, we must assume it's still functioning." Zeus looked at her with a frown.

"I'm curious as to why nothing happened to us while we were there."

"I don't know," Raeta said, perplexed. "Perhaps we weren't there long enough."

"We've got to discover what it is, Raeta. We have seven people –" Zeus stopped abruptly. Raeta looked at him puzzled.

"What is it?" He gave her an odd look.

"We have nine people who were there, Raeta. I didn't realize until just a moment ago that Will and Martin were also there when the disappearance occurred." They lapsed into a long silence. Each considered the events since their first approach to Earth. An old enemy had gotten the jump on their return, fearing they would be revealed to the humans. They would also learn they were a part of another people, defeated in war and exiled to space.

Raeta believed what had happened had been something beyond the control of the Kraken and the Grays. She decided to say nothing as she had only a shadow of evidence that was ominous and elating. To be rid of the Kraken meant her people were finally free. But an entire planet's population as the price was much too horrible a cost.

Aubrey came to the sister's cabin after a week in space.

"Have you learned anything from the girl?" he asked. Janis paced while Ophelia sat looking calm.

"Only vague distraught feelings," Janis replied. "I got some sort of blurred vision that was incomprehensible."

"It's the fear her feelings convey that's frightening," Ophelia said. "It's such a primal fear that it's hard to understand."

"Can you give me some idea of what?" Aubrey asked. Janis stopped and faced him.

"The only way to even come close to describing it is that her whole being felt the fear," Janis replied. "It was a profound fear she couldn't understand."

"But you still have no idea of what caused it?" Aubrey asked.

"Should we discover it," Ophelia said, grimly. "We may wish we hadn't. At least, that's the impression I felt from the girl."

"Whatever it was, it enveloped the Earth," Aubrey said. "There hasn't been any radio transmissions picked up since we left.

If somebody was left, I had hoped they might have gotten a radio and broadcast for help."

"Whatever it was, it was sudden," Janis said. Ophelia shook her head.

"I don't think so," Ophelia said. "The results seem abrupt to us, but it must have been a process that had been going on for sometime."

"What led you to that conclusion?" Aubrey asked.

"If the Grays had known what was going to happen, do you think they would have remained on Earth?" Ophelia asked. Aubrey conceded her point.

"They didn't know," Ophelia continued. "And no ships left that base." Janis gave her sister a quizzical look.

"If the Kraken planned this, why didn't they warn the Grays?" Janis asked.

"The Kraken simply withheld the information from the Grays," Ophelia replied.

"To what purpose?" Aubrey asked. Ophelia shrugged.

"Your guess is as good as mine," Ophelia said. "Nobody, not even Zeus' people, know what The Brotherhood is really after. What we've been getting was for our consumption."

"You mean disinformation?" Aubrey asked.

"It's the only thing that makes sense," Ophelia said. "This whole show with the Grays was to convince us that they were behind it. Now we know they weren't."

"Then who or what is The Brotherhood?" Janis asked. Aubrey regarded her with a frown.

"Who the hell knows," he said. "Those malformed hands were meant to mislead us, make us believe those people were the Kraken. The attack on the complex was the same sort of ruse."

"You're starting to understand, Mr. Blaine," Ophelia said. "If they had known about that complex all along, they could have destroyed it anytime. Instead, they waited until we were there and in contact with Zeus' ship." Janis was confused.

"I don't understand their reasoning," Janis said.

"Join the club," Aubrey said. "Nobody does." The idea came to Janis in a flash, and she knew it had to be the truth.

"The strange ones, ancient ones, the Gray told me of," Janis said. "They're the Kraken. Not even the Grays knew their motivation." This brought her uneasy looks from Ophelia and Aubrey.

The rest of the voyage, Raeta worked but produced no results that might solve the mystery. It was disconcerting to think that the people brought aboard the ship might be all that was left of the human race, and it was a subject broached by no one. Only the girl seemed unaware she might be the last child of Earth. It was a sullen idea that felt cold, and wished she could forget.

As they neared Olympus, Raeta began sending reports of what they had found on Earth and the results of her investigation. She had expected a quick reply, but it was some hours before she got an answer, and only a perfunctory one. From it, Raeta got the impression that those on Olympus were just as shocked about what had happened as they were, and were stalling for time to study her report. She acknowledged the communication and went to Zeus.

He rubbed his beard regarding her with a puzzled expression.

"That was all?" he asked, incredulous at such a terse response. Raeta nodded.

"I think they're as mystified as we are."

"And you believe they don't have any idea of what happened either?"

"Yes, Zeus. It must have been a shock to find that a world can be depopulated in what seems the blink of an eye." He looked at her with a furrowed brow.

"Raeta, I feel you have some idea of what happened. You can tell me, and I'll say nothing." She considered his request before deciding to answer.

"What I think is irrelevant to what might be discovered." He got a slight smile.

"I know. That's why I'll keep it to myself." She frowned and locked her gaze on him.

"While we were on Earth, I noticed some of the ship's instruments were registering some odd harmonic frequency. I checked and found it coming from all directions. I didn't think much of it until I made an orbit of Earth." His eyes widened in surprise.

"You made an orbit before we left, Raeta?"

"Yes, Zeus, I felt it was necessary."

"What did you learn?" She inhaled deeply as a look of uncertainty came to her.

"The planet is enveloped in that frequency. What it is, I don't know. I've never saw or heard anything like it."

"Could it have caused the depopulation?" She bit her lip.

"I prefer to wait until I've had more time to study the data."

"Do you plan telling the Pantheon, Raeta?" She shook her head.

"Not until I've studied it with other scientists. I must have independent confirmation the phenomena is there. It's possible the instruments were picking up waves from a natural source."

"But you don't believe that?"

"No, Zeus. The field was too focused. It was something unknown producing that frequency." Zeus nodded and patted her arm.

"Keep me informed of what you find and any relevant data other scientists might discover, Raeta. If The Brotherhood's behind this, we're not only going to have to be cautious, we're going to have to be alert for an attack."

"I don't think we have anything to worry about, Zeus. The same thing must have happened to The Brotherhood." He gave her a surprised look.

"The Brotherhood destroyed itself?"

"That's the way it appears," Raeta replied.

"Do you think they knew what they were doing?" Raeta smiled.

"I think they have gotten too smart for their own good." Zeus frowned.

"Unfortunately they took most of the human race with them," he said.

TWENTY-TWO

Martin told Raeta he wanted to help with the investigation. The Pantheon agreed their scientists needed all the help they could get. Yet no one had put forth a viable hypothesis as to what had happened to Earth's population. Raeta felt the odd frequency was behind it, but decided to keep it to herself until someone else drew the same conclusion. The reason for her silence was the seeming improbability of her assumption, that if proven, she knew what had happened.

Ophelia and Janis worked with psychologists and neurologists trying to help the girl, Sandra Kortner. Everything that came from her was in a confused state and hard to interpret. They decided to see if they could discover what she had been exposed to and found her nervous system had been subjected to some sort of electromagnetic pulse. This was disturbing because it had been believed this could only be produced by a nuclear weapon, but there had been no evidence of any such event having occurred. They were left to explain a phenomena unknown to them. What they were unaware of was that it was the sort of evidence Raeta was searching for.

The probes put around the Earth confirmed that a few people remained scattered in isolated pockets throughout the world. There had been no decision made about what, if anything, to do to aid these groups. Will wanted to go after them, arguing that they needed to discover why these people hadn't been affected. The Pantheon wasn't willing to risk it. They felt it might be a trick of The brotherhood. Will didn't buy that, but abided by their decision, after a fashion. He began to plan a recon on his own. Exactly whom he was going to get to help him carry it out, he ignored at first. But the more he planned, the more impatient he became to implement it. Will decided to take a chance and speak with Raeta. He had no idea how she would react to the proposal that she help him steal a ship and return to Earth. He wouldn't ask her to go, just help him get away.

It was a week before he found her alone in the lab. She looked up when he came through the door.

"What brings you to the lab?" He glanced around.

"Are we alone?" The question pricked her curiosity.

"Yes," she replied, with a coy smile. "What have you got in mind?" At that moment, Will was struck with fear of failure, but he needed her help.

"What have you found out about that frequency envelope, Raeta?" This seemed rather an odd question coming from him. He had never asked about the research before.

"It's produced by something on the surface, Will. Just what it is still remains undetermined. Why?"

"I believe I know what's causing it, Raeta. I need a ship to return to Earth to prove it." She looked at him with a cocked eyebrow.

"The Pantheon said no one's to return until we know what's causing the frequency." He could tell she was interested, but how far she would go remained to be seen.

"I don't stand a chance of convincing the Pantheon I know the cause. If I can convince you, will you help me get a ship?" She regarded him for a moment then nodded.

"All right, Will, convince me." He inhaled deeply knowing what he was about to say would sound unbelievable.

"I believe it's caused by HAARP. I don't know how, but feel certain that's the source." Raeta didn't let it show but it hadn't taken much to convince her.

"What makes you think HAARP is the cause?"

"Simply because there is no other explanation. It's the only thing that could cause such odd phenomena. Nobody knew what HAARP might do. The scientists who designed and built it were only guessing as to its effects, and it looks like they guessed wrong."

"That's not very scientific, Will." He turned from her shaking his head.

"No, I guess it isn't," he said, without looking at her." Do you have a better explanation?" She couldn't help the smile that came easily to her.

"I've come to the same conclusion." He spun and faced her, hope growing in him.

"Then you'll help me?" She stepped close to him and gazed into his eyes.

"Only if I go with you." This was something he hadn't counted on and was unwilling to put anyone else at risk.

"This could prove very dangerous, Raeta." She held a steady gaze on him and folded her arms.

"What are you planning to do, if you get back to Earth?"

"Land as close as possible to the HAARP control center and try to shut it down."

"I want to study the frequency it's producing, Will. If you want a ship, I'm an accessory that comes with it. Take some time to think it over. But if you go, I go." He regarded her knowing she wouldn't change her mind. He was reluctant because he had no idea what they might come up against

"Raeta, I don't know what's there. I don't want to put you at risk." She cocked her head and narrowed her eyes.

"What do you think is there, Will? And don't tell me you don't have some idea or you wouldn't have said what you just did. I want to know what you think is dangerous there." If he wanted a ship, he had no choice but to tell her. He exhaled and looked at her.

"I believe the disappearance was caused by the Grays." She stared at him with amazement, never having considered that.

"Why would they do such a thing?"

"To save the human race from The Brotherhood. Just how they done it, I haven't any idea, except that they modified HAARP somehow. When we were on Earth before, we didn't detect that frequency. Don't you see, Raeta? It all fits." She smiled.

"When do you want to leave, Will?"

It was Aubrey who noticed Will's absence and went to Zeus to see if he knew where he was. Zeus had been looking for Raeta, and it seemed to him no coincidence they had both disappeared.

"Where the hell could they be?" Aubrey asked. Zeus had his suspicion but wasn't certain.

"We should check to make certain the ships are accounted for." Aubrey's eyes widened in amazement.

"You think they may have headed for Earth?" Zeus frowned.

"It seems a fair assumption, Aubrey. Two of the scientists Raeta has been working with told me she expressed disappointment at not having more time to study the frequency envelope around Earth. We know Will wanted to go after the people, so I would say that's where they're headed."

"We have to get them back, Zeus." Zeus' eyebrows shot up.

"Do you think either would acknowledge communication? They've left against the directive of the Pantheon." Aubrey was crestfallen because he knew Will too well.

"You're right, Zeus, they wouldn't. It's unlike Will to slip away. They must have discovered something for them to act in such a cowboy way, especially Raeta."

"She had a strong attraction to Will, Aubrey. I doubt he could have talked her into this venture."

"She went willingly?" Aubrey asked. Zeus nodded.

"What can we do, Zeus?"

"Report it. There's nothing else we can do."

"How long do you think it will be before they discover we're missing, Will?"

"Long enough so they won't send a ship after us – I hope."

"They won't. The Pantheon decreed no ships approach Earth until more is known about the phenomena." Will gave her a sharp look.

"That means you're in trouble, Raeta." She smiled.

"No more than you. We chose to defy the decree."

"What do you think they'll do when we return?" She looked at him with a serious expression.

"What makes you think we will?" He looked at her, alert to her tone and not liking it.

"What have you done, Raeta?" She gave him a sweet smile and put a finger to the edge of a lip.

"Did I forget to mention we won't have the power to escape Earth's gravity?" Will felt like strangling her, but held his anger in check.

"Why the hell would you do such a thing?" Raeta folded her arms as her expression became serious.

"Two reasons, Will. One, I want to study the effect of the HAARP frequency." She stepped close to him, almost touching her body against his.

"Two, I've been wanting something from you." He frowned as he regarded her. He hadn't been mistaken when he believed she was becoming aroused in the complex.

"What is it you want, Raeta?" She pressed against him.

"Do I need to make it obvious?" Before anymore was said, they felt the ship suddenly decelerate. Raeta went to the instrument panel and began checking to see what the problem was. Scanning the panel she saw no malfunction.

"What is it?" She turned wide eyes to him.

"I don't know. The instruments are showing everything is normal." The ship steadied drawing her eyes back to the panel. She became bewildered.

"Whatever is causing this is outside, Will. There's no malfunction in any of the systems." Will went to the port and looked out, but could see nothing out of the ordinary.

"I don't see anything. Have you checked the proximity sensor?" She glanced at the screen but nothing showed.

"Nothing." The ship lurched again causing them to lose their footing and Raeta fell into his arms just as a violet flash engulfed Them.

Zeus and Aubrey had reported the unauthorized absences of Raeta and Will to the Pantheon. All were disturbed at their flight.

"Why do you think Raeta left, Zeus?" Hera asked. He inhaled and looked from her to his grandfather.

"I feel she discovered something about that envelope and wanted to get proof."

"And Will Vaughn?" his grandfather asked. "Do you believe she talked Will into going with her?"

"I can answer that better than Zeus," Aubrey said. "I think it was a mutual agreement. Will wouldn't have left without informing me unless he had a good reason. He discussed nothing with me. That leads me to believe Raeta and Will reached a definitive conclusion." A murmur of voices filled the great hall.

"When might they return?" Poseidon asked. Zeus had been hoping for that question. He exhaled loudly as he turned to Poseidon.

"They won't." This caused a loud outburst among the Pantheon. Hera raised her hand for silence.

"Why do you say that, Zeus?" Hera asked. A grim set came to him.

"According to the record, the ship's batteries were only energized with enough power to reach Earth and limited atmospheric flying." This was a shock to Aubrey.

"How the hell did that happen?" Aubrey asked.

"It was deliberate," Zeus replied. "Whatever they were going for, they weren't planning on coming back."

"Why did they act in such an irrational manner?" his grandfather asked.

"I have no idea," Zeus replied. "I do know Raeta is too good a pilot to have missed undercharged fuel cells. She took off knowing they couldn't' return. I doubt Will was aware of it."

"We've got to send a ship after them," Aubrey said.

"No," Hera said. "I have faith in Raeta as I believe you have in Will. They've gone for a definite purpose. Until they communicate, we must bide our time and trust in what they consider a vital mission." Old Zeus had been keeping an eye on Aubrey.

"You do trust Will, don't you?" Zeus' grandfather asked. Aubrey didn't hesitate to reply.

"Of course. It's just not knowing why they went that disturbs me."

"As it does all of us," Hera said. "But they knew what they were doing. When they have succeeded, they will contact us."

Raeta and Will faced the tall Gray.

"Why have you brought us here?" Raeta asked. Will put an arm around her waist and pulled her against him.

"Don't talk, Raeta. Form the question in your mind." She looked back at the Gray and thought her question. It was an odd sensation when the Gray's thought entered her mind. It felt like a massage with light fingers against her consciousness. She quickly rethought her question.

"It is time you knew the truth about those you call The Brotherhood," the Gray thought. "They are a race from the far side of the galaxy. They have been conquering worlds and destroying races for millennia. My race made contact long ago. They threatened our world with destruction unless we cooperated with them. Some of us were forced to do things we otherwise would never have done."

"How did they threaten you?" Will thought.

"To send an asteroid onto our planet," the Gray replied. "At first, we were incredulous, but they showed us they could easily do what they said. We had no defense against such a large object."

"What have you done to Manipulate HAARP?" Will thought. Admiration came from the Gray.

"I am glad you understand," the Gray thought.

"Raeta wants to investigate it. I guessed it was somehow responsible for the disappearance of the people."

"We altered the power of its grid. Earth's people are in a different time. They have no conception anything is different. We sealed them, with most of our people, in a parallel time.
It had been determined The Brotherhood would be unable to locate the source of the temporal shield."

"You can manipulate time?" Raeta thought, awed.

"It is relatively simple once you know how to control the waves of time space," the Gray replied.

"What about the people that were taken?" Will thought. "What made them different?"

"Some cannot be taken through the temporal shield," the Gray thought. "Why remains a mystery to us."

"We must get to Earth," Will thought. A surge of alarm and sadness came from the Gray.

"You intend battling The Brotherhood, Will Vaughn?"

"They must be exposed for what they are." The Gray nodded.

"You are determined to carry out your plan," the Gray thought.

"Do not seek them where they were."

"Where have they gone?" Will thought, alarmed he wouldn't be able to find them.

"The few who remain have transferred to the base you were watching."

"What about the people they took?" Will thought.

"They are kept as experimental units at the base," the Gray replied. "One of my people made a minor adjustment to the converter and warned your people how to act. None have been harmed."

"That's good to know," Will thought. "Any advice you can give us?"

"Be cautious. Though they are few, they are still dangerous."

"You'll return us to our ship?" Raeta thought.

"While we have been communicating, we have transported your ship," the Gray thought. "It is in orbit, all you need do is land. Do not shut down HAARP unless you are successful in defeating The Brotherhood. Otherwise, the population will be enslaved."

"Just how dangerous are they?" Raeta thought. The Gray's thought was grim.

"They have destroyed many worlds, many races. They will not hesitate to destroy Earth and every living thing."

The Gray's last thought was foremost in their minds as Will and Raeta took their seats at the instrument panel. She looked at Will with a worried expression.

"Are you certain we should go through with this, Will? After what we've heard, it means risking the planet."

"Do you think those people would be better off in another time?

No, Raeta, The Brotherhood has to be stopped and we're the only ones available. They can't be allowed to go on threatening worlds." She had an uncertain look that became a confident smile.

"We better get going if we're to put an end to them, Will." He returned the smile and turned his attention to landing. They were released from the Gray's ship and began the descent into the atmosphere. Will was trying to think of someway to keep Raeta out of harm's way. He was willing to put his life on the line, but wasn't willing for her to do likewise. After all, putting himself in danger was his job.

TWENTY-THREE

The Gray entered Janis' mind as she slept, communicating its conversation with Raeta and Will. When she woke she knew what had to be done. She told Ophelia, and they went to see Zeus. He listened, and decided that Aubrey, Schiffer, and Martin be told.

"Someone has to go after them," Janis said, folding her arms. "They don't realize the danger they're going into."

"Who would you suggest we send?" Zeus asked. Janis was wondering how the Gray had been able to communicate from such a distance, but the thought of Will pushed it from her mind.

"Me," she replied. "The Gray said only a few of the race we call The Brotherhood are left. If they're eliminated, it will mean the end of the threat to both our worlds, Zeus."

"Would the Pantheon be willing to risk a ship for that, Zeus?" Ophelia asked. He regarded the sisters thinking how much he would like to see an end to The Brotherhood.

"It may not be easy to convince the Pantheon," Zeus said. Janis got an impatient look.

"One ship is all that will be needed," Janis said, testily. Zeus regarded her solemnly.

"I'll get you an audience with the Pantheon, Janis," Zeus said. "Just don't get your hopes up."

"That will do, Zeus," Ophelia said. "Thank you."

Zeus accompanied the sisters before the Pantheon. Janis regarded each member without emotion, her eyes stopping on Hera, who she felt was more sympathetic.

"I've not come before you to plead for Will and Raeta," Janis began, her voice strong. "I'm here to plead for the lives of the people of your world and mine." A murmur filled the chamber.

"One ship is all you need send," Janis continued. "You have within your power to be free of The Brotherhood. If you fail to act now, you risk The Brotherhood acting against you. Is your world worth a ship? Consider what must be done." Janis bowed her head to Hera and turned away.

"You have a plan, Janis?" Hera asked. Janis turned back to her.

"Send a ship to Earth and defeat The Brotherhood." An eruption of voices filled the chamber as Zeus and the sisters turned to go.

"Remain, Zeus," Hera said.

"We need your thoughts on this proposal." Janis and Ophelia went through the tall bronze doors and went back to their apartment, where the other Earth people had gathered. Janis had been feeling a loss since Will had left with Raeta. She didn't want to continue feeling this way and hoped to be chosen to go.

The answer from the Pantheon was not soon in coming. The hours seemed to drag as the Earth people awaited their decision. Ophelia felt for her sister, sensing the hurt she felt at Will's action. Yet Ophelia agreed with his action. It had been necessary, as they all had been doing nothing.

"Raeta must have discovered something important," Aubrey said, pacing.

"What?" Schiffer asked. Aubrey shook his head.

"I wish I knew. Will doesn't act without orders unless he feels they would hinder him." Aubrey stopped and regarded Schiffer.

"Why didn't he say something to one of us?" Janis asked. "Don't he trust us?"

"He thought he was protecting us," Aubrey replied.

Zeus came through the door with a grim expression he turned on Janis. Seeing his face caused her to lose heart that the Pantheon had agreed.

"They didn't buy it, did they?" Martin asked. There was no change in Zeus' expression.

"They agreed to send a team," Zeus replied, in a monotone. Ophelia sensed Zeus' sympathy as he looked at Janis, but didn't understand it.

"A surprise raid," Aubrey said, rubbing his hands together. "That sounds like our bag of marbles, Chet."

"If you two are going, so am I," Martin said.

"Janis and I are ready," Ophelia said. Zeus shook his head.

"You and Janis must remain here," Zeus said. "Only you can communicate with the Grays. Should we fail, this world is going to need your help." Janis turned away to cover her disappointment.

"Raeta talked Will into going," Janis said, angrily.

"No one talked anyone into anything," Aubrey said. "They planned it together." Ophelia stepped beside Janis and put an arm around her shoulders as the first sob escaped.

"I'll be leading this little foray," Zeus said. "We leave in twelve hours."

"And we just sit here on our asses," Janis almost screamed, angry tears spilling down her cheeks. Zeus stepped to her and took hold of her arms.

"Ophelia and you may prove the last hope our worlds have," Zeus said, gently. "They won't risk either of you." Ophelia put a hand on Zeus' arm and he looked at her.

"We understand, Zeus," Ophelia said. "I'll take care of her." Zeus looked sad and nodded.

"We'll bring Will back," Aubrey said. Janis gave him a blazing look.

"Dead or alive?" she asked, angrily. The four men turned their eyes from her knowing there wasn't any way to answer with certainty. Zeus turned to the men.

"We have preparations to make," Zeus said. They followed him out as Janis collapsed sobbing.

Raeta eased the ship through the turbulence above the Arctic icecap.

"Head southeast," Will said. "I'm certain we'll have no problem spotting HAARP." She leveled the ship and turned it in the direction he indicated. It was only minutes before they saw the vast array of flat antennas stretching over the landscape. Will pointed to a group of three buildings.

"Set down near that building, Raeta," Will said, pointing. "That must be the control center." She guided the ship to a gentle landing in front of the building. As she began shutting the ship's systems down, she glanced at Will.

"What if one of The Brotherhood is here?" she asked. Will pulled a pulse weapon from his pocket.

"He won't get a chance to tell his friends."

"We may have been seen already."

"I don't think so, Raeta. If so, we would already have visitors."

They stepped out into the cold afternoon making Will wish they had coats. They saw nothing moving, making the landscape seem lifeless. Raeta shivered and Will put his arm around her.

"Let's get inside." She glanced at him with an uneasy look.

"I don't like this, Will." He gave her an upstanding nod.

"I didn't like it when Martin and I went onto the base and found it like this, it wasn't as cold though." He opened the door and stepped in, Raeta followed.

The place was silent except for the slight whir of the surveillance camera. They turned to it as it watched them. They moved down a short hallway that intersected one running perpendicular.

"You're the scientist, Raeta. Which way do we go?" Will wasn't aware that he had whispered. She looked in both directions and pointed left. He now followed her to a metal door with a no admittance sign on it. She glanced over her shoulder.

"This must be the main control room," she said, also whispering. Will reached past her and opened the door and looked in. It seemed like the men who had been here had only stepped out for a cup of coffee. Will saw the body lying by the mainframe. He went in and heard a sharp gasp from Raeta when she saw the body.

It was tall and spindly with pale yellow skin stretched over bones. Will used his foot to roll it over. The face was long and narrow with only slits for eyes, a wide flattened nose, and thin strips of flesh that passed for lips. The back of the skull was elongated and arched that held it about an inch off the floor. The small holes, where ears were, had some sort of fluid caked below them. Will looked at Raeta as she turned her face to him.

"I believe we've found a Kraken, Raeta." Overcoming her initial disgust, she knelt beside the body and lifted the small eyelid and examined the fluid from the ear. She stood and looked at Will.

"My guess would be it died from some kind of extreme pressure." Will snapped his fingers.

"It must have died when the Grays manipulated the time space displacement. In such a confined space, the pressure in here must have been unbelievable."

"There's not much we can do here, Will." He had been considering what to do about her as he didn't want to take her to the Arizona base. If there was trouble, and he expected no less, he didn't want her getting hurt.

"Now that you're here you can study what you want about HAARP." She gave him a sharp look.

"I am not staying here alone, Will. This thing might not be dead. Just because it has no pulse and respiration doesn't mean it's not alive." He got a determined look and frowned.

"Raeta, I don't want to take you into a situation that's going be dangerous." He took the small transmitter from his pocket and handed it to her. She looked from him to it.

"What's this for?"

"You can send what you learn about HAARP back to Olympus. It might prove of some value to them." Her expression turned hard as her eyes narrowed.

"I told you, Will, I'm not staying here alone." He had felt she would prove stubborn. He recalled a similar incident with a woman in Munich, and thought this problem could be solved in the same way.

"You're determined to come?"

"Yes. I won't let you abandon me such a desolate place." He nodded and smiled.

"Okay." Without any warning, he slugged her and caught her before she hit the floor. He picked her up in his arms.

"Sorry, Raeta, but you should learn to compromise." He carried her to a soft chair in the front of the building and put her down. He went back and plucked the transmitter from the floor, stuck it in her hand, and stood looking at her.

"Where I'm going, Raeta, I have to concentrate on what I'm doing. I can't afford to have you along."

When Raeta came around, she was groggy but it passed quickly. She leaped to her feet and ran to the door. A wave of despair and fear washed through her when she saw the ship was gone. She had never thought Will would do anything like this. She had to face the fact that she was stuck in a place that made her feel insecure. The sun was setting and the air was becoming frigid.

Raeta stepped back inside and closed the door. At least she would be warm and have light. That's when she decided to transmit what happened, but without any hope of rescue until Will returned – if he returned. Raeta hoped someone might get here in time to prevent Will from the foolish action he was determined to take against The Brotherhood.

Aubrey, manning the ship's radio, had just received Raeta's transmission. He shook his head, annoyed at Will's imprudent decision to go after The Brotherhood on his own.He knew Will was being impetuous because he had no way of knowing help was on the way.

That made it imperative they get to the Arizona base as soon as possible. He informed Raeta they were on the way, but said nothing about picking her up. He couldn't be certain Zeus would want to get her before going after Will.

When Aubrey came on the bridge, Martin sat at the pilot's station, Schiffer manned the sensor console, and Zeus was calibrating the ship's weapons system.

"I just got a transmission from Raeta." They turned to him, Zeus looking surprised. Aubrey smiled.

"Where are they?" Zeus asked.

"It seems Will's abandoned her at the HAARP site," Aubrey replied. "He's gone on to the Arizona base." Even Zeus couldn't suppress a grin at the thought of Will getting away from Raeta.

"I'll bet it wasn't easy for him to leave her behind," Zeus said. Aubry's smile grew.

"She didn't say how he done it, but she's awfully damned steamed about it."

"I haven't any doubt of that," Zeus said, and got a grim look. "If he left her behind, he must be expecting difficulties."

"That's what I was thinking," Aubrey said, losing his smile.

"He can't fight them alone," Martin said. "How much longer till we get to Earth?" Zeus turned and checked some instruments and turned back to them.

"I'll increase speed so we can arrive in twenty-four hours," Zeus said.

"That might be too late for Will," Schiffer said.

"There's nothing more we can do," Aubrey said. "He went knowing there wasn't any help he could count on, so he must have a plan in mind."

"Let's hope he can keep his ass in one piece until we get there," Martin said.

"Contact his ship," Zeus said. "Tell him we're on the way and ask him to delay any action until our arrival."

"Sounds good," Aubrey said, and went back to the radio.

Will made straight for Arizona, staying low and not bothering to avoid cities as he had before. He kept going over a loose plan in his mind, but knew he couldn't make any decisions without looking over the situation first.

He felt bad at hitting Raeta, but knew it had been the only way to convince her to stay behind.

He had no illusion that what he was getting into would be easy. The only thing he had on his side was surprise and experience of working in hostile environments. He wondered if he had ever been up against The Brotherhood before. From what he now knew, he had no doubt they must have crossed paths before, but this time he knew the real enemy.

Janis had been unable to get to Zachary and Klast before Zeus and the others left. When she told them what was going on, they were both of a mind to speak with someone in charge. Janis was successful in getting a private audience with Hera. Klast and Zachary tried, without success, to be allowed to follow their friends. Hera was wise as to whom really wanted to go, and didn't blame Janis, but the situation might easily get out of hand. She didn't want to see Janis harmed, or worse, taken prisoner by The Brotherhood.

"I sympathize with you," Hera said. "But the situation will become critical when Zeus and his team make their raid. We have taken the precaution of putting the fleet on alert as we have no way of knowing what to expect."

"You can't just let them die," Janis pleaded.

"I don't believe they will, Janis," Hera said. "Zeus is too good a commander to expose his team to unnecessary danger."

"Will isn't a part of his team," Janis said. "He's gone off with Raeta, acting like a damn fool trying to stop The Brotherhood without help."

"Raeta's a level-headed woman," Hera said. "She'll be able to keep will from doing anything foolish." Zachary shook his head and frowned.

"You don't know Will," Zachary said. "When he gets it in his mind to do something, nobody's going to talk him out of it."

"Then we can only hope he's intelligent enough to wait for Zeus," Hera said. "Raeta knows better than to intrude into a Brotherhood stronghold without more help than Will."

"It's not Raeta you have to worry about," Zachary said. "Will's a headstrong son of a bitch. Chances are he'll dump Raeta first chance he gets and head off on his own."

"It's true I don't know him very well," Hera said. "But he didn't strike me as being a fool."

"Please, Hera," Janis pleaded. "Let us go after them." Hera regarded Janis with a helpless expression knowing well what she was feeling.

"I'm powerless to grant your request, Janis. If it was up to me alone, I would let love rule. But I'm one voice among twelve and have little sway among them." Zachary stepped forward and took Janis in his arms as tears flooded from her eyes. She turned and pressed her face against him. He gave Hera a nod.

"Thank you for seeing us, Hera," Zachary said. "We had to try for Janis' sake."

"Believe me, I understand how she feels," Hera said.

"We'll take her to her sister," Klast said. Zachary turned and left pressing Janis to him. She was sobbing loudly as Klast pulled the door to Hera's private quarters closed.

TWENTY-FOUR

With a second night coming on, Raeta was very uneasy at having been alone so long. She wished Zeus would arrive but estimated it would be another twelve hours. She was almost convinced the alien was dead, but still had qualms. She tried keeping her mind on other things, but always came back to that body. She decided to find out what she could about it.

She found a dispensary that also had a lab, got scalpels, plastic gloves, and specimen containers. Stepping in the room, she stood staring at it. What would she do if the creature suddenly stood up? Raeta began to sweat as she tried to convince herself it was dead or she would have known better by now.

The alien still lay where it had fallen, and that was a relief to her. She quickly knelt beside it and started by taking a skin sample and the caked substance from the ear. She took a second skin sample from the arched part of the skull because it appeared different. With her samples, Raeta went back to the lab and prepared her slides and took them to the microscope. She was quickly engrossed in work and oblivious to what was a distinct sound in the hallway. As she studied the samples, she was amazed. Raeta was convinced she was seeing very primitive cells, almost protocells. But how could something so ancient have not evolved over millennia? It intrigued her and kept her working until she became aware of the sound outside the dispensary. She turned on the stool and stared. It was an irregular tapping that seemed to come from all directions.

Raeta got off the stool and went slowly to the door. She leaned forward and peered in both directions. The sound seemed equally loud from both directions. She wished Will had left the pulse weapon with her and felt a sudden anger at her fear. She turned back to find something to defend herself with. She found few things to use as a weapon, and settled for a scalpel. She went back to the door, stepped into the hallway, and listened.

The tapping sound remained constant and she couldn't ascertain where it came from. She started down the hallway toward the main entrance turning her head from side to side to discern direction. It continued all around her. Raeta was experiencing fear like never before. It was more upsetting because she had no control over it.

She stopped by a desk and looked around. She bent over and looked at the phone system, but the sound wasn't coming from it.

Raeta thought it might be coming from the main control room and her heart leaped at the thought of the alien. She quickly discarded the thought because the sound was all around and could only be coming from the outside. The sound had remained unchanged since she first heard it and Raeta felt it might be electronic but couldn't think of anything electronic that tapped. That wouldn't explain how it was all over the building. She went back to the main control room, opened the door and peeked in. The alien lay in the same position, that gave her some small relief.

What was making the sound remained a mystery. As Raeta moved away from the control room, she became aware of another sound, one that was growing louder. Like the tapping, she was unable to locate it. It sounded like rising wind and she assumed it was coming from outside, too. Yet the tapping continued in its baffling way.

She hurried to the main entrance believing if the wind was rising, like she heard, the building might be blown away. By the time she got there, she saw a shadow drop from the sky and the wind ceased. Only the tapping remained, now very loud in the sudden stillness. Raeta looked out a window at the dark, empty landscape visible in the feeble glow of the outside lights. She saw something moving at the edge of the dim glow. She was able to discern two vague forms coming toward the building.

Her first thought was that it was The Brotherhood aliens coming to check on the dead one. A sharp surge of fear quickly became panic and she desperately looked for someplace to hide. She went to a desk and crawled under it. As she pressed against it, her heart was pounding and her throat dry. She swallowed hard when she heard footsteps and the door opening.

Will set the ship down a mile from the base and used the desert darkness as cover. Even here he wished he had a coat, but knew that was the least of his worries. When he got a close look at the base, he could see movement around two adjacent buildings. He saw a shape he identified as an alien, like the one they had found at the HAARP site, standing guard at the building nearest to him. He felt that must be where the people were being kept.

As he started a round about approach, he saw only the one alien, but knew there were others. He moved along the fence to the main gate.

When he got there, he saw the alien was no longer in front of the building. Will became alert and sidled past the guard shack. Still unable to see anything moving, he became cautious. Could they know he was there? That didn't matter. He was here, and if he was correct, the people were in the building to his left.

Will had to be certain before he attempted to enter. He looked to his left and right, saw he was alone, and dashed to the nearest corner of the building. He pressed himself against the wall and waited. When everything remained quiet, he started toward the lighted window at the end of the building. He crouched below the window and listened. Slowly, he stood beside the window and bent his head forward and took a look in.

He was surprised to see the group from the cave. He saw Cathy sitting by Mitch like they were meditating. The others seemed to be in a torpor. Will decided to get Mitch and Cathy out. The others would have to be brought out later. He wanted to know what had happened to Cathy.

He slipped the pulse weapon into his belt, took hold of the window and tried to push it up. It was stuck! Then with a loud squeak, it jerked up. Will moved quickly away from the window. Everything remained quiet. After a few minutes, he went back to the window and slid it up noiselessly. He climbed on the sill and swung his legs over. Not one of the people bothered to look up at his entrance.

He went to Mitch knowing if he could wake him up, he could help get Cathy out. He shook Mitch's shoulder.

"Mitch! Mitch! Goddamnit, wake up." Will spoke urgently in a low voice. Mitch's head began to loll from side to side and a slight moan escaped him. Will shook him a little harder and his eyes fluttered then opened. At first, Will noted Mitch's eyes seemed glazed. Mitch focused on him and blinked a couple of times and lifted a hand to Will's shoulder.

"Will? Is it really you?" He motioned for Mitch to be quiet.

"I'm going to get Cathy and you out of here," Will whispered. "But I need your help with her. Do you feel up to it?" Mitch nodded and got to his feet, swayed, and put a hand over his eyes.

"What's wrong with me?" Mitch asked, as Will held his arm to steady him.

"Don't you recall anything the aliens have done to you?"

"I don't remember anything from the time we were taken from the cave."

"Help me get Cathy out the window." They each took an arm and pulled her to her feet, but she didn't respond the way Mitch had. They carried her to the window.

"You climb out and I'll hand her out to you." Mitch slowly pulled himself up on the sill, slid his legs over, and lowered himself to the ground. Will lifted Cathy in his arms and handed her out feet first. Mitch took her and lowered her to the ground. Will climbed out, and again they each took one of her arms and pulled over their shoulders, and slipped an arm around her waste, and hurried away from the building.

"Where are we going, Will?"

"I got a ship about a mile from here. We'll take her there and see if there's anything we can do for her."

"I haven't been able to raise, Will," Aubrey said. "He must be away from the ship. Under the circumstances, I feel certain he would have acknowledged my transmission."

"What makes you think that?" Martin asked.

"I used a special code that only Will and I know."

"Keep trying," Schiffer said. "If he comes back to the ship, we don't want him to miss getting the message." Aubrey glanced at Zeus.

"What are we going to do about Raeta?" Aubrey asked.

"We'll land and get her," Zeus replied. "I don't much care for her being alone at that base."

"You're right," Schiffer said. "The area around HAARP is desolate and uninhabited."

"What do we do with her if we get into a fight?" Martin asked.

"Raeta's capable of taking care of herself," Zeus said. "It's unfortunate that Will wasn't aware of the help she might have been."

"He was thinking of her safety," Aubrey said. Zeus looked at him and frowned.

"I don't doubt that," Zeus said. "But you've got to admit going off alone wasn't the smartest thing he could have done."

"I agree," Aubrey said. "But Will's always had a tendency to work alone. He's also got the unfortunate habit of trying to keep people from being harmed."

"We're approaching the pole," Martin said. "Strap in. This could get rough." Zeus took the pilot's seat as Martin moved into the next seat.

"Everybody ready?" Zeus asked. He got three affirmatives, and turned the ship down and the shock of turbulence rocked the ship. He was hard pressed to keep control until they were well within the atmosphere, then leveled the ship.

"Which way to HAARP, General?" Zeus asked. Schiffer loosened his straps and moved beside Zeus to see the ground below.

"Southwest. You can't miss the large array of antennas," Schiffer said. Zeus got an incredulous look.

"That may be true in daylight, General, but it's almost dark." Schiffer gazed out the windscreen and saw a dim glow to their left and pointed.

"There, Zeus," Schiffer said. "That dim glow. HAARP is the only thing with lights for hundreds of miles." Zeus turned the ship toward the glow and began losing altitude.

"Is there a place to land?" Zeus asked.

"Inside the grid by the main control center," Schiffer replied. "That's as close as we can get." Zeus took the ship lower, making out individual lights. He was rewarded by the bottom of the ship brushing against treetops.

"Take her up, Zeus," Aubrey said. Zeus had already done so.

"You're going to have to be careful," Schiffer said. "This area is wilderness." Zeus was concentrating on getting the ship down. He made a couple of sharp maneuvers and settled the ship into the cleared area in front of the main building.

As Zeus put the ship's systems on standby, Martin and Aubrey stepped to the windscreen for a look at project HAARP.

"My God!" Martin exclaimed. "It looks so desolate."

"That's why this area was chosen for HAARP," Schiffer said. Zeus stood and pointed out the windscreen.

"Is that the main building?" Zeus asked. Schiffer gazed into the dim area.

"Yes," Schiffer replied. "The one next to it is the generator housing."

"How can you be sure Raeta's in the main building?" Aubrey asked. Zeus turned to him.

"What building would Will have left her in?" Aubrey smiled and nodded.

"Right, Zeus."

"I'll get Raeta," Zeus said. "Is there any defensive mechanisms around here?"

"No," Schiffer replied. "The isolation was considered enough of a deterrent to keep people away." Zeus started for the hatch.

"I'll tag along," Aubrey said.

They headed for the lighted building. Zeus couldn't be certain Raeta had seen them land, but knew she should be expecting them. He and Aubrey glanced in the window before Zeus opened the door and stepped in. Aubrey followed and closed the door with a shudder.

"Raeta? Are you here?" Zeus called. They heard a scrambling behind a desk and was startled at the noise. Raeta stood exhaling a sigh of relief.

"Zeus! Am I glad to see you. That noise is frightening." She went forward and embraced him, putting her head against his chest and pulling herself tight against him. Zeus looked at Aubrey and smiled as he held her. Aubrey smiled and patted her back.

"It's just the wind making tree branches hit the building," Aubrey said. Raeta was embarrassed and stepped away from Zeus.

"You aren't frightened by the isolation are you?" Zeus asked. She lifted her head and regarded him.

"Not by the isolation," she replied. "But by the body of a Brotherhood alien. It's in the control room. That hasn't been easy on my nerves."

"A Brotherhood alien?" Zeus asked, giving Aubrey a surprised look.

"I'll show you." She led them to the control room and opened the door. They stepped in and looked down at the body.

"So that's what they look like," Zeus said. "Have you been able to learn anything about them, Raeta?" She nodded.

"I studied some tissue samples." Raeta felt excited as she continued.

"These aliens are incredibly ancient. It's hard to believe, but it appears they haven't evolved in millions of years. From the cell structure, I discovered they've remained in their primitive form throughout their entire racial history."

"Is that why there are only a few left?" Aubrey asked.

"I believe so," Raeta replied. "They're on the verge of extinction."

"Why did they take over the Earth, Raeta?" Zeus asked. She got a grim look.

"I believe they're trying to create a hybrid of themselves. To breed, Zeus! That would give them the chance to evolve into a new life form – and mean many more years of trouble for the galaxy."

"How can they do that?" Aubrey asked. "I mean, I don't see any…" He looked at Raeta who cocked an eyebrow.

"I don't know," she said. "But if they're successful, we're in for a terrible war." Zeus stared at her knowing what she had said was the most frightening thing he had ever contemplated.

"Let's go after Will," Aubrey said. "Any success they might have had must be at the Arizona base."

TWENTY-FIVE

Will and Mitch bent over Cathy giving her a cursory examination. She remained in what, to Will, seemed a coma and her breathing was irregular.

"What's wrong with her?" Mitch asked. Will looked at him.

"I don't know. But her condition doesn't seem good."

"Isn't there something you can do for her, Will?" Will looked at her and frowned.

"Maybe – if I had some idea of what's wrong with her. Not knowing that, I don't dare try anything." The signal of an incoming message sounded loud in the ship. Will went to the communications panel and opened the receiver switch.

"Will, can you hear me?" Aubrey's voice was loud and clear. Will pressed the transmit switch.

"I read you, Aubrey. Where are you?"

"On the way to your location. Leave your switch open." Will pushed it into the open position.

"I hope you have someone with you with medical knowledge," Will said. "I got a woman away from The Brotherhood but she's comatose and her breathing is raspy. How long till you get here?"

"We'll be there in a few minutes. I don't know if anybody here has medical knowledge. I'll check." There was a short pause before Aubrey's voice came again.

"Raeta knows basic medicine and should be able to help her."

"Good," Will said, and turned to Mitch. "Help is on the way. Are you certain you don't know what happened to her, Mitch?"

"Like I said, I don't remember a thing after the raid on the cave. I wish I did. It would help Cathy if I could." Will patted Mitch's shoulder.

"Raeta will help her."

"Why don't you see if you can wake any of the others, Will?" He had been thinking of doing that. He was curious as to what had happened to the alien he had seen. He looked at his watch and made a quick assessment of how much time he would need to get there and back. Those people were going to need medical help, too.

"I'll see what I can do, Mitch."

Will headed back to the base at a run. He went through the main gate and to the building where the people were.

Looking in, he saw them just as he had left them. Instead of climbing in, Will moved to the next building where he moved to the window. What he saw wasn't what he expected and it surprised him. Six of the aliens were in the room, and all appeared to be dead. They lay face down, just like the one in the HAARP control room. Were they dead, or was it a trap? Will decided there was only one way to find out.

He moved to the door, took the pulse weapon from his belt, and slowly pushed it open. It banged against the wall and he stepped in ready for any movement from the aliens. Will stepped to the nearest, bent down and pressed his fingers against what he presumed was its throat. He felt no pulse and could see it wasn't breathing. He stood and returned the weapon to his belt. What the hell is going on? he wondered. Someone else would have to figure that out.

He went back to the people and tried waking them, he had no luck with the first three, then came to Linda. He shook her shoulder and got a soft moan from her. He gently shook her again.

"Linda, can you hear me? Wake up." Her eyes fluttered and opened. She didn't seem to recognize him, then flung her arms around his neck and pulled herself against him.

"Oh, Will, I knew it wouldn't be long before you came for us." It was clear she didn't know how long it had been since being taken from the cave. He gave her a hug as he remembered she was first to volunteer to cooperate with him when he joined the group.

"It's all right, Linda. Can you stand?" He helped her to her feet but her legs buckled. They were too weak to support her so he carried her.

He saw the large ship land as he was on his way back. When he was almost there, Martin came to him and looked at Linda lying in his arms.

"I'll take her, Will," Martin said. Will gave her to him and followed them to the ship.

In the ship, Will saw Raeta examining Cathy. Martin put Linda down to await an examination.

"There are more people who need tending," Will said. Raeta finished her examination and looked at Will.

"I'm not certain," Raeta said. "But I think this woman is pregnant." Zeus stepped beside her.

"Did the aliens do this to her?" Zeus asked. Raeta got a hesitant look.

"I can't be certain without medical equipment and a doctor," Raeta replied. Mitch got an angry expression and stepped forward.

"If Cathy's pregnant, then it's Will's kid." Everyone looked at Will.

"Wait a minute. There's no way she could have gotten pregnant by me."

"How can you be sure, Will?" Raeta asked, in a pissed off tone. Will frowned.

"I just know," Will replied, angrily. "Now what's this about the aliens might have done this to her?" Raeta explained what she thought they had been trying without taking her eyes from Will.

"You don't have to worry about them," Will said. "They're dead."

"How do you know?" Aubrey asked. Will got an annoyed look.

"I saw them less than half an hour ago. You want to see the bodies?" Aubrey shook his head. Zeus turned to Raeta.

"If we can get this woman to a hospital, you can use Earth technology to ascertain her condition," Zeus said.

"I won't have a problem with the equipment," Raeta said. "But I'm not a doctor."

"This base has a hospital," Will said. "We take Cathy and Linda there."

"Of course," Aubrey said. "We have every medical facility we need right here." Zeus turned to Martin.

"Fly us there, Martin."

After almost two hours, Raeta finished her tests and had discovered what could prove a serious threat. She hurried to tell the others.

"The woman isn't pregnant," Raeta said. They regarded her with puzzled looks.

"What is her condition?" Aubrey asked.

"She's affected by a sort of neurological…" Raeta struggled for the word she wanted.

"She's in an endergonic state."

"What the hell is an endergonic state?" Aubrey asked.

"Basically it's a state having to do with the biochemical system requiring the absorption of energy," Raeta explained. "She's absorbing her tissue to form another living form."

"She's becoming alien?" Zeus asked.

"No," Raeta replied. "Her comatose condition suggests that her system isn't able to absorb whatever they put in her. That's why Will couldn't rouse most of the people. In this state, it's impossible for them to become conscious."

"What about Mitch and Linda?" Will asked. The question gave Raeta a shudder, and she couldn't speak for a moment.

"They shouldn't be conscious," Raeta finally replied. "The only way for them to be conscious is if their systems were able to absorb the alien substance."

"Meaning what?" Aubrey asked, uneasily. Raeta got a grim look.

"They must be carrying symbionts," Raeta said, as a cold chill ran her spine.

"Shit!" Will exclaimed, as Schiffer looked around the waiting room.

"Where are they?" Schiffer asked. Everyone looked around.

"They were just here," Martin said.

"We have to find them," Raeta said. "And fast! I don't know what the carrying term is. If they get away, this could become a new home world for them." Aubrey quickly took charge.

"Form teams," Aubrey said. "Search the hospital."

"They couldn't have gotten far," Zeus said.

"What about the ship?" Schiffer asked.

"It's locked down," Martin replied.

"They must be in the hospital," Aubrey said. "And we need them alive."

Raeta and Will took the nearest stairwell. When the door shut behind them, he took the weapon from his belt and got a cold look from Raeta.

"We're to take them alive." He frowned and returned her cold look.

"I don't intend killing them, just wounding them – slightly, if it becomes necessary." He took her hand and they moved cautiously down the stairs. When they reached the ground floor, he opened the door and looked up and down the corridor. It was empty as Raeta stepped past him and turned into the corridor.

"This way," she said, starting for the exit as Will got a perplexed look.

"What makes you think they came this way?" She stopped and turned to him with a look of superiority.

"It's the nearest exit. If they've left the building, this would have been the way they most likely would have come." Will frowned, uncertain as to her reasoning.

"We can't be certain of that."

"No, Will, we can't," she said, in an icy tone. "But if I wanted to get away from here quickly , this is the way I would have come." He saw she was pissed about him leaving her. He wasn't sure how much the rap on the jaw counted for, but knew she would get over it.

"All right, Raeta, we'll check outside." They went to the exit and Will pushed Raeta behind him before he opened the door. Outside, they looked across the empty base as chill night air blew around them. He turned to Raeta.

"If they came this way, they're in the desert now. Let's go back upstairs."

Hera had called the sisters to a private audience in her chambers. Neither Ophelia nor Janis knew what it was about. They were ushered into Hera's presence and found her pacing, her brow furrowed in concentration.

"You wished to see us, Hera?" Ophelia asked. She stopped pacing and faced them with a look of concern.

"I wish to ask a favor of you," Hera said.

"What?" Janis asked. Hera took a moment to compose her thoughts.

"Our team arrived on Earth over a week ago," Hera began. "Since then we've had no contact with them.
I hoped you might contact the Grays and see if they have any information about them." Janis and Ophelia exchanged glances.

"At this distance, I'm not certain we can make contact," Janis said. It was the first the sisters learned of the lack of contact with the Earth team. It was ominous and unsettling to both.

"Any idea why they haven't kept in contact?" Ophelia asked. Hera got a grim frown and averted her eyes.

"I have only the blackest of pictures in mind. Zeus knew it was important to keep us informed."

"You think they may be dead?" Janis asked, struggling to keep emotion from her voice.

"That's the picture I have," Hera replied. "But I'm not certain it might not be a communication malfunction."

"We'll try to contact the Grays," Ophelia said. "If we're successful, we'll let you know." Hera stepped forward and placed a hand on each of their shoulders.

"I appreciate your help. Feel free to return here as soon as you know anything."

Raeta and Will heard screams as they stepped out on the floor where the search had begun. They heard crashing and clatterings in a room and broke into a run. Stopping at the door, they looked in with surprise. Aubrey and Schiffer were holding Linda's arms as she struggled furiously.

"You have to let me go," Linda screamed. "I have so much to do."

"What's wrong with her?" Raeta asked.

"We don't know," Schiffer replied, angrily. "We found her hiding in one of the rooms and chased her here. She's been carrying on like this since then." When Linda saw Will she calmed down. Aubrey gave Schiffer a puzzled look.

"Don't let go of her, Chet," Aubrey said, as Will stepped in front of Linda.

"Tell me what you have to do, Linda?" Will asked, in a gentle tone. She kept her wide brown eyes on him, making a quick glance at the men holding her arms.

"I am of the first ones, Will. You must help me leave here so I can start our new race," she replied, in a calm voice with an undertone of urgency.

"Where has Mitch gone?" Will asked. She shook her head wildly, her long hair flitting in Aubrey and Schiffer's faces.

"I don't know," she replied. "He said we should separate. I never got a chance to get away. Please, Will, you must help me."

"Has Mitch gone back to the cave?" Will asked.

"He only said that we had to get away from you people or you would destroy us." Raeta came back in the room with a syringe. Will put a hand on Linda's arm and smiled.

"I'm going to help you, Linda. Let Raeta give you the shot to keep you calm so we can plan what must be done," Will said. Linda smiled, expressing confidence at his assurance. Raeta moved beside her and gave her the injection. In a few minutes, Linda was out. They took her to a room and put her in bed.

"What do we do with her?" Schiffer asked.

"Restrain her," Raeta said. Will glanced around.

"Where are Zeus and Martin," Will asked. "They should have been back by now." Aubrey and Schiffer looked alarmed.

"We haven't seen either since we separated to search," Aubrey said.

"Raeta, you and the general stay here," Will said. "Come on, Aubrey, we've got to find them."

They found them in the front lobby. Zeus was getting up rubbing the back of his neck. Martin was sprawled on the floor out cold. Will lifted him and began bringing him around. Will helped him to his feet as Aubrey faced Zeus with an urgent expression.

"What happened?" Aubrey asked. Zeus turned his head and kept rubbing his neck.

"He was waiting for us," Zeus replied. "Caught us from behind."

"Mitch got away?" Will asked, alarmed. Zeus nodded.

"It might be impossible to find him," Zeus said, putting a hand on Will's shoulder.

"We've got to stop him," Zeus said, alarmed. "He's going to find more people like himself and the woman. People who can carry the symbiont."

"What about the others from the cave?" Will asked. Zeus got a sad look and shook his head.

"The alien substance they ingested is killing them," Zeus replied.

"No!" Martin shouted. Zeus patted martin's shoulder.

"I'm sorry, Martin," Zeus said. "There's nothing to be done for them."

"I think I know where Mitch went," Will said.

"Where?" Aubrey asked. Will's lips tightened as he recalled the layout of the cave.

"The cave where we hid out," Will replied.

"We have to go after him," Zeus said, emphatically.

"That won't be easy," Will said. "The cave has branches like a maze. He could hide, let us pass, and slip into another one. There's too few of us for such a search."

"What are we going to do?" Aubrey asked.

"The only way to get Mitch is to draw him out," Will said. "Especially if he thinks there's no danger of capture."

"How do we do that?" Schiffer asked. Will thought for a moment, contriving a hasty plan.

"I'll ask Raeta to go with me," Will said. "She can have a syringe ready to use when he least expects it."

"You have to be careful, Will," Zeus said. "We don't know if he's attained alien powers."

"You want me to come along?" Martin asked. Will shook his head.

"I don't think he'll feel threatened by Raeta and me."

"What if he gets past you?" Aubrey asked. Will patted the weapon at his belt.

"I have no intension of letting him do that, Aubrey." Martin gave Will a horrified look.

"You're going to kill him?" Martin asked, in a tight voice.

"Not if I can help it," Will replied.

"What about the woman?" Zeus asked.

"We got her," Aubrey replied. "She was given a strong sedative. Raeta and Chet are with her." Zeus looked at Will.

"Raeta doesn't know you want her to go with you?" Zeus asked.

"I'm going to ask her when we go back upstairs." Zeus got a stern look.

"You know she won't refuse, Will. I want you to take better care of her this time."

"Don't worry, Zeus," Will said. "If I could have left her at HAARP willingly, I would have. But you know how tenacious she is when she has her mind made up." Zeus' frown deepened.

"I also know she's liable to take unnecessary risks," Zeus said. "I don't want you to allow her to do anything foolish."

"Going after Mitch isn't much of a risk," Will said. "Two men would have less of a chance than Raeta and me."

"Why?" Martin asked.

"Women are easier to subdue than men. If I'm right, Mitch will try to kill me and take Raeta away."

"You're taking a big risk with her," Aubrey said.

"I know. But we don't have a choice."

"You better hurry," Martin said. "No telling how long he'll remain in the cave, if that's where he went."

TWENTY-SIX

Will explained his plan to Raeta emphasizing the risk to her. She turned to Zeus who shook his head.

"It's your decision, Raeta," Zeus said. "This is something no one can advise you on." She was silent for a few minutes, and the men remained silent. She turned to Will.

"What makes you think he went to the cave?" she asked.

"It's the one safe place Mitch knew," Will replied. "It would be the perfect place to take someone for what he has in mind."

"Do you think he's human enough to reason with?"

"I don't know," Will said. "But there should be enough of him left open to suggestion."

"What are you going to suggest, Will?" Aubrey asked, uneasily. Will had been considering that problem.

"I'll offer him safe passage to wherever he wants to go. I doubt he'll believe me, but it will give us time to act while he's thinking it over."

"What if he has telepathic ability?" Zeus asked.

"I don't think that's possible," Raeta replied. "This person is being used for breeding, a container for the symbiont to grow in."

"You expect to walk into that cave, have a conversation, and sedate him when he doesn't expect it?" Schiffer asked, incredulously. Will nodded.

"I can't think of anything else, General," Will said.

"I see no alternative either," Raeta said. "We can't allow the aliens to breed into a new race. That became their primary objective once they realized they were becoming extinct." She looked back at Will.

"I'm ready to go, Will. I just want to get this over with." He regarded her with a sad expression.

"I don't like taking you in there, Raeta, but it's necessary." She got a cynical smile.

"Like the necessity to leave me at HAARP?" Will stared at her without answering.

For some reason the sisters didn't understand, they were able to contact the tall Gray quickly. It was unaware of what was happening on Earth, but would try to learn what the situation was and let them know, but it had no idea as to how long it would take. The sisters sent the information to Hera.

"I wish there was something more we could do," Janis said.

"Even if we were on Earth, there would be nothing we could do."

"But I feel so helpless just waiting, Ophelia."

"I feel the same. It depends on what Zeus, Will, and the others accomplish that counts."

"Maybe we should try to contact Will." Ophelia shook her head with a patient look.

"He doesn't have the ability to pick up our thoughts, Janis. We have to wait for the Gray to get back to us." An attendant of Hera's came and told the sisters Hera had news and wanted to see them. They followed the young woman to her quarters.

They found her looking less stressed than earlier. She greeted them warmly.

"We heard from Zeus," Hera said. "Not all of what he transmitted is good news."

"Has something happened to Will?" Janis asked, in a staccato voice. Hera regarded her with a wan smile.

"Nothing's happened to him – yet. He and Raeta have gone in pursuit of a man carrying a symbiont grown in him by The Brotherhood aliens. The aliens are all dead."

"If they're dead, why can't we return to Earth?" Janis asked.

"The man they went after can transfer an alien substance to other humans, making them carriers of symbionts. Unless he's stopped, there will be a new race much more powerful than their predecessors," Hera replied.

"Why did Will have to go after him?" Janis asked. Ophelia put an arm around her shoulders and regarded her with a serious demeanor.

"Because it's his job," Ophelia said.

Will set the ship down below the cave, shut down the systems and locked them, in case Mitch got to the ship. Will inhaled deeply and turned to Raeta feeling his fear of failure.

"Before we go, Raeta, I want to say I'm sorry for what I did at HAARP. But I was thinking of your safety." She regarded him with a pronounced frown.

"Next time, let me worry about my own safety." This wasn't to her liking because she suffered from claustrophobia, and didn't tell Will. Going into a dark, confined place like a cave was going to cost her. He noticed her hesitancy.

"I don't like doing this either, Raeta. If you don't want to do it, I'll understand."

"No. I'm going with you. You need me and I won't let you down." Will's eyes narrowed at her tone of voice.

"There's something more, isn't there?" She lowered her eyes and remained silent.

"This is no time to keep secrets, Raeta. Our lives, our worlds, are depending on us." She turned a helpless expression on him. Will felt sorry for her without knowing why.

"I'm claustrophobic." He had a sudden picture of her reaction in the darkness of the complex, and got an angry look.

"Christ! You picked a hell of a time to tell me."

"I'm going! I can control it."

"Control it my ass. I've never known a claustrophobic who could control it." She gave him an angry glare as a firm set came to her lips.

"I'll do what we came here for. Worry about your part, Will, I'll do mine." The resoluteness in her voice gave him pause for thought. He reached out, took her hand, and nodded.

"I know you will, Raeta. Let's go."

Outside the ship, Will looked up the rocky face to the entrance of the cave. This wasn't the type of job he usually tackled, but these were extraordinary circumstances. He started up the rock face, Raeta followed. He began moving up a familiar path. Raeta kept slipping, but doggedly stayed with him. He stopped, took hold of her hand, and helped her up the last few feet. She stood beside him breathing hard. Will looked at her.

"Still determined to go through with this?"

"Yes. I told you, I'll control it. Stop worrying about me, I'll be fine." He looked at her with a new found admiration.

"Okay." He stepped to the rock face and began wriggling through the fissure. Inside, he pulled the flashlight from his pocket and turned it on. Everything was just the way he remembered when Martin and he had left. He heard Raeta grunt a couple of times as she worked her way through the narrow opening. When she was through, she took hold of his arm and looked around.

"It doesn't look like anyone's been here recently, Will."

"Mitch wouldn't have bothered anything." He put his hand over her's and on his arm.

"Stay close. This place is easy to get lost in." Her grip tightened on his arm and he patted her hand. She looked at him and he thought how pretty she was in the glow from the light.

"Don't worry. You won't lose me." They went forward a few feet and stopped. Will kept the light on the lantern hanging on the wall as he took out a lighter and lit it. The light gave her some relief from the anxiety she now felt, but wasn't sure why Will had lit it.

"What are you doing?" Will glanced at her.

"Lighting up the place. We won't be able to find him with a flashlight. I'm going to light all the lanterns because I don't want him coming up on us in the dark." Reata swallowed hard and nodded as beads of perspiration formed on her forehead.

"Let's move to the next one," she said.

One by one, Will lit lanterns as they moved deeper into the cave. The only sounds were the ones they were making. If Mitch was here, Will wanted to be certain he heard him. Lighting the fifth lantern, he was certain they were being watched. He said nothing to Raeta as it was obvious she was fighting to control her claustrophobia. He caught a subdued outline in the faint glow at the side of the cave wall, but Mitch remained undefined among the shadows.

As they went deeper, Raeta was beginning to feel she was losing out to the panic that was flooding her, but she concentrated against it. Will was beginning to feel uneasy as he hadn't heard a sound. He had never cared for a silent adversary. Lighting the seventh lantern, he turned to Raeta.

"We'll wait here for him." Her face was covered with sweat and her skin had taken on an ashy pallor.

"I don't think he's here," she said, in an unsteady voice. "There's been nothing to indicate anyone's been here lately." He leaned close to her and whispered.

"He's been watching us for the last fifteen minutes." This caused her to start sharply and look at Will with a fearful expression.

"Are you certain?" Will nodded.

"I've seen him in the shadows a couple of times." Raeta glanced quickly around into the suffocating gloom. Will was looking too, but more carefully.

"Mitch, I'm willing to make a deal. Are you interested?" His voice echoed away through the subterranean passages.

Minutes passed with no answer coming from the inky depths. He heard Raeta gasp as she gripped his arm and pointed to movement. Will couldn't make out if it was Mitch, but knew it could be no one else.

"We've come alone, Mitch. There's only two of us." Still he got no response. He felt Raeta begin to tremble and put an arm around her.

"I've got to get you out of here."

"No, Will." He could see the turmoil in her eyes and felt helpless at her refusal. If it had been him, he knew he would have gotten out long ago. She tightened her grip on his arm.

"We're here," she said, a tremor in her voice. "Let's do what we came for."

"We're not going to wait much longer, Mitch. If you want to talk, better do it now." At the sound of his strange voice, Raeta started.

"I'm not making any deal with you, Will. All you want is to destroy me."

"That's not true, Mitch. We want to help you. We've got Linda in the hospital and she's already getting better." Raeta gave him a shocked look, and he quickly shook his head.

"I know how humans are. Anything you feel to be a threat you destroy."

"And I suppose those aliens never killed a human?" Will asked.

"We haven't. We've let your own kind do the killing. They always seemed to get pleasure out of doing it." Will didn't like hearing Mitch talk like he was no longer human, but why had he expected anything different?

"You and Linda are the last two, Mitch. If you –"

"Are you sure of that, Will?" That question from the darkness shocked Will, but he continued with no change of voice.

"If you want to survive, you better goddamn well listen to what I have to say."

"Oh, I'll listen, Will," Mitch replied, his voice coming from a different location. Will knew he was moving, looking for an opening. The shadows around them made for good concealment for someone who wanted to remain out of sight.

Raeta noticed something that made her panic grow as she tugged on Will's arm and pointed. The lanterns were going out! As they darkened, the gloom became palpable to Raeta.

Will took her arm and they moved against the wall. She shuddered violently as her back touched the cold rock. Will put his arm around her and pressed her against him as he took out the flashlight. The last lantern went out leaving them standing in what seemed like solid darkness. Will switched the light on and turned it around. When Mitch was not to be seen, that settled it for Will.

"We're getting out of here, Raeta." He kept them moving along the wall using it as a guide to the mouth of the cave. Will kept stopping to listen, but whatever Mitch was doing, he was doing it silently. He saw daylight through the fissure.

"We're almost out, Raeta." A hard blow smashed against Will's head dropping him into unconsciousness.

"How long have they been gone?" Martin asked. Aubrey looked at his watch.

"A little over two hours," Aubrey replied. He didn't like Will taking so long with a simple plan. But experience had taught Aubrey that simple plans had a unique way of becoming complicated, depending on who the players were. In this case, it was an alien hybrid race trying to survive at the expense of humanity.

"We better go after them," Martin said. "That cave is riddled with side shafts where a man could easy conceal himself and attack without warning."

"Will wanted us to wait," Aubrey said.

"Goddamnit! They could be dead," Martin said. "We don't know what Mitch is capable of."

"Settle down, Doctor," Schiffer said. "Will's quite competent in his line of work."

"I, too, am beginning to wonder if that was a wise move," Zeus said. "Something might have gone wrong. I don't think it should have taken this long to give a man an injection." Aubrey was inclined to agree, but wanted to give Will the time he had asked for. Aubrey experienced something new – impetuosity.

"You could be right, Zeus. Let's get the hell up to that cave and see what's happened." Schiffer was surprised hearing that come from Aubrey.

"What about Cathy and Linda?" Martin asked. Aubrey knew someone had to stay with them.

"You stay with them, Chet," Aubrey said. "I need Martin because he knows that cave and Zeus might have to do some tight piloting." He saw a flicker of disappointment come to Schiffer.

"All right, Aubrey, but get your asses back here quick. That guy might show up and try to free his girlfriend, and I'm too old for fist fighting." Aubrey got an understanding smile.

"We'll be back as soon as we can, Chet."

Boarding the ship, Zeus took the pilot's seat and began bringing systems on line. He lifted the ship into the air and looked at the red glow of the mountains in the glow of the eastering sun. He was concerned about Raeta but said nothing, hoping to find her safe.

He sat down beside the smaller ship and they filed out and looked up at the rugged face they had to climb.

"Lead the way, Martin," Aubrey said. Martin started up the lower rocks for easier passage to the cave. The morning was cool, but they were soon sweating from the exertion of climbing. When they stood at the fissure, everything was quiet. Aubrey looked through the fissure but saw no light in the cave.

"I don't like the looks of this," Aubrey said. Martin and Zeus were uneasy.

"We can't go in without lights," Martin said.

"We're not going in very far," Aubrey said. "Just far enough to call for Will and Raeta." As Aubrey started through the fissure he discovered he needed to shed a few pounds, but made it into the cave. He was confronted with total darkness. If Will was all right, he should see light.

"Will? Raeta? Can you hear me?" Aubrey called. He listened intently but couldn't be certain he heard anything. He turned his head from side to side listening, and he heard it again. There was no mistaking a painful moan. Aubrey couldn't see anything in the darkness and took out his penlight. The glow it gave was feweble in the immense darkness and he kept it pointed down. Moving slowly, he found Will with blood caked on the side of his face. He knelt beside him and turned the light around.

"Where are you, Raeta?" No response came from the darkness. At first, Aubrey thought she might be hurt too, and made a quick sweep of the area around Will. When he didn't see her, his worst nightmare clarified in his mind.

"The son of a bitch has her!" he exclaimed, harshly. He went back to Will and lifted him to his feet, returned the penlight to his pocket, and started pulling him toward the fissure. He pushed Will into the opening.

"Martin, Zeus, pull Will through." He saw them take hold of him and begin working him through. Aubrey was wondering where Mitch had taken Raeta, and concluded they had to be in the cave. They could only have left on foot. This was a big desert and hot as hell during the day.

He saw them pull Will from the fissure, Aubrey began working his way out.

"Where's Raeta?" Zeus asked, as he started helping Martin take Will down to the ship. Aubrey nodded at the cave.

"In there." A determined look came to Zeus.

"We'll have to go in and search for her," Zeus said.

"We don't have any lights," Martin said. "There are a hundred places Mitch could hide with her."

"We're not going to abandon her," Zeus said, sharply.

"We're not going to," Aubrey said. "Do you have portable lights on the ship?"

"Yes, high intensity lamps."

"Good. You stay at the ship and tend to Will. Martin and I will search for Raeta."

"Are you crazy?" Martin asked, incredulous.

"I will be if we allow him time to transfer some of that alien shit into her," Aubrey said. "Let's get Will to the ship and get a couple of those lights." Without anymore protest, the three of them slowly took Will down, and Aubrey looked back at the cave.

"If that alien bastard is in there, I'll kill him," Aubrey said." He's been too much trouble to mess with any longer." As he looked at the cave, Aubrey fingered the plasma weapon in his pocket.

TWENTY-SEVEN

The tall Gray learned that all The Brotherhood aliens were dead, but the sisters already knew that. It also told them two Earth people were known to be carrying alien symbionts that could produce a new race, unless the symbionts were destroyed. One of the two had been trapped at the Arizona base while the other had gotten away. This one Will had gone after. That was all the Gray knew. Although the Gray was trying to keep up with developments, it had to await the final outcome, too.

The Pantheon was relieved to hear of the demise of the Brotherhood, but anxiety at the prospect of a more powerful hybrid race. Hera had again sent for the sisters.

"I've heard nothing more from Zeus," Hera said. "The last report said they had the woman carrying a symbiont, but the man had escaped." Janis had hoped to hear more about Will.

"Until this crisis is resolved, I fear we will hear nothing more from Zeus," Hera added.

"We appreciate your courtesy and concern, Hera," Ophelia said.

"I'll inform you as soon as I have anything new," Hera said. The sisters returned to their quarters where Janis would spend more agonizing hours waiting.

In the ship, Zeus found Will had a fractured skull and his condition was bad.

"We need to get Will to the hospital," Zeus said.

"Who is going to be the doctor?" Aubrey asked. Martin looked from Aubrey to Zeus.

"We can't let him die," Martin said. Zeus took the only option he could think of. He placed Will in the navigator's seat and turned the healing ray on him.

"This only works once on an individual," Zeus said. "But it might stabilize him." He stepped away from the chair as the yellow beam engulfed Will. It faded after a few minutes and Zeus stepped beside Will and examined him. He glanced at Aubrey and Martin.

"It helped, but he needs medical help as soon as possible." Aubrey and Martin knew the closest medical help was Raeta.

"It's time we went for the doctor, Martin," Aubrey said.

When Raeta came to, she found herself in darkness and a surge of panic filled her.

"Will?" she whispered.

"He's not here," came that strange voice. "I don't think you'll ever see him again." The words made her uneasy.

"What did you do to Will?" The odd warbling laugh that filled the darkness alarmed her.

"I smashed his head in with a rock. He's dead." A pause from the darkness.

"You don't have anyone to count on."

"Why didn't you kill me?" Raeta slipped the syringe from her blouse pocket.

"You will aid in producing the new race. You should be honored to be among the first."

"I won't cooperate."

"I don't need your cooperation. As soon as the symbiont bursts forth from me, it will come to you. You will carry it while the others develop." Raeta had a paroxysm of fear. The idea of some alien thing crawling toward her in the dark was the most terrifying thought she had known. But she was curious about how the process worked. If she could locate her captor, she was going to stick the syringe in him.

"It will destroy you when it's born?" again, that laugh sent a tingle up her spine.

"Of course. But it will then live in you while it becomes part of our new race. Only the birth host dies. You won't. It will become one with you."

"If it needs hosts to reproduce, what happens when there are no more hosts?"

"The new race will be quite long-lived. From our beginning, we won't need any birth hosts for more than a millennia. By then, we'll be breeding humans for this very purpose." The idea was repulsive to Raeta.

"Why did you destroy the man that wanted to help you?" She waited to hear where he was and move in that direction.

"We were the first sentient race in the galaxy. It, and everything in it, belongs to us. We need no aid from inferior races such as you humans. We need you only to fulfill our needs." Raeta didn't move, as it was clear that he was moving as he spoke.

"How did you determine you were the first race in the galaxy?"

"I didn't say we were the first race," the voice replied, clearly annoyed. "I said, we were the first sentient race.

That gave us the right to conquer, rule, and destroy. We have seen many worlds, studied many races, and found them all to be inferior."

"If you're so superior, why do you fight from darkness? Why not open conquest?"

"War is terrible. We have seen it on countless worlds, and caused most of them. We have no need to fight and conquer when we can control races to do the destroying and dying for us." A moment of silence and Raeta was startled by a sharp cry of pain.

"What's wrong?" She dreaded the answer from the darkness.

"It's close to my birth time." Ratea quickly understood it had been the symbiont speaking.

"It's only a couple of hours before our new race will be born." These words filled her with an unreasoning panic. She had to find a way out of this dark hell. For Raeta, it was escape or have something alien come for her, use her body to create an alien race.

Schiffer was almost dozing when he heard the bed thump. He was on his feet staring at Linda as she screamed and twisted in agony. He had no idea what was wrong with her and decided not to take any chances. He thought of a weapon, but a hospital didn't offer a variety of options. Schiffer thought for a moment. When Linda screamed again, he rushed from the room desperately looking for anything he might use. Her screams became more agonized as he went to the desk and made a quick search, finding nothing useful. When a scream faded into a strange gurgling, followed by silence, Schiffer saw a pair of crutches standing in a corner. He grabbed one and pulled the cap from the bottom. It wasn't sharp enough to do any harm, but it would keep anything away from him.

He went back to the room and found Linda's bed covered with blood that slowly dripped to the floor and soaked the sheet that covered her. He saw something moving under the sheet. Cautiously Schiffer stepped beside Cathy and pressed fingers to her throat. She was alive. He moved to Linda and done the same. She was dead.

Whatever was under the sheet was moving toward her head. He backed away holding the cruth like a rifle. He saw a yellow tip emerge from under the sheet. Schiffer stared, fascinated as the thing came into the open just below Linda's chin.

It looked like a cat-sized snail, and he at first, believed that was what it was. But he had never seen a snail that yellow or so damned big.

Its antennae began waving in his direction causing Schiffer to back to the door. He realized Cathy was in the bed next to the thing and decided it had to be destroyed. He moved toward it holding the cruth in front of him as if it held a bayonet. When he was close, he stretched the crutch out and poked the thing. It emitted a loud squeak and tried to move back under the sheet. This gave Schiffer an idea. He moved to the foot of the bed and pulled the tucks of the sheet free. He slowly began pulling the sheet up toward the thing. He didn't think it could harm him, but Schiffer wasn't going to take the chance that it might do worse.

He was ready to capture the thing in the sheet. His eyes widened as he wondered what he would do with it then. He needed some sort of container to put it in. Again, hospital equipment dictated what he could use. He got the bedpans from the units beside each bed and put them on the floor by Linda's bed. He prepared to do what he didn't want to.

Schiffer took hold of a corner of the sheet and put it over the thing. It began moving away from the sheet

"Shit!" He threw the bottom of the sheet over it, stepped to the head of the bed, grabbed the bloody part of the sheet and threw it over the thing. He grabbed it and dumped it quickly into the bedpan, dropped the sheet, and quickly lay the other bedpan atop the other one. He carried it to the desk, grabbed a roll of tape, and began taping them together.

When he felt it had been secured, he breathed a sigh of relief. He went back to the room and saw Linda without the sheet covering her. Schiffer had been in some horrendous battles, and seen awful wounds, but none had prepared him for this. Her body had been literally ripped open from her pubic hair to just below her breasts. Her insides were a mass of slimy yellow and red glistening in the light. It was too much, and he turned away and vomited.

Martin offered Aubrey a pulse weapon.

"Zeus thought we might need these," Martin said. Aubrey shook his head.

"I already have one." Aubrey regarded Martin for a moment.

"We're getting the girl from that alien son of a bitch." Martin nodded looking grim.

"You know this place. Where do we start?" Martin looked around knowing he didn't know this cave as well as Aubrey thought he did. Any direction would be a guess.

"This way," Martin said, heading into the cave. The branch they entered was a close, confining space with barely enough space for a person to squeeze through. Jutting rock caused them some contortions to get past before facing a dead end. Aubrey looked at Martin with an annoyed expression.

"Now which way?" Aubrey asked. Martin turned to him recalling an opening they had passed by.

"Let's try that branch we passed."

It was wider, but not by much.

"Do you know where the hell you're going?" Aubrey asked. Martin glared at him with a stern expression.

"No. This goddamn place is like a maze."

"We've got to find Raeta before that damn alien does anything to her. How do you propose we search more quickly?"

"All we can do is check each branch and hope we find her."

"Hope, Martin? We can't hope. We've got to find her and kill that alien." Martin became angry as he faced Aubrey.

"Mitch isn't an alien. What happened to him was no fault of his own."

"I'm sorry," Aubrey said. "I know he was a friend of yours, but he's not friendly any longer. He'll kill us if he gets the chance." Martin knew Mitch was no longer anyone's friend, and he didn't want to think about what he might do to Raeta.

"I know," Martin said, sadly. "We'll just have to keep going. There's no other way." Aubrey patted his shoulder.

"Then let's keep moving."

They went from one branch into another, but found no trace of Raeta or Mitch. It was beginning to be frustrating for Aubrey when they heard a cry of agony.

"Where did that come from?" Aubrey asked.

"Sounded like it was straight ahead," Martin replied. "But this cave has funny acoustics. It could have come from anywhere."

"Let's go on." They moved past the dark rock wall turning their lights around to make certain they were alone. When they heard another scream, they knew they were closer.

"You were right, Martin, they're ahead of us."

"Mitch sounds like he's in awful pain." Aubrey nodded.

"Yeah, but it's what's causing it that worries me."

"Let's hurry. We might get there in time to help him." Martin moved quickly ahead.

Raeta pressed herself against the rock wall, running her hands over it to see if she could climb. Being higher would keep the thing away from her – she hoped. But the rock offered no handholds. She could hear Mitch writhing and crying out in torment. She was glad there was no light, as she had no desire to see what was happening to him, nor the thing that was causing it. Each cry of pain caused her panic to grow. But when she heard the awful tearing sound, Raeta felt sick. Mitch's last cry faded in a gurgle and the place filled with silence.

Raeta couldn't help the terrified whimpers now escaping her. There was an alien creature in the darkness not far from her, and it would be coming for her. She tried to quiet her racing heart and gasping breath. She had to if she wanted to be able to locate the thing and stay out of its way. A sudden terrifying fact revealed itself to her. Mitch had been able to see in the darkness; she couldn't. What if the creature could see her? She was at a disadvantage and wished she had Will's flashlight. But Mitch hadn't given her the chance when he knocked her out.

Raeta moved along the wall feeling her way. Her hand pressed against nothing and she fell slamming hard against the floor. She rolled onto her back and listened.

"Raeta, where are you?" The voice came from behind her, outside the chamber she was in.

"Here! In here! Please hurry." She quickly got to her feet and pressed her back against the wall. She didn't know who was coming, but thought it was Will. She wished he would come faster.

She felt something brush against her foot and quickly moved, but away from the opening. She thought she saw light out in the cave.

"Please hurry," she screamed. "There's something in here trying to touch me."

"We'll be right there," the voice said, and echoed away. She stood still and listened, then moved again. She could now see two lights in the cave and they gave a dim glow where she was.

She looked down, desperately searching for the thing. She thought she saw movement by her foot and hurriedly moved away. Raeta realized that the thing was between her and the only way out. She didn't think she could be more frightened. Knowing help was on the way, but hadn't yet arrived, a new surge of terror filled her.

She kept moving along the wall hoping she was keeping away from it. Then the lights vanished, leaving her again in total darkness. This made Raeta desperate as she tried making her way back to the opening. She heard the thing moving along the floor. It didn't sound very fast. Maybe she could keep away from it. What had happened to the people coming for her?

She felt carefully along the wall so she wouldn't fall again. If she did, the thing might be on her before she could get up. Just as her hand touched the opening, the chamber was filled with light and a welcoming arm slid around her waist. She seemed to melt against whomever held her. She closed her eyes and felt a relief that was better than the terror she had experienced.

"Son of a bitch! Would you look at that thing, Martin." Raeta turned her head and opened her eyes. She saw an ugly yellow snail-like slug moving across the floor toward her. She screamed and pressed her face against Aubrey's shoulder. A bright flash, followed by a sizzling sound, filled the cave.

"It's all right, Raeta. The thing's dead." She turned her face up and saw Aubrey was holding her.

"Jesus Christ!" Martin exclaimed. Aubrey turned his light in the same direction. Mitch had been torn open from his pubic hair to just below his sternum. His insides were a mass of yellow and red jelly. Raeta started to look but Aubrey pressed her head against him.

"No, Raeta. You don't want to look. Come on Martin, let's get the hell out of here."

"Will! How's Will? That man said he killed him."

"Will's in bad condition, Raeta," Martin said. "But he's not dead."

The walk out of the cave was in silence. When she wriggled out of the cave, she had never known what a joy it was to take a deep breath of fresh air in bright sunlight. She gave Aubrey an embrace and then Martin.

"I'm very grateful you two came along when you did." Aubrey smiled.

"It was the least we could do," Aubrey said. "Besides, you're too damn good looking to be an alien."

TWENTY-EIGHT

Back at the ship, Raeta immediately began treating Will's wound. He had an ugly gash on the backside of his head that didn't look good at all.

"We've got to get him proper medical attention as soon as possible," she said. "I'm limited in what I can do for him. The longer we wait, the less his chance of surviving."

"As soon as we drop Martin and Aubrey at the hospital, we'll head for home at the fastest possible speed," Zeus said. Raeta gave him a doubtful look.

"How long will it take, Zeus?" she asked.

"Four, maybe five days. We don't have a choice, Raeta. There's no one here who can treat him." Aubrey looked down at Will's pale face.

"I never should have allowed you two to go to that cave alone," Aubrey said. Raeta put her hand on his arm.

"You can't blame yourself," she said. "Will and I chose to go." He looked at her with the saddest expression she had ever seen.

"Once we get him to Olympius, he'll be fine," Raeta said. "You'll see."

When Zeus set the ship down at the hospital, Raeta was first out. As Zeus stepped beside her, she spoke.

"I'm going to need medical supplies. I won't be long." She hurried ahead as Zeus, Martin, and Aubrey followed her into the hospital. They went to where Schiffer was. Aubrey took one look and knew something had happened.

"What's wrong, Chet? You look green around the gills."

"I saw what that thing did when it came out of that woman. I've never seen anything so goddamn horrible in my life, Aubrey." He remembered the corpse of Mitch and felt thankful he hadn't seen it happen.

"We know, Chet. We found the man in the cave after his slug came out."

"How's Cathy?" Martin asked. Schiffer looked at him with some relief.

"She seems to be resting, now it's away from her. I think that damn thing was disturbing her. Where's Will?"

"He's been hurt pretty bad," Aubrey replied. "Zeus and Raeta are going to take him to Olympus for treatment."

"What did you mean, it's away from her now?" Zeus asked. Schiffer got a sick look.

"I caught the thing in a couple of bedpans. I got them taped together at the desk."

"If it's all right with you, I would like to take it back to Olympus for study," Zeus said.

"I don't care if you fry that ugly thing in shit," Schiffer said.

"Can you get it for me?" Zeus asked. "We've got to get going. Raeta's probably waiting by now."

Zeus came hurrying in with the taped up bedpans. Raeta was cleaning the dried blood from Will's head. She glanced at the bedpans.

"What have you got?" she asked.

"The slug that came out of the Earth woman." A dark fear filled her.

"Keep that thing away from me. I've had more than enough from one of those things." Zeus put in a locker and electronically sealed it. He took the pilot's seat and made preparations for liftoff.

"I'll make this easy, Raeta, so you won't have to strap him in." She glanced at him.

"When we get outside Earth's atmosphere, I'll send a medical report on Will's condition," Raeta said. "That way everything can be ready when we arrive." Zeus took the ship up slowly and headed toward the pole while gaining altitude.

The Gray had given the sisters the good news that the alien threat was over, HAARP would be shut down, and Earth's population restored. The general population wouldn't know about the secret invasion that befell their planet. The Gray made no mention of Will or any of the others and gave Janis reason to be nervous.

"Why didn't it tell us anything about the team?" Janis asked. By team, Ophelia knew she meant Will.

"Maybe there was nothing to report," she replied. "After all, they've been successful and are probably on their way back." Janis began pacing, her brow furrowing in concentration. Ophelia got up and came to her. Janis stopped and they faced each other.

"You know he won't be able to pick up your thoughts, Janis."

Janis looked at her sister and Ophelia knew she wasn't about to listen to her.

The young woman came to them and told them Hera had news. Janis had a bad feeling flood her.

"It's about Will, isn't it?" Janis asked.

"I'm not aware of why Hera wishes to see you," the young woman replied.

"We'll learn what it's about from Hera," Ophelia said, giving Janis an annoyed look. "Why must you have such black pictures in your mind, Janis?"

"I know something's happened to Will. It's a strong sensation I can't get rid of."

"Put it aside until you know the facts," Ophelia said. "Don't put yourself through misery until you have a reason."

They followed the woman along the resplendent corridor to Hera's quarters. She opened the door and they went in. Hera wasn't there and Janis turned to Ophelia.

"I wonder where she is."

"Maybe something unexpected came up," Ophelia suggested. Hera came in through a side door and stopped in front of the sisters, her face devoid of emotion. Janis clutched her hands to her breast.

"Something's happened to Will, hasn't it?"

"He was wounded by the man who carried the symbiont," Hera replied. "He's in bad condition and is being brought here for treatment." Janis couldn't stop the tears and didn't trust herself to speak.

"How bad is his condition?" Ophelia asked.

"We won't know that until he's been examined by doctors," Hera said. "The ship should be here soon. I felt you would like to know before they arrived."

Aubrey picked up the phone and put it to his ear.

"Blaine."

"Any word yet?"

"I haven't heard anything since Zeus left, Chet."

"I wouldn't have believed this was possible, Aubrey. Everything's just like it was, except for Will being gone."

"I know. It's been over a week and I've not been able to establish communication with Olympus. I guess it's moved beyond the solar system. But I sure would like to hear from Raeta or Zeus."

"All we can do is wait," Schiffer said. "I've got a meeting with the president. He wants HAARP dismantled, but I'll be damn if he knows why."

"If I hear anything, Chet, I'll let you know." He put the phone down and turned the chair to the window. What the hell had happened? Had that damn slug gotten loose in the ship? Aubrey couldn't believe that. Zeus was too smart to get careless with something like that. He had to find a way to get a message to Olympus. The sisters, Zachary, and Klast were still there.

Aubrey had thought of approaching a supervisor he knew at NASA to try to communicate with Olympus, but knew it would raise many questions he didn't dare answer. The door opened and Crist came in.

"Sir, there's a young woman insisting on seeing you."

"Tell her to come back later. I'm not seeing anyone."

"She said someone called Hera sent her." Aubrey was out of the chair charging past Crist.

She had silky red-brown hair, gray eyes, and was the loveliest woman Aubrey had ever seen.

"How can I help you, Miss?" Aubrey asked. She bowed her head and brought her eyes back to him.

"We should speak in private," she said, in a voice that gave Aubrey a tingle. He motioned to his office and followed her.

Seated and alone, Aubrey was anxious to hear about Will.

"How is Will?" She quickly turned her eyes down.

"Hera sent me to you because Zeus' ship has disappeared. It was twelve hours from Olympus when Zeus last reported. Since then, there's been no contact."

"How long ago was that?" Aubrey asked, concerned.

"Three days." Aubrey looked puzzled.

"What does Hera expect me to do?"

"She would like for you to return to Olympus with me. You have more experience in searching for lost people than we do. Hera pleads for your help in finding Zeus and his passengers." The idea that Will was lost came as a hard blow to Aubrey. He wanted to help, but had no idea what Hera expected of him. He had no experience in searching for people in space.

"Hera must understand I've had no experience in a case like this." The woman got a glowing smile.

"Thank you for agreeing to help. Hera will be pleased." Aubrey took a closer look at her and noted she looked familiar.

"What is Zeus to you?"

"He's my father. I am Selene."

There had been consternation when Zeus' ship failed to arrive. Ships were sent to search its last reported position. No trace was found. Everyone in the Pantheon was wondering what could have happened to it. When Janis heard the news, she had to be sedated. She had become hysterical, and not even Ophelia could calm her. Ophelia had suggested to Hera she send someone to get Aubrey. Hera had chosen Selene to go.

Ophelia and Hera stood silent.

"That ship has to be out there, Hera."

"I don't understand. Our ships are kept in the best working order. We haven't had an incident like this in a very long time."

"Whatever happened, maybe Mr. Blaine can get to the bottom of it. I only hope Janis can come to terms with the loss of Will." Hera got a surprised look.

"I'll count none of them lost until I know for certain what happened to that ship." Ophlia looked at her with a sad expression.

"Hera, you're forgetting Will's condition. Zeus said if he didn't get medical help he would die." Hera lowered her eyes.

"I had forgotten, Ophelia."

"All we can do is wait and hope for the best." Hera regarded Ophelia.

"Please try to contact the grays. Maybe they know something about the ship." Ophelia nodded.

"I'll try. I'm sure if they knew something they would have contacted me."

After reporting their position and estimated time of arrival, Zeus noticed something happening to the controls. He switched to manual control, but they were frozen. He glanced at their course and saw they were deviating by eight degrees. Zeus struggled with the controls, but it was useless. He glanced at Raeta as she changed the dressing on Will's head.

"We've gone off course, Raeta." She turned an alarmed look to him.

"What's wrong?" Zeus shook his head.

"I don't know. The controls are frozen on a setting that's taking us eight degrees off course."

"Switch to manual."

"I have, but it makes no difference."

"Where are we headed, Zeus?" He regarded her grimly.

"Into deep space. There's nothing I can do to stop it." He tried to contact Olympus, but something was jamming communications.

The ship had been on its altered course for two hours without any deviation when Zeus noticed a strange blip on the sensor screen. Whatever it was, it was immense.

"Raeta, take a look at this and tell me what you think it is." She came beside him and looked at the sensor. Her eyes got big as she realized the size of the object.

"I've never seen a profile like that," she said, awed. "It has to be over five miles long and definitely an artificial construction." She looked at Zeus.

"No wonder communications are jammed." Zeus was also impressed by what was on the sensor and began considering it might be a Kraken ship.

"Who could have built such a ship, Zeus?" He shook his head.

"I wish I knew. She moved her hand to the communications console and began to transmit what she hoped would be understood as an emergency call.

"What are you doing?"

"Trying to contact that ship. Whoever's running it drew us off course and they're pulling us in." She got only the crackle of static.

"Lower the shield on the windscreen, Zeus. Let's have a look at it." As the shield lowered, they beheld a behemoth only a few miles from them. Its size made their ship insignificant in comparison. They could see a few lights along its white hull.

"It appears abandoned," Zeus said, making an intense observation.

"Then how can it be pulling us in?"

"It must be automatic, Raeta." She stared at him in alarm.

"Why would it want to pull us in?" Zeus gave her an impatient look.

"Our questions will be answered after we're aboard her."

They were drawn relentlessly toward the great ship. In the last mile, its vast size became more imposing. They watched a light on its side begin to flash and a hatch open.

"That must be the landing bay," Zeus said. Raeta heard a soft moan from Will and went to him. She bent beside him and caressed his cheek. She glanced at Zeus who was watching the ship. She quickly kissed Will.

"I hope we can get Will help on that ship. If he doesn't get proper care soon he'll die."

"We'll know soon, Raeta. Look at the size of this landing bay." She hurried back beside Zeus. The brightly lit bay looked to be over half a mile across, and empty. Their ship was drawn to the far side and set down so gently neither of them felt the impact. They felt vibrations through their ship and knew the great hatch was closing.

"How will we know if we can breathe the air, Zeus?" He glanced at her and shrugged.

"Good air or bad, it's the only place we have to go. I estimate we're over fifty-seven hours from Olympus." She was aware of what that might mean for Will.

The vibrations ceased and they waited, judging the time it would take to fully pressurize the huge bay. After waiting what they agreed was enough time, they went to the hatch. Zeus glanced at her as he depressed the release and the hatch began to open. The air was cold but breathable. They stepped out of the ship and looked around. No one was coming to greet them. They walked around their ship hoping to see someone. When no one appeared, Zeus turned to Raeta.

"Let's see if we can find the medical center. You're going to have to treat Will."

"This is an alien ship! How will I know what to use, or how?" Zeus gave her a grim look.

"Will's life is in your hands, Raeta. What we find here is all there's going to be. You're just going to have to do what you can. Nobody can expect more than that." She regarded him solemnly as she nodded. Zeus put a hand on her shoulder and gave a gentle squeeze.

"Let's get Will."

As Aubrey drove, with Selene beside him, he had a nagging thought of never seeing Will again. He glanced at her.

"Where did you land?"

"In the woods by the sisters' house. Do you know where that is?" Aubrey nodded. It seemed an awful long time since that night Will, he, and the teams had taken Janis.

"How did you get to Washington?" She gave him a surprised look.

"I walked."

"From there?" She nodded.

"How were you able to find me?" She took a small instrument from her pocket and extended a delicate hand so he could see it.

"This is a medical DNA tracker. When you were on Olympus you left skin samples. Once they were identified, this device was programmed to search for your DNA pattern." Aubrey shook his head in wonder.

"You people always amaze me." He turned the car down the drive to the farmhouse and around to the rear of the house. He shut off the engine and looked at Selene, wishing he were twenty years younger.

"I hope I can be of help, Selene. I've only done my searching here on Earth." She got a confident smile.

"Hera wouldn't have sent me if she didn't have faith in your ability. Now that I've met you, I share Hera's confidence." Aubrey smiled weakly and shook his head.

"I'm glad someone has confidence in my ability. Over the past few months, I've lost a lot of self-confidence."

"Let's go to the ship," she said. They got out of the car and Selene led the way into the woods. Aubrey recalled it had been this woods Ophelia had escaped into. He felt an urge to see Will, followed by a sorrowful feeling.

They came to the clearing where the ship sat and Selene opened the hatch and they boarded. He took the seat next to her at the control panel. She was very efficient as her agile fingers skimmed over the controls and the ship was rising quickly into the sky. Once she had cleared the trees, she wasted no time putting on speed. It was breathtaking for Aubrey at just how fast the little ship shot through the sky and into the blackness of space. He had never thought he would be returning to Olympus, but the circumstances filled him with sadness.

TWENTY-NINE

As Zeus and Raeta carried Will along one of the passageways, she began to see something that gave her some small hope.

"Does this look familiar, Zeus?" He glanced around and looked at her.

"Should it?"

"Take a close look at the construction." He studied it as they continued. He began to see what Raeta meant.

"It looks almost –"

"Exactly! This is put together just like the underground complex in Yucatan." Zeus couldn't hide his surprise.

"That would mean this was built by the same people." She had a hopeful look.

"How much is known about our ancestors? The ones that remained on the home world." Zeus realized they had no data. No one on Olympus had bothered to try to contact them again.

"We've got to find something with alphabetical symbols, Raeta. If this ship was built by our people, everyone on Olympus is in for a shock." They proceeded along the passageway looking for clues to the origin of the great ship. They came to an intersection that had a plaque on the bulkhead and stopped. It was their alphabet and showed the way to the medical facility.

They turned down the indicated passageway and lifted Will's feet from the floor so they could hurry. When they went into the sickbay, Raeta was stunned at how advanced the equipment was.

"This is incredible, Zeus. I've never seen such advanced medical technology."

"But can you use it?" They put Will on the table and moved around looking at the instruments. Raeta gently moved her fingers over a medical sensor screen. After a few minutes, she was confident she could use the equipment and turned to Zeus.

"I feel certain I can use this facility to help Will. But we have to get the main power functioning."

"I've a general idea of where the central power switches are. You prepare Will and I'll see about getting it on." Zeus hurried out while Reata found the locker with medical gowns. She put one on and went back to the panel checking to make certain she knew what each instrument was for.

She started when a surge of power activated the panel. One screen lit up naming it as an anatomy computer. She went through it until she found what she needed for Will. As she studied the detailed view of the skull, she discovered an adjacent screen that gave medical techniques for treating any injury. She studied intensely for a few minutes and picked up the instrument the screen had shown her to use. She checked its power and found it functional. Raeta went to Will and began working the instrument over the wound. She was amazed at how rapid the healing proceeded.

She had finished before Zeus returned. When he came in, she was taking off the medical gown. He stared in surprise as she smiled and nodded at Will.

"He's going to be all right, Zeus. I can't believe how advanced this equipment is, the technology is remarkable."

"You're finished?"

"Yes. It's only a matter of time until he regains consciousness."

"You stay with him, Raeta. I'm going to see if I can find the bridge without getting lost. We've got to be able to operate this ship to take us to Olympus."

After Aubrey got acquainted with Selene, he decided to find out what she knew.

"What do you know about Will?" She gave him an odd look, cocking her head.

"He is a descendant of the first Zeus. He was wounded trying to get Raeta away from the hybrid on Earth. The one sister, Janis, seems to be very much in love with him."

"What do you mean he's a direct descendant from the first Zeus?"

"His genetic line remains unbroken," Selene replied. "He carries DNA from our first leader, Zeus, as he was known to your ancient Greeks." Aubrey thought for a second when something occurred to him.

"What about Ophelia and Janis?"

"Their lineage is unbroken also. They are descendants of Athena."

"Then it's true your people helped make the human race what it is?"

"Of course," Selene said. "I've made a thorough study of our colonies on Earth in those ancient times. If we hadn't intervened, there would be no human race. Your ancestors were adapted to what they became. There was no need for them to have evolved further."

"One of your colonies was in the Middle East?" Aubrey asked.

"That was the earliest colony, where your race was created. They aided in mining for gold so that Olympus was able to sustain us."

"Where did The Brotherhood originate? And how did they get to Earth?"

"I have no answer to your first question," Selene replied. "They may have followed us there, or accidentally discovered your planet. It's certain that if they hadn't been stopped, there would have been a terrible war." Aubrey asked the question he had wanting to ask all along, and see her reaction.

"Selene, what do you know about the Grays?" She hesitated for a second, but it was enough for Aubrey.

"I'm one of the few on Olympus who know about the ones you call the Grays. Not even father is aware of my knowledge."

"Can you tell me where they come from? I promise I won't tell anyone. I just want to know the truth." She regarded him for a moment.

"You really won't tell anyone?"

"I promise, not a word to anyone," Aubrey replied.

"Only a select few of us telepaths have had contact with them. I acted as a booster so the sisters could communicate with the Grays on Olympus. They are curious, friendly, and helpful. They are from a future parallel Earth. They travel into different universes studying how different Earths developed." She paused and took a breath.

"They do not interfere with parallel worlds. Here The Brotherhood forced them to intervene so they might produce symbionts." At the mention of the slug, Aubrey recalled where one was.

"Your father had a live slug on his ship, Selene. Do you think it may have caused his ship to disappear?" She thought for a few seconds, then answered confidently.

"I doubt it. Father would have made certain it was safely contained." Aubrey let out a long, slow breath.

"That's what I thought," he said.

Hera had been informed that Selene was only a day from Olympus and Aubrey was with her. This gave her fresh confidence that Zeus' ship would soon be found. She decided to go and tell Ophelia. The sisters were surprised when she came to their quarters. Hera's message seemed to revitalize Janis. Ophelia wasn't going to get any false hope, as she didn't know what to expect from Aubrey. She felt he could do no more than what was already being done.

"I don't understand, Hera," Ophelia said. "What makes you think Blaine can find Zeus' ship?"

"He's very close to Will. That should be sufficient for him to locate the ship." Her reasoning escaped Ophelia.

"How? Your search has found nothing."

"There's a strong bond between the two," Hera replied. "This, I believe, gives him a means of ascertaining where Will is."

"What sort of bond are you talking about?" Janis asked, becoming interested. Hera was aware that what she thought was only a slim hope, but better than no hope at all.

"It's difficult to explain," Hera began. "I believe with the both of you, Blaine may be able to locate Will."

"You mean by telepathy?" Janis asked.

"Yes," Hera replied. "Those two seem acutely aware of how the other thinks. It might be possible to at least see what Will is seeing." Ophelia didn't say it aloud, but knew it might work – if Will was alive. Right now, that seemed a thin possibility.

"We'll do anything we can," Janis said, eagerly. Ophelia glanced at her sister and back to Hera.

"Yes. We'll do whatever we can," Ophelia said. "When is Selene due to arrive?"

"Less than a day. Have you heard anything from the Grays?"

"Nothing," Ophelia replied. "I get the feeling they're no longer close by."

"That may be because of our distance from the sun," Hera said. "Maybe they can't travel far from Earth." Ophelia hadn't considered that as an explanation.

"Do you want us there when Selene and Aubrey arrive?" Janis asked. Hera thought it would be better if she spoke to Aubrey alone first. He, too, was probably wondering what she had in mind.

"That won't be necessary," Hera said. "I'll explain to Blaine what we wish to attempt. We can meet later. I want you both calm and ready to use all of your telepathic ability."

After Hera left, Ophelia felt she should prepare Janis for failure. It wasn't something she wanted to do, but felt obliged to do so for Janis' sake.

"I'm not hopeful about this, Janis." She saw anger flood her sister's face.

"Why not? You think Will is dead?"

"The chance of finding them after this long aren't promising." Janis pulled her shoulders back taking a defiant stance.

"Until I see Will's body, he's alive. Nothing you can say can make me believe any different, Ophelia."

"I'm not saying this to hurt you, Janis, just make you aware of the circumstances." Janis' expression softened and she stepped forward and embraced Ophelia.

"I know. I'm sorry. I didn't mean to get angry." Ophelia returned the embrace knowing how it would affect Janis if Will wasn't found.

"We better prepare ourselves, Janis. What Hera is asking isn't going to be easy."

Raeta came on the massive bridge and saw Zeus looking over the control panel. He glanced at her as she stepped beside him.

"How's Will doing?" She got a glowing smile.

"He'll be fine. How are you coming at learning the control system?"

"Another couple of days and I'll know it well enough to take us home."

"Have you found the communications system, Zeus?" He glanced over the entire control panel with a puzzled look.

"I haven't come across anything that resembles a comm system. It's odd, almost as if the ship had no need for communications."

"What reason could there have been for that?"

"I don't know. But we're going to scare a lot of people if we get this ship to Olympus without finding someway to let them know it's us." One thing had been bothering Raeta and she felt it was time to ask.

"Have you checked to see if that thing's still alive?" He looked at her just as she shuddered.

"It still bothers you?"

"Very much. I would feel safer if it were outside the ship." He couldn't help his grin.

"You've nothing to worry about, Raeta. I checked the container and it's sealed. I didn't bother to check to see if it was alive."

"As long as it's locked up I feel safe. What are you going to do with it, Zeus?"

"We can learn a lot by studying an alien life form." She pondered his answer and decided that was research she wanted no part of. Zeus pressed a switch on the panel and a screen just above them began to glow.

"Wonder what this is?" Zeus asked. They watched the screen fill with colors and begin to define a shape. A rather handsome man, Raeta thought, was looking at them with a serious demeanor.

"I'm the last onboard. The others have gone down to our new home. By unanimous vote, I was elected to set the ship adrift as we are all tired of space. I've an automatic tractor beam on. Should any ship pass within a specified distance, the tractor beam will bring them aboard. Should some of our banished kindred find this ship, be advised there's no home world to return to. It was destroyed by a large asteroid the Kraken sent down on us. All the survivors were aboard this ship. There's no communications system simply because there's no one to communicate with. I'm leaving in the last shuttle, and pray the enemy never find us again." As the image faded, Raeta and Zeus regarded each other in silence. Neither had words to express what they were feeling.

"Looks like this is our property, Raeta." She got a puzzled look as her brow furrowed.

"Why didn't they take their technology with them?" Zeus got a lost look and shrugged.

"Maybe they thought it would give them away to the Kraken. Too bad we don't know how long this ship's been adrift or where it came from. If we did, we could visit them."

"We can learn much about our people, Zeus. They must have a library onboard."

"See if Will's able to get up. I need you both on the bridge because I can't pilot this ship alone."

When Raeta came into the sickbay, she found Will pacing.

"What are you doing up?"

"I feel fine, just a little weak in the legs. Thought exercise would take care of that. Where the hell are we?"

"If you lay back down, I'll tell you." He smiled.

"All right, I'll lay back down." He was amazed at the story of their discovery.

Hera accompanied Aubrey and Selene to the sisters' quarters. They were eager to hear news about Earth. When Aubrey told them everything was normal, except for some inexplicable disappearances, they were elated.

"I would like to keep a record of this experiment, Hera," Selene said. Hera looked at the three before her.

"Do you have any objection?" Hera asked. They shook their heads.

"Very well, let's begin." The sisters each held one of Aubrey's hands and they joined hands.

"Mr. Blaine, you concentrate on Will," Ophelia said. "Janis and I will act as transmitter and receiver." Selene leaned close to Hera and whispered.

"I'll give them the boost they need." Hera glanced at her and nodded.

"We're ready," Janis said. They closed their eyes and began to inhale deeply and slowly. Aubrey focused on Will's face along with the question of where he was. Aubrey began to feel an odd sensation in his hands but quickly pushed the distraction from his mind.

Minutes passed, and Aubrey was aware of no change discernable to him. He saw the bridge of a ship and it startled him, but he kept focused. Janis spoke.

"Will's on his way here," Ophelia said, sensing Janis' excitement. The concentration was broken by Janis' elation. They let go of Aubrey's hands and looked at Hera. They and Aubrey were smiling.

"I didn't think this would work," Aubrey said, and gave Selene a wink. Hera, too, was smiling, but she had an important question.

"What about Raeta and Zeus?" Hera asked.

"I got the impression they're all right," Ophelia replied.

"What I saw wasn't the bridge of Zeus' ship," Aubrey said. "The bridge I saw was much larger." A sudden fear surged through Hera.

"A large ship?" Hera asked, apprehensive. "It wasn't a Kraken ship, was it?"

"I got no sense of danger," Aubrey said, and looked at the sisters. "What about you two?"

"None," Janis replied. "I felt only relief."

"Where could they have gotten such a ship?" Selene asked, looking puzzled.

"We'll have to wait until they arrive to learn that," Ophelia said.

"Could you discern how long before they arrive?" Hera asked. Ophelia glanced at Aubrey and Janis.

"I felt it was only a matter of days," Ophelia replied. Janis and Aubrey nodded.

"We must prepare for their arrival," Hera said, giving way to her excitement. "There's much to be done."

The days seemed to pass slowly for Janis as she looked forward to Will's return. For others on Olympus, they were preparing for the arrival. The fact that it was an unknown ship made for some anxiety. How would they know it was the ship they were expecting? Might it not turn out to be an enemy vessel? Hera assuaged the Pantheon that it could no longer be an enemy vessel, the Kraken was dead. Still she could not allay all of their trepidation.

An excited attendant awakened Hera.

"What is it?" Hera asked, sitting up quickly.

"A gigantic ship is approaching Olympus," the attendant replied. "I thought you would like to be in the control center when it comes into orbit."

"Yes, thank you, Aleah. Please inform the sisters and Earthmen. I'm certain they'll wish to be present, too." She hurried off to alert the others.

They were soon gathered in the main control room, the Earth people stood off to the side to keep out of the technicians' way.

"This is fantastic!" one of the technicians exclaimed, loudly.

"What is it?" Hera asked, curious. He looked at her awed.

"The size of that ship. It's almost six miles long and over a mile wide. I wonder who built it?" Aubrey glanced at Janis and Ophelia with a surprised expression. Zachary and Klast stood with their mouths open. The sisters couldn't conceptualize something so huge, so it had little impact on them.

"My God!" Aubrey mumbled. "It must have cost several fortunes to build."

"She's in a stable orbit," a female technician said, calmly.

"How long before they can come down? Hera asked. The technician who had spouted the dimensions grinned.

"It will probably take them longer to walk to the landing bay than it will take them to get down here," he replied.

A few moments of subdued excitement passed as everyone discussed the size of the ship now in orbit. The calm voice of the female technician sounded clearly above the din.

"A small ship has left the larger one and is entering the atmosphere." A tense wait began as she called off the altitude. They saw the ship settling on the landing pad. Janis started to move when Aubrey took hold of her arm. She turned to him with a surprised expression. Aubrey smiled.

"Don't let him know you want to see him so badly," Aubrey said. "Let him come to you." Ophelia smiled at his advice, and felt he was right. Janis looked at Ophelia who nodded.

"Are you certain?" Janis asked.

"Trust me," Aubrey said. "I know how Will thinks. He'll be expecting you to come running into his arms." That was exactly what she had been planning to do. Now she wasn't so sure Aubrey didn't have some telepathic ability.

On Zeus' ship, Will and Raeta stood behind him looking out at the crowd. Zeus glanced at them with a smile.

"Think we were missed?" Zeus asked. Raeta put a hand on his shoulder and smiled.

"You certainly were," she replied. Will saw Janis, Ophelia, and Aubrey standing with Zachary and Klast. Raeta noticed his expression as he looked at Janis. She turned to him.

"Are you glad to see her?" He looked at the serious expression on her pretty face.

"Yes, Raeta." She got an understanding smile.

"You better go to her, Will." He got a puzzled expression.

"I can see you love her," Raeta said, and nodded upward. "With that ship, I'll have lots of work to do. I wouldn't be able to spend much time with you." Will looked at her, and back to an anxious Janis, and there was an Earth for them to return to.

THE END

www.ingramcontent.com/pod-product-compliance
Lightning Source LLC
Chambersburg PA
CBHW030327030726
47499CB00003B/677